MONS GRAUPIUS

MONS GRAUPIUS

M.G. ANDERSON

A mountaineer's tale of long-ago Edinburgh,
before the Beatles changed everything.

Book Design & Production
Columbus Publishing Lab
www.ColumbusPublishingLab.com

Print ISBN 978-1-63337-055-5
E-book ISBN 978-1-63337-056-2

Printed in the United States of America
1 3 5 7 9 10 8 6 4 2

For Ernette and Bobby

"Let us, the last free men on earth, shielded by remoteness and seclusion, uncorrupted, unconquered, be ready to fight for freedom, proving at the clash of arms what heroes Caledonia has been holding."

Calgacus defending Scotland at the battle of Mons Graupius against the Romans in AD 83

"Montavi semper liberi (Mountaineers are always free)"

Motto of West Virginia
A Better Translation: "Mountaineers are always children."

Chapter 1

The Sycamore

Last night, I dreamt that I had returned to Edinburgh. I was walking through St. Margaret's Park at the very spot where Bonnie Prince Charlie spent the night carousing in the little village of Corstorphine prior to his triumphal entry into the capital. I was with my lover, an ethereal embodiment of no one in particular, kicking up crinkled leaves blown about by early autumn breezes that held no hint of the dank chill to follow. A moody thunderstorm dogged our steps, crackling and lighting our path, spasmodically spattering us in quick, short-lived showers. As happens in dreams, my companion's identity swithered through a flurry of possible acquaintances, not settling on anyone. We had moved into the shelter of the ancient sycamore when a swarm of white pigeons fluttered out from the nearby dovecote to hover over us. The tree, a cherished feature of the village, was haunted by a Pale Lady waiting for her lover, whose life had been claimed at Flodden Field. I was appropriately equipped for the expedition, wearing a white flowing dress that billowed and swished most satisfactorily. My lover kissed me. I opened my eyes and saw his wide open, calculating and sincere as Judas. Something told me it was not safe under the tree; I stepped out a few paces. Suddenly, a flash of lightning struck the tree. My lover, bathed in a blue flame, turned to dust before my eyes. My body, bathed in icy sweat, jerked awake, and in that instant I knew him.

I sat up. According to the Romans, vivid dreams signaled great (often ugly) changes ahead. The lurch in my stomach, however, told me they were most likely caused by the Grappa I had taken as a preventive measure to ward off the minor irritations of the school trip I was shepherding.

Everywhere we went in Rome, my flock was plagued by rampant youths following us from place to place like ravenous wolves setting their prey, and of course, girls being girls, both the lookers and those to whom nature had not been so charitable preened themselves for the youths' benefit. At night I checked the cupboards and under the beds to make sure no impulsive Lotharios had managed to break through the chastity cordon. In the daytime my young lambs, heedless of culture and history, minced and chattered past the immortal works of art in the Eternal City as if they were on a catwalk, which in a sense they were.

"Miss Fiorelli, if the pope speaks Latin, can he only speak to the likes of you?" I smiled at this mild, possibly unconscious barb, but a single Classics mistress in her mid-thirties must expect to be treated as an oddity—a muse-um piece if you like.

"Learn your gerunds, Donna, and you too can have a chat with him." Me playing up to the part, you see, giving off the faintest whiff of spinsterdom, tweed-set and pearls, an image whose relationship with the truth was not entirely peripheral. I am told the years have been kind to me, ruffling my cheeks with the balmiest of breezes, my looks not en-tirely withered; for even faded beauty leaves its trace, while my keen sense of fashion keeps me alert so that the vagaries of youth rarely catch me off guard. On the other hand, the loutishness held to be de rigueur in this day and age receives no welcome in my little imperium, making me a positive dinosaur of punctiliousness in the schoolroom, and therefore a target for the trendy, bead-wearing, swearing type of teach-er who empathizes with the youngsters and is nowadays so terribly popular. I, a mistress of the old school, have never empathized.

I was not always thus. Once I was silly, giddy and fun to be around, but a certain someone saw to that, and in a sense my story is simply that—how something sweet turned to something sour. Why was I dwelling on this? The newspaper I had casually turned over at breakfast told me. Something about the date pricked at my memory, like an archeological trace of a previous existence. It was ten years to the day of my aborted "wedding." I was such a complete-ly different person that the memory only slightly unsettled me, like the embarrassing moment that pops up, warms your cheeks and then recedes without trace.

Unaware of my somber mood, my pupils were joshing each other and chuckling like young tourists everywhere. They stopped their wittering and laughing when we stopped by Michelangelo's Pieta just inside St. Peter's. Of an instant twenty jowls stopped in mid-mastication. A glimpse into Earth's most tragic moment: Mary tenderly holding the dead Christ across her lap. The pale marble held them in its thrall.

"It's beautiful, isn't it?"

"Yes, Trudy."

"His mam, she looks awful sad." This came from Julia, an innocent so wide-eyed you wondered at her mother letting her out of the house.

Her friend standing next to her said, "But Jesus, he looks so peaceful. And his mam so young and pretty."

Know-all, Bellaine, just had to say, "It was the medieval thingimmy, you know. Virginity was like a preservative, kind of like Oil of Ulay, sort of." She tailed off tamely, aware of overstepping the line in admitting to listening to teacher.

Just at this moment when Art finally caught their attention, a sluggish crocodile of reluctant teenagers trailed into the Cathedral, and, in the way fate reserves its irony for the susceptible, who should be their guide but the author of all my bad fortune. He seemed unchanged. The face was still handsome even though the cheeks had billowed out to a discernible puffiness, which considering the service they had seen was fair enough. As usual he was talking entertaining balls, serving up to his overawed protégés these great works of art as props for his solipsistic humor.

"Now look at her clothes, Tracy."

"What about them, Mr. Mulvaney?"

"No go for a go-go, them floppy kaftans. Get in everyone's way." And here he paused; standing next to him was a girl whose jeans were so tight I wondered if they were strangling her, his eyes fixed on the vortex where the denim was being sucked into her body. "Wouldn't do for some of us, eh Donna?"

"Oh, do stop it, Mr. Mulvers!" Donna giggled coyly.

This seemed to cheer both groups up, for their jaws relaunched into chomping mode. Soon, one or two of my girls began coyly looking over their shoulders. Yes, their admirers were still there, and that disturbing exposure to culture was now a memory.

It was then that he caught sight of me. For a moment he looked like a naughty wee boy caught piddling in the bushes, then that almost-forgotten cocky smirk took over.

"Why it's Moira Fiorelli! Hi, Moira. How's it going?"

I stiffened; my pupils giggled. I'm sure in their dizzy little minds they didn't believe I had a Christian name.

There and then he started to chat me up as if I was still eighteen and green as a gooseberry. "That Virgin Mary kind of reminds me of you." Never mind the blasphemy, I was blazing at the brass-neck of him trying to chat me up right in front of my girls, and after everything. Needless to say, my pupils were loving every minute, me red-faced and him smoother than a snake like he was back in one of his Rose

11

Street Pubs and I once again the foolish virgin.

Eventually I managed to force myself away from him, but not before he managed to wheedle the name of our hotel out of me. Well, not me exactly—one of the girls blurted it out as I pretended to have misheard him. At once she caught my glare, realized what a clanger she had dropped, and started to cry—her way of unloading responsibility. I was not looking forward to dinner that night and the inevitable awkward questions. With any luck he would lose or throw away the fag-packet he had scribbled the address on. I steered my awkward column out into the bright sunshine of St. Peter's Square.

"Now, girls, onwards! To the Forum!"

"Please, miss, our feet hurt!" The unrehearsed chorus came surprisingly well-harmonized.

"You'll forget all about it when you see the spot Julius Caesar was murdered." If that didn't get them nothing would, but then I always overestimated their interest in anything prior to last night's telly.

Unfortunately my memory took me back considerably further.

Chapter 2

The Patrimony of St. Celestine

There are few things more annoying than, after shelling out for the bio of some fallen celebrity, to find the first fifty pages consumed with tales of her playpen and the name of her favorite pet pig, to say nothing of the antics of her drunken uncles. How many sixpences would be deducted from the asking price if we could leave the green room and get straight into the bit where she strides onto the world's stage. Unfortunately (and this makes my declaration ring a bit hollow), to make head or tail of my story I have to inflict something of the same on the reader.

My parents came over from Italy at the end of the war, and with immigrant energy made a go of a small restaurant business specializing in fish and chips. Deciding to run the gauntlet of native snobbery and cap their success, they installed me at St. Celestine's Academy for Young Ladies at Lauriston, on the grounds of the Celestinian abbey near Cramond on the nether skirts of Edinburgh. Our presumptive founder was St. Celestine, a perfect sweetie of a saint, but sadly a hopeless pope pushed out of office by grasping clerics. The Middle Ages needed sainthood in its rulers like it needed the Black Death. This then was our role model.

The building was celebrated as one of the finest examples of the Scottish Renaissance. Above the windows were gargoyles carved in stone, each and every one representing facial expressions relating to or consequent upon dabbling in the seven deadly sins. The twenty-three different forms of misery seemed a trifle overdone, but the portrayal of bellyaching gluttony was scrumptiously well-observed. All the teachers and former pupils of the school were immensely proud of this—Scotland's only contribution to the Baroque—but unaccountably they always shuffled past the portrayal of lust without comment.

The school was rebuilt in the mid-seventeenth century as a refuge for unmarried young ladies of gentle disposition. Between the lines, that should read as "unsaleable spinsters who could no longer be dumped off into nunneries." This unforeseen consequence of the Reformation made for depressing occupants, and as a result there were few neighbors. When, in the nineteenth century, the homely maids were removed to provide for a school, they bequeathed a magnificent sweeping landscape of woodland and fields that ran down to the sea, untarnished by intruding habitation. The old potato- and plough-land was dug up to make hockey pitches with one of the finest backdrops of any playing field in

Midlothian. We were often accused of cheating, as even the hardy bruisers we were playing would take their eyes off the ball now and again to sniff the glorious sea air and enjoy the sublime view of the Forth and Inchkeith Island.

On our left the ground dropped away to the post-card-pretty village of Cramond and the wooded River Almond. When the wind blew from the west we breathed in the unique tang of the river. Nowhere else have I come across that peculiar blend of riverbed, seaweed and sea that is so spicy and evocative, a perfume so much more engaging than some of the nasty stuff sniffed nowadays, that I am surprised no cosmetic opportunist has marketed it under the byline Lauriston Lady or maybe Femme d'Almond.

The view to our front was superb—the Firth of Forth that at times could be almost as blue as my native Tyrrhenian Sea set under the misty and faint hills of Fife. On our left was the finest achievement of Victorian engineering, the Forth Bridge, which always had a freshly-painted, glowing red-brick color. Painting that huge Meccano toy must have been a labor of love wrapped up as work.

Nowadays everybody boasts of how much they hated Latin. What use are ablative absolutes they say, giving the picture of a golden-haired little cherub being brutally lashed into learning pluperfects passive by a bewitched demon who every so often screams out, "Construe!" to her unwitting and unwilling charges. Me, I loved it, but I was lucky in having an inspired teacher. And here I come to the point.

Her name was Miss MacPherson. Even as I write this,

I see her strong outline set against a window through which sunlight always poured, with twenty pairs of eyes transfixed on her. Here there was no flippancy. To Miss MacPherson the Roman world was the world. In lessons she was always demanding, always austere. These moments of learning were, she claimed, the golden, most sunny hours of our youth-tide. I was only one of many who were her devotees, yet fearful of her displeasure. She was one of those few who needed no bolts from Jupiter to exact obedience. The merest frown as she read your homework could lead to tears in the playground, for no emotion was permitted within the walls of her temple. Praise could lead to dizzy surges of pleasure and simmering envy from the other girls.

She was trilling as she did when borne aloft on the flight of passion. "Now, girls, someday you may meet your Aeneas, a young man, high-minded yet passionate." Then she murmured sotto voce, "All men are not Aeneas," and we were left to wonder what she meant. "If you are unfortunate enough to be caught in a compromising situation, as Dido was in a cave, remember..." I think she meant to say "remember Lauriston," but began to point to her elegantly sculpted bosom, then something stopped her tongue. I often wondered about that. Was she, who bared her soul to us on a daily basis, hiding this one snapshot of the past? If it were me who was compromised, it wouldn't be just his clothes or weapons that went in the fire. I would get even I am sure. Would I immolate myself? Would my love ever reach such tragic heights as Dido? I woke up from this reverie as Miss

MacPherson rather sharply asked me to translate, but made up for my apparent lack of attention by the perceptiveness of my translation.

"Brilliant." Miss MacPherson was trilling admiration of an oddly intense timbre; Aeneas had just bumped into his discarded ex in Hades, an embarrassing situation anywhere, then proceeded to dig himself deeper into the mire, squirming out excuses, each one more pathetic than the last, just like a man. I put a lot of feeling into my rendering of the encounter. Surprising, for I had no experience of men in any shape or form outside of my immediate family. But I must have got something right.

"Now, girls, Moira has captured the flavor of Virgil's poetry. You can almost taste the Mediterranean in the breeze." High-flown rubbish of course, but Miss MacPherson was like that. I suspected that she still mourned the Ides of March.

She used to tell us that when she found the twentieth century too wearisome she would repair to Agricola's Roman Fort just next to the school and refresh herself with the air of antiquity. At the lesson's end she invited me to spend the lunch break with her, standing on the very spot where she was positive Tacitus' uncle, Agricola, had stood twenty centuries ago.

"From this very outpost of the Pax Romana, Moira, two thousand years ago, Agricola set out against the Caledonians." There must be an element of the banal in me, for I fear that I found standing toe to toe with Miss MacPherson on an old brick surrounded by nettles a bit on the strange side. She pointed past the glittering Forth, through and beyond the Kingdom of Fife. "To meet on the field of Mons Graupius, locus incognitus, somewhere. My ancestors on one side, yours on the other." This unlikely historical recreation she delivered with complete conviction. "Our leader was Calgacus, a man fit to stand alongside Wallace; the day the first in a long line of lost causes."

She recited a list of names, most of them lost to me ruminating on my chums, Rosie & Co.—living riotously on mince pies and tatties, flicking out illicit-kiss curls on their foreheads while jiving to the strains of "See You Later, Alligator." The damp cress sandwiches I was allowed to share were hardly a match for that.

"...Flodden and Culloden. As a Latinist and a Scot I have mixed feelings about that particular attempt to civilize us, especially now wi' such a parcel o' rogues in a nation." This last bit was done out in Braid Scots. "I suppose that must be your mission too, Moira. Mind you, a chip shop is hardly a Coliseum."

I always had difficulties with adult "jokes." With this one I still don't know. Realizing I hadn't the foggiest what she was on about, she shook that fine mane of hair coiffured on the lines of the empress Faustina, sighing, "Keep up the good work," and she touched my scalp. I felt a perceptible tingle as she breathed, "Stay true." I was not in the least bit alarmed, but nonetheless, on this rock, the laying on of hands...

She got off our brick, and we returned to school, teacher and pupil. Between us walked an awkward silence.

Chapter 3
Mince Pies

"Twae fish suppers, hen. You scrumptious wee darlin'."
The Lauriston Lady side of me flinched, but the one who
knew where my bread was buttered dug up a smile while
ladling a pile of sizzling chips onto last night's Edinburgh
Dispatch. School? It was important, but I learnt there was
more to life when I helped my father out in his chip shop.

The chip shop was his pride, but no one dared call it
that in his presence, and we referred to it with Edinburgh
daintiness as Fiorelli's Fish Restaurant—in capitals. It sold
fish and chips from a counter about the length of a pool table,
approached by an aisle whose flanking pews were milk bar
stalls with Formica tables and chairs. It was, after all, only a
chip shop, but (and here I smile) it was our bread and butter.

When I think of it now, I don't think of the slap of last
week's Sunday Post wrapped round a fish supper landing on
the counter, the Saturday-night punters reeking sweetly of

pints of heavy, discussing Hearts or Hibs; nor of my father at the back, stripped to his vest, sweating heavily as another bucket of sliced potatoes was poured into boiling fat to begin their metamorphosis into golden chips. The memory that I cherish is biting into a hot mince pie, the delicious hot grease dribbling down your cheeks, spoiling your blouse. To eat that crusty, spicy, dusty mess with a bottle of American cream soda was—well, scrumptious, if that is not too English a word—and was like dining at the Ritz. To me they evoked the true culture of Italo-Edinburgh. The pathetic emasculations called Scotch pies that masquerade as the descendants of our mince pies do nothing but sadly recall the riches of our youth. But then, the picture house up the road is also gone, the palace of our youthful dreams, replaced by yet another supermarket.

I became less snooty when I had to watch and then copy one of our servers expertly wrap a fish supper in last week's Sunday Post with a few quick flicks of her wrist. She could do all this while casually chatting to the customer about Heart's result that day. I wondered why she was so much better at dealing with real life, having left school at fifteen, when I had spent two expensive years learning to integrate dy and dx. I did not even know what dy and dx were or what integration and I suppose disintegration were supposed to do, while she could cook, place bets on horses, and roll cigarettes with one hand while gutting fish with the other. I could get no clues as to her secret in life from our chats in the little back room where we spent our breaks. Esme's conversation revolved around friends "falling pregnant" and drunken boyfriends bashing them up. We could not even discuss our mutual love of dancing, for in those class-ridden days even the dance halls were segregated. She had been once to the Carousel, which was patronized by my friends, but found it too tame and the boys anemic. Their chief failing was that their coiffure lacked the healthy springy quiff of her drape-suited co-pilots of the jive. She took me once to the Palais de Dance, her favorite spot, but I found it over-stimulating and felt isolated and vaguely threatened, as if I were with a strange tribe in another country.

Before Esme got married her greatest ambition had been to get off with one of the numerous American servicemen who used to strut and chew gum round our city. They were the only people who radiated style and confidence in those days. But she faced stiff competition in that quarter as illustrated by the only joke she told me.

"What dae ye call a pair of Kirknewton Panties?" (Kirknewton being a US air base.)

"No idea."

"One Yank and they're aff." I laughed, and naturally Dad chose this moment to come in.

"What's so funny?" he scowled. If he knew what we were laughing at I could kiss goodbye to seeing my pals on Saturday. So he left muttering reproachfully something about "flibberty-gibberty girls" and "time-wasting blethering."

In point of fact, I was quite shocked at the offhand way

she could discuss immorality. I was still under the impression that Scottish ladies were Vestal Virgins, and from then on for a long time thought promiscuity synonymous with the lower classes. Esme was astonished how incompetent and cack-handed I was at all practical matters. "I bet it's all playing the harp and needlework at your hoose, eh Moira?" It's funny the notions one half have about the other.

When I tried to interest her in higher things, as Miss MacPherson called them, Esme started looking at her nails and wondering when her pal Bella was coming on shift. On the one occasion when I managed to interest her in matters cultural it was the tear-inducing story of how the deaf Beethoven had to be turned round to receive the thunderous applause for his greatest work, the Chorale Symphony.

I said, "He could not hear his own supreme masterpiece."

Visibly moved, she replied, "Aw, that's awfy sad, and to think if it was noo he could get a free hearing aid from the doactor!"

I attempted to follow up this encouraging response by suggesting the two of us go to a concert of the same Beethoven in the Usher Hall. "No thanks, Moira," she said. "Thon story was gey nice, but it's still a load o' mung—the music, ken."

That very night she had made arrangements to go and see Terry Dean, a soon to be redundant rocker. My disappointment was tinged with relief at the rejection of my impulsive invitation. Fancy my friends seeing me with Esme.

So, laughing, I said, "Esme, you are a Philistine."

"No I am no', I'm Scottish," she replied indignantly.

I did not, as it may seem, treat her with contempt. Her approach to life was so much more mature than mine. "There are times to bend wi' the breeze," was her comment whenever I clashed with parental authority. She was particularly well-informed about seamy moments in life's glorious pattern, where my education and upbringing had cocooned me. For instance, Esme was right on the nail about men. "Men," she coughed between puffs of her cigarette, "are only interested in one thing: getting their phud!" You could have knocked me over with a feather duster. I was not used to people being so direct. That expression was an extremely gross piece of Edinburgh slang to denote that which men most prize prising open and which the wise virgin keeps under lock and key. She was miles away from my conception of men as courteous Sir Galahads, always walking on the outside of pavements to protect me from the splash of puddles even on the driest day. The only warnings I had from my pre-Esme days were beware of the man who carries a wad of bank notes in his back pocket as he is bound to be a Glaswegian, and avoid at all costs anyone with a Windsor knot in his tie, the sure sign of a shyster.

Chapter 4

The Breezy Pentlands

My father was not always a serious man of affairs. There were certain signs that told you a change was on its way. When he sang "O Sole Mio" or "Santa Lucia" you could not be absolutely sure, as he often did this leaning over the gurgling fat as part of his role as the genuine-article Italian chef. He had a look that said, "Ask me what's going on today," and he answered, "Mi arrangio," meaning "to get by" or "go on the scrounge" like a genuine Neapolitan scugnizzo—then you knew for a short while we were on holiday. On such days, if he was especially happy and relaxed, there was the possibility of an excursion. The trip itself could be a bit of a gamble. There could be some fearsome outing to a place of culture such as a museum or a castle, of which there were a fair number around, all in varying degrees of decrepitude, all peopled by the same languid ladies with lorgnettes. These expeditions often ended with feigned sickness on my part and bad tempers all round.

However, if he decided to go al fresco that was a different thing altogether. Dad's favorite outing was traipsing over our local hills, the Pentlands, only a cheap bus ride from home and chips. He used to claim that going there reminded him of his high days during the war when he used to hide from the fascists with his own partisan band way up in the Apennines. I didn't know about that. My own theory was that the Pentland breezes chased the aftertaste of chip fat out of his clothes. But I used to enjoy his war stories as we tramped the shaly purple paths up from Balerno and then bog-plodded over Bell's flat-topped Hill.

One of our best-loved tales was the one about the time the Germans made a rastrellamento, a sweep search of his village, and he had to hide in the hay loft. The Tedesco patrol went up the ladder, and one of the soldiers was stabbing about with his bayonet into the piles of hay where my dad was hiding. Apparently the bayonet was being pronged all round the straw, missing Pappa by inches until he punctured his calf. Our father never said a word or even flinched. He told us that the word Italia was sewn across his lips. The German did not prod any more as he evidently had hay fever and was spluttering and sneezing almost uncontrollably.

Sometimes when he told the story he added that when the soldier went back down he was given a rocket, as the front of his uniform was covered in sneeze and bits of straw. Goodness knows how he worked this out, as Dad had not a word of German. It was a good story that apart from thon wee embellishment never varied in the telling. I could not help feeling that the fact that the Tedesco must have noticed blood on his bayonet was never satisfactorily explained.

It was strange also that we first heard this saga whilst sipping tea in Habbies Howe on the Biggar Road just a fortnight after the showing of Reach for the Sky in the local flicks. A remarkably similar incident befell Douglas Bader. He was less brave than our Pappa for he surrendered after a few preliminary pokes in the hay.

Anyway, his tales formed an interesting background as we clambered over stiles and sweated our way up the rough grass and heathery slopes of Caerketton or Allermuir. The stories were so enthralling and he had such a lively way of telling them that if he forgot the thread I could always fill in for him. In fact sometimes I used to say in disappointment, "You told it differently last time," whenever he varied from the set text.

You may think that these Pentland days would have been very heavenly to me with their Viking brew of saga and adventure. Not at first—I had to be dragged every foot of the way, causing my parents and brother just as much misery as I was inflicting on myself. The reason was that, although I was independent in many ways, I was very aware of how others saw me. Quite simply, hill-walking was a square's game. What I was doing was about as trendy—a word as yet unborn—as wearing Auntie Beanie clothes. What was de rigueur was to spend all weekend practicing putting on make-up and dancing with a tinny gramophone to Little Richard,

Bill Haley or the Kalin twins in your room, with shopping for clothes in Princes Street an occasional treat. Fortunately, at school we all wore the same uniform of maroon blazer and navy skirt topped by a little cake-box hat so that rich and poor, square and hip would all be the same under a sartorial communism that hid anyone's non-conformity. That we were the storm troopers of a new youth culture was something that escaped our notice till we read about it twenty years later.

However, Dad must have known what he was doing, for gradually I found myself looking forward to these hill outings—always to the Pentlands—and I realized that I was only making a token homage to the rites of adolescence by putting on a dab of lipstick, and that just to annoy Pappa. I realized how much I liked the hills one Saturday night just before I went off to the dancing. I had just put the final touches to my makeup and admired myself in the mirror when I went downstairs. The whole family was round a map on the dining table. Dad was tapping the map with his pipe stem and checking the compass bearings. "If we get caught in the mist on top of Allermuir we need to know the route down to the reservoir." This for a trip we had done umpteen times, where Dad could have guided us blotto and in the dark.

"Enemy coast ahead and bandits at eleven o'clock, skipper." I had just seen The Dam Busters film, and laughed. The others looked at me in that curious way groups have for outsiders or intrusive drunks. By going out on the town I had excluded myself. I dimly grasped that I had missed the point. What I was witnessing was not a briefing but a knight's first communion before going forth to earn his spurs. It was a profound ritual modeled on, but not mocking, the Catholic mass. Mamma then took up the Credo, "Cheddar or ham on your pieces." The response, "cheese" or "ham," was irrelevant, as the item nearest to hand had already been slammed onto the bread. The opening of the map was the Elevation of the Host, with "How many miles to West Kip?" as the moment of transubstantiation. Too fanciful? Nowadays you would say that putting the flask of coffee into the sack was the foreplay to the act. A metaphor which, thank goodness, would never have occurred to my family or myself in that innocent era.

By going out I felt out of it, yet still caught up in the fervor of their little ceremony, so much so that when dancing I bored boys silly by prattling on about hill-rambling. This puzzled them, as they could not make out if I was trying to put them down. It was so much different from the usual patter of the dance hall. No one realized that I was talking about what interested me, when that was the last thing you were supposed to mention. You talked about what you supposed the other person supposed you would talk about. Boys talked about getting into fights and how steaming they were, and were surprised when the girls were not impressed. The girls said and did nothing beyond providing a discouraging or encouraging audience. Rambling on about rucksack boots treading the springing heather, I must have been considered a freak.

Soon, quite soon, I had the bug myself and wanted to

go out even when Dad did not, with likeminded friends or sometimes alone. Clattering down the steps of the bus in our heavy boots at Hillend, the Pentland terminus, with as nonchalant an air as we could muster, we tried not to look too embarrassed under the unbelieving stares of the passengers and the conductor in his role as corporation wit. "Mind you dinnae get lost for we're no coming in a search party. Ah ken yer goin to snuggle up wi' one of thae shepherds the night."

But soon that was well behind us, and we took our first step onto the heather and our first breath of hill air. If you're a climber you will know what I mean. From Allermuir to Alpamayo, Ben Nevis to the Punta Zocca, that first step is magic, like the thirsty drinker's first sip or the curtain rising on a play. If you feel that, you are a mountaineer; if not, not. It really is as simple as that. It defies explanation.

The hills gradually, almost insidiously, were becoming such an obsession that when not actually on them I was reading about them and those giants who dared to challenge them. My favorite bedside books were W.D. Mornay's *The Pre-Raphaelite Mountaineers of Scotland* and its companion volume *Don't Bring Your Compass in the Cuillin*, both of which took the place of Holy Scripture. From my bedroom window I could see steep, craggy Caerketton with its screes dripping down to R.L. Stevenson's cottage at Swanston. When I read of these iron-fingered Teutons who conquered the great Alpine Nordwands, I conjured up a picture of Caerketton as my own private Face Nord, where I could do gripping feats of Alpinism under the eyes of toute Edinburgh.

Coated under winter snow, the crags standing out black and menacing—they had an air of inviolability. Whether Edinburgh would have its collective telescope trained on me emerging through storm and avalanche to Caerketton's icy summit is another matter. Mountaineering is not a subject normally associated with peering through lace-trimmed curtains.

Fantasies apart, the walk up Caerketton was a pleasant stroll, comfortably done—icy or not—in half an hour. There you had a choice of viewing. Look north, and there under its smoky haze was Auld Reekie; beyond lay the Forth, grey or blue according to light or season, and then the hills of the Kingdom of Fife. To the south, across the plain of Penicuik, the hazy Moorfoots shimmered insubstantially. No one I knew had been there, and this unattainability was to me the stuff of magic.

From purple-bowered Caerketton it was only a quiet dander to the great dun dome of Allermuir, where you might bump into stern-jawed members of Edinburgh's climbing fraternity out for their Sunday communion with the hill. You could tell they resented my presence for they frowned at my breezy bobble cap. "Noddy comes to the mountain," I heard one say as I pranced off towards Castlelaw and its Iron Age fortress. He must have been talking to the summit cairn, poor man standing there lonely with his childhood memories of Enid Blyton.

One evening my best pal, Rosie, and I set out for a midnight hike intending to bivouac on the tops. I had read many accounts of the incomparable Alpine sunrise. Dawn over the Pentlands promised to be a celestial experience. In my imagination a heavenly choir would accompany dawn's rosy fingertips as the gently-touched crest turned from grey to gold, while a silvery mist unwrapped the sun's warming rays as we ate our breakfast.

Things did not work out that way. Rosie had not read my books, and looked on the whole business as a lark turned miserable as we shivered in the cold night air. "I never knew there were so many minutes in the night." This was said about nine o'clock in the evening, still a long way away from the witching hour, never mind our glorious dawn. And, "My teeth chattering are keeping me awake." I hoped that Hermann Buhl in his icy Alpine bivouacs had something more substantial than our ex W.D. sleeping bags, else he would have no more toes before he was thirty.

"There's your dawn." It was annoying that she should wake me up when I had fallen asleep only five minutes before. Sure enough, night was being chased away. Black turned to grey, with limited visibility in the mist, and that was that. Just down the hill the sheep, who had seen it all before, were placidly munching their breakfast grass.

"Perhaps it's always better in the pictures."

"Perhaps."

But we cheered up when we had to trespass past the reservoir keeper's cottage to get on the ridge to Turnhouse Hill. There was little danger we would get yelled at at five in the morning, but being naughty was exhilarating. We tiptoed past the white painted gate, holding our breath till we were past the old Covenanting Battlefield on Rullion Green, clambering up the steep sheep grass onto the first point on the ridge. The mist was just beginning to splinter off into puffy clouds.

Some folk will try to convince you that the finest ridge on the mainland is the Aonach Eagach in Glencoe. Hapless creatures from south of the Solway may impertinently suggest Crib Goch, but none of them have sampled these spiky mounds of earth and grass that stretch from Turnhouse Hill to the Kips, the Pentland Matterhorn. For here on Edinburgh's southernmost boundary was the ridge walk sans pareil, where you danced lightly for mile on mile between earth and air, between the sea to the north and the great plain to the south, stretching to the Lammermoors and Moorfoots.

I met a man in the placid surroundings of a Habbies Howe teashop who said that with the Pentlands on our doorstep no Edinburgh hillman need look any further. In fact he got quite tremulous about it, thumping the table and accusing those "Glencoeites" of shirking by abandoning the Pentland mosses to the sheep. The delicious cream and slaveringly jammed scone perpetually on the verge of being bombed by his fist seemed to be having a chancy time of it. I was quite relieved when he finally ate it. With all the scrimshankers safely away in Glencoe there would be more space for him to savour the heather-infused atmosphere and accompanying sheep, or so I supposed. When I outlined that little consolation to him I was accused of being selfish. This particular gauntlet I refused to pick up, being lulled into complacency by the delicious glut of cream and pastry set in front of me. The aficionado of the Pentlands was dressed as if for a hard day at the office, in a suit and Watsonian tie. The only concessions to the hill were a pair of brogues, plastic mac, and a little knapsack in lieu of a briefcase. A little later he was standing on the doorstep cursing the tardy arrival of his wife. He had a lot to put up with.

"He's not a bad bloke really." This was my companion, an Irishman, whose foibles were large enough to make him tolerant of others. But it was obvious that the man was doo-lally, listening to him muttering, "Cairnpapple, Carnethy Scald Law, scald me with thy passion. Nectar Avaunt thee. Let me drink at the burn of Bavelaw. May my bones be put to rest on the unbrushed midden of Craigenger." But he had a point.

This point of view was certainly not shared by the man kipping by the Cairn at the top of Carnethy hill. He was nestling in a little hollow in the boulders, a student by the look of his tatty anorak, thick spectacles and pale face. It was six o'clock on the morning of our dawn pilgrimage, and the clouds were dissolving. All the heavy-laden greys and browns of the hill and loch were transformed and uplifted into soft pastel shades: blue, pink and bright green, making a moment no hillman would miss.

Rosie shook him. "C'mon, mister, don't miss the ethereal soufflé of sunrise on water," said she, taking the micky out of my mountain diction. She assumed he would be grateful for two angels inviting him to open his eyes to such a splendid vision of daybreak in the hills, but instead got a fright, for the guy woke up with a start and would have assaulted us but for the confines of his sleeping bag. Instead he assaulted our ears with language for which St. Celestine had ill-prepared us. With "wee lassies no right to be on the hills" ringing round the summit cairn we left him to his slumbers. We wondered what such a torag was doing in the hills, and then forgot all about him as we began the long plod up Scald Law, the highest summit in the range, till finally on the top we lay down and drank in the view of azure ridges rolling down to the border country.

These then were the blue remembered hills of home, steeped in memorials of our history, a modest bus fare away from my own doorstep, tasty morsels to whet your appetite for bigger things and always a pleasure to come home to. A place to get wet feet, weary thighs, and happily, contentedly tired. A place whose memories would never grow cold.

Chapter 5

Working in George Street, Partying in Sauchiehall Street

"Moira, can you get me that file on Wango-RTZ, West Indies?"

"Yes, Mr. Meikle. Does there seem to be a problem there?"

Here I was all of eighteen years old and gainfully employed in one of the insurance offices dotted along George Street. Edinburgh's Regency New Town was punctuated by these sober edifices, whose granite neo-Augustan columns gave it that air of unyielding gravitas which makes all other cities, Glasgow especially, seem like comic relief. Meikle, the "man over me" as he liked to call himself, wore the puzzled frown that perennially adorned his features whenever a "problem" arose. Promoted beyond his depth by virtue of his former-pupil tie and nineteenth-hole cheer, he resorted to bullying his subordinates to do his work for him. He had just vented his spleen on a poor effete Anglo-educated graduate whom, nerves shattered by the lambasting, was dropping files and printouts all around. In the woolly hinterland he called his brain, he probably saw that as a patriotic act that would increase his popularity. In truth he was disliked, but this was disguised, as most people were frightened of him or at least did not want the tremors of his temper to disturb the genteel atmosphere where people only got passionate about golf.

Me he did not bully, as once or twice he had seen me putting my peers in place with a show-stopping display of Latin temperament such as to put Maria Callas on notice. He also fancied me in that sickening way one's father's friends have, leering down into your cleavage while patting your knee in an avuncular fashion. You knew that all the while their little titillation was being recycled into their mental passion file. Their wives would be pleasurably shocked by a surprise rogering that night, little knowing that for a moment their faces wore the mask of Moira Fiorelli.

As I have hinted, I did not like him, but even the strong have to use bullies as allies. So I let Meikle explain while suffering his beery-cum-pipe-tobacco exhalations. "Interesting case this, Moira. Seems an employee of theirs was eaten by a shark caught by a fisherman, and bits of body disgorged. Claims depend on disputed identification. No moolah till dental records verify it."

"What, the man's or the shark's?"

"Whit?" The frown was momentarily split by dawning intellect. "Oh, very good, Moira."

Surprisingly few people tried jesting with Meikle, being too frightened of a volcanic explosion to stay long enough in his proximity. Encouraged by my amiability, Meikle lingered longer to savour the lacy outline of my bra. I could feel the rest of the office hating me for this, but who cares. I needed a favor, and this superannuated wing-forward was the one to oblige. I swiveled round en face and caught his guilty peek, looked fleetingly stern just to let him know, then swiftly changed gear to show he was forgiven, let that linger before I put on my winsome pleading look, combining this with just a hint of further delights.

"Ergh, Mr. Meikle?"

"Yes, Moira?"

"Could you do just a teeny favor?"

"Well, let's hear it." This was his bluff no-nonsense voice.

"Let me go an hour earlier tonight." I was all butter not melting in the mouth.

"Miss Fiorelli, you know the company's very strict policy about staff time-keeping."

I knew then that I'd got it. His stuffy little speech was only a token, and all I had to do was put on a meek look to show I knew he was the boss and wasn't he just masterful. When he asked what it was for I did not even bother lying, but told him I wanted to catch the train to Glasgow with my pal Rosie to get to my cousin's party. Honesty was the best policy; if I spun him the usual Granny's funeral one he would know I was taking him for a ride.

"Well, in that case, I'll tell staff department you've gone sick, that it's..." I watched fascinated as he dared himself to say it was my period, and let him have a prurient vicarious intimacy with me. But the Permissive Society was not yet born, and his Presbyterian birthright and downright cowardice won as they always would. "...That it's the cold weather seems to affect you."

"Thank you, Mr. Meikle. You're so kind and understanding." I was fairly fulsome in my thanks. Turning round I reddened as little blasts of envy and enmity from my colleagues hit me. I was not so skilled in manipulation to do it without generating a fair amount of body heat. Heat, as you know, rises, so my rosy face nicely complemented my cream-of-ivory blouse.

....

"Tutti frutti, aw rutti!" was bouncing off the walls of the Glasgow apartment in party mood. Our cousins the Cannelottis were celebrating their victory in the Glasgow Ice-Cream Wars, where rival gangs of Glaswegian mafiosi had fought it out to control the bicycle-operated ice-cream vans of the city. Now their Hokey Pokey vans selling cream sliders and cones had established bridgeheads in the dreary housing schemes of that city. I had been elected to represent the Fiorellis at the festivities and had brought Rosie along with me for moral support. In the morning we intended to clear our heads early and take off to the hills.

It was one of my few trips to that great city on the Clyde, built on the tobacco and slave trade and now eking out its wages by shipbuilding, another industry showing signs of decline. To us it was almost a foreign visit, greeted by miles upon miles of red-stone tenement, each with a strange, cold, aromatic mélange oozing from their front entrances. Going up the dank, dark tenement steps, hollowed out by a century of footsteps, I managed to sort out the mingled smells by some visual clues. On the ground floor a dog was cocking its leg against a door, which I hoped was only a broom cupboard. Farther up, my feet crunched over bits of broken glass, and I spotted a tattered label with a jaunty Johnnie Walker striding out confidently on a Regency morning.

Eduardo Cannelotti—now Eddie McCann—opened the door, welcoming us in with what sounded like a burst of Neapolitan; seeing my puzzlement he switched to Glaswegian. Despairing, he put his version of Standard English to use, and at last we grasped where to put our coats, where the bathroom was, and that we were to come in and join the fun.

The fun consisted of standing around in groups, a glass in both hands, laughing and shouting at full stretch under the umbrella of sound from Little Richard.

"Why two glasses?" I enquired of one bearded party-trouper.

"So as you ken whit your drinkin'." He held out a fist full of glistening dram. "The right hand tae get you steamin'." He looked as if he was well on the way to that objective. "The other tae pace yersel wi'," said he, indicating what looked like a firkin of ale. "Onyway it saves fighting around the bar." That was the truth, sober or not. The drinks area was a jungle of elbows, with underfoot a vegetable patch of soggy fag ends—all the signs of a lively party.

"C'mon Tam," someone called out, and my friend disappeared into the crush to laugh and anecdote loudly with his pals in another corner.

"Ah well, here goes," said I to Rosie, and "Ta" to another who handed us a large glass of cold pale ale.

"Eh, no thanks." This being Rosie refusing the proffered dram.

The donor had taken time off from entertaining his own little group of handmaidens. Whilst his hands delivered the rations, his eyes leisurely paced up and down our bodies, finally giving us a smile each before returning to his story. Eddie came back and took us round to each significant group, introducing us briefly. The introductions were received in the usual way: a drunken "Well, hallo there," a smile, and then we let them get on with it. The party was a mixed bag of business people, shady types and a few self-styled intelligentsia. The latter could easily be recognized, as male and female alike wore the same listless, baggy sweaters. There were also representatives of the different races populating the west of Scotland: Italians, Poles, one Asian—possibly a medical student, while the dark-haired guy who had given us our drinks was emphatically Irish. The waves of the party having drifted us back into his ken, we could now at leisure observe his technique of keeping court, which was to hold people at the other end of the room up to ridicule. Just when the aggrieved twigged what was happening, the jester would change gear with a ridiculous story about himself.

He laughed and pointed a beer can. "See Kenny o'er there." A dozen eyes focused on an innocent tweedy type, pencil in top pocket, looking a wee bit lost. "His ma told him never trust women at these parties. 'Keep yer troosers weel anchored wi' baith belt and braces' were her final words." True enough his jacket was open just enough to reveal a greying elastic hint of suspension. "Go on, Dierdre, get him to open his jacket and expose Scotland's last great secret."

Laughing, Dierdre stepped over to Kenny who looked up in alarm. "Now, as I was saying, I can always tell when I am really ill. I look at her lingerie catalogues." He pronounced this as if he loitered over the pages. "If I'm sickening, not a flicker. But if I'm on the road to recovery, the old battery charges up."

"What does your wife—lady friend—think?" I said.

"She calls it my domestic doctor. A slip in time keeps me fine." He and his little gang now turned on me, laughing.

"Oh, clever," I said. He irritated me and somehow made me feel a fool. What a repulsive person, treating others as butts for anecdotes. I wondered how he treated women, but seeing his amused eyes unbuttoning my blouse I had my answer.

"C'mon Rosie, I think we should go."

"Where to? We're staying the night aren't we?"

She was enjoying herself talking to a young doctor, I

think—who else would wear a spotted bow tie with just a shirt and a pullover?

Eddie caught my arm, saying, "You must try one of our Canny Ices. They're great."

Tempted, I sampled the snow-white confection, peppered with multicolored chocolate seeds. "Mmm! scrumptious. Wi' a great punny name," I laughed.

Now that my ear was more attuned to his talk I could see that Eddie was a fine mixture of Latin and Celt. We spent a long time talking ice cream, which may sound boring but I am always fascinated by our family business and its technical side. It always mesmerizes me the way the Hokey Pokey man can coat and wafer a slider with a sleight of hand like a conjurer. Hoc est pocus meum. Eddie's Canny Ices were so popular that there were always queues outside their ice-cream parlor even in the depths of winter. To loving care in their making they had added their own special ingredients. Being part of the family, I was admitted into the secret, guarded with all the mystique clinging to Bonnie Prince Charlie's recipe for Drambuie. In our case Garibaldi was supposed to have given it to an ancestor of ours (for services rendered during the Risorgimento) while on his ship to Caprera, at which very moment our esteemed forebear was puking up over the starboard rail—but I think this was added to the story to make it more credible. This cloak-and-dagger business always seemed to me a piece of phony baloney, as it shouldn't take a forensic chemist five minutes to break down the formulae for both Drambuie and Canny Ices, but family loyalty keeps my lips sealed. There was no doubt that Eddie's ices, delicious and creamy to the palate, had more to them than your average factory ice, and they certainly didn't give you wind in your stomach like the mass-produced blocks of chilled margarine palmed off on the general public.

All in all I enjoyed the party. An added bonus was that I managed to snub the lecherous Mick, whose tentative pass at me was ruined by stumbling on the beer-slop floor. "Another slip in time," I replied rather wittily, giving him one of my ice-queen special looks from eyebrow to toes. I am not sure that it registered for he just grinned quite a bit more slack-jawed, but he was probably canned by then.

The next morning Rosie and I left in fine fettle, not forgetting to thank Eddie. "Come over for a hot supper in Edinburgh," I joked. He looked blank. I must learn to talk more slowly. "Pie and chips, not ice cream."

He smiled wanly, the perfect host to the last.

Chapter 6

The Cobbler and His Wife, Jean

"Two returns to Arrochar."

"That'll be ten bob, hen."

I hated that expression, which always made me feel like clucking back. I was about to give the conductor a Morningside rebuff when he pointed to my rucksack lying beside us on the back seat, and, knowing that these conductors could make things difficult, even throw you off the bus for carrying contraband, I swiftly altered my expression to poor helpless sweetie. But all he said was, "Sees, you've got a Rangers rope there!" pointing at a brand new blue and white rope tucked through the flap of my rucksack. I fervently hoped he was not a Celtic supporter and would not insist on me carrying a green rope, as anything was possible with their football-crazed citizenry. But it was merely a sample of his wit, and after a chuckle to himself he walked back up the bus to entertain more responsive hens.

"Dinnae stick your noses in the air like that or you'll trip o'er yersel'," was the conductor's cheery farewell as we got off the bus into a cold, bleak November drizzle, and tramped up the gloomy and boggy hillside onto the foothills of the Cobbler, the oddest shaped mountain in the British Isles. Its outline is supposed to represent a cobbler bending over his last—that is the north and central peaks respectively—while the left-hand, south peak is his wife Jean looking on, but to me the shape always seemed more like an upturned old-fashioned ladies boot. Today the only rock we would see would be the one we bumped our noses against. In the mist, huge towering lumps turned out to be clumps of bog-grass when approached, while Highland cattle changed into dripping sheep. As we were meeting a friend at the little campsite on the bank near the Narnain Boulders, we had to press on, and by sticking to the path beside the burn we would not go far wrong.

Our boots kept squelching and slipping on the muddy path. The mud contained curious silvery specks, making our clarty boots sparkle with stardust. "Cinderella boots," laughed Rosie. "Well, Prince Charming better be waiting for us."

I was not in a good mood. The dreich day, the bus conductor, this exhausting slimy slog were all conspiring to make me grumpy. The Buttermilk Burn bubbled and frothed with a creamy wake on its swollen downward path while we trudged up through the soggy rushes feeling hot and clumsy with our exertions. To take my mind off this trudge I began musing about my wee chum. I like to think of her as she was that November morning, especially in the light of what became of us. Smaller than me, with matching dark Latin looks, she haled originally from Ireland with, she claimed, Spanish blood donated by a sailor washed up with the flotsam of the Armada. Knocking on the door of an ancestress, he was welcomed with more than open arms. Wild dark curls signaled Rosie's bubbly personality. I never saw her almond temptress eyes without their mischievous gleam. Boys came after her in droves. When she wanted to, she could give them what for. I remember one shaken suitor, subsequent to dismissal, telling me how she used to throw furniture at him. "And I still don't know what I am supposed to have done." Well, once would have been enough for me, but I noticed they always came back for more. Very, very seldom had we been rivals, going in for a different kind of fella. Lucky for one of us, or so I thought on that innocent morning.

I managed to get Rosie interested in climbing. "What are the fellas like?" she said when I suggested coming down to the club.

"Oh, the usual—like dogs on heat, but good looking with it."

"Great, show me the ropes."

She always denied this anecdote. "I climb for higher reasons," she maintained somewhat haughtily, to which I add, "She means bigger fellas." This slander was almost funny the first half-dozen times she told me.

Anyway, whatever the road that brought her there,

quite quickly she could scamper up rock with silky skill, finishing with a winsome smile that said, "Amn't I the lucky girl to have so masterful a guide?" after her Bergfuhrer had clumped up, frutching, fighting and shaking on every move. In the interest of historical truth, I have to say my first forays in the vertical were substantially different.

One trip to the Lakes, I stood frozen midway up Little Chamonix at Shepherds Crag, stuck to the rock like ivy, weeping in terror for over two hours. Strung along the crag I could see other bodies unable to move from tittering at my plight. I would have remained there to this day if a guy had not soloed up to me, unsticking my hands and feet from their holds and replacing them higher up, at the same time shouting to my belayer, "Take in." At the bottom of the crag a chorus of Volga boatmen swayed and sang, "Heave, haul, haul away." A great time was had by all but one.

"Och, Jamie will be there. He's an all-weather mountaineer." How she could always be cheerful was a riddle, irritating at times.

Quite soon we were on flat ground searching for the rendezvous boulder under which the adventurous, or those who had mislaid their tent, might sleep. This Howff had the added attraction of hosting problems on its walls so you could practice climbing before bedtime. Bouldering was the nearest thing to physical chess. Unraveling the problem with your feet almost touching the ground sharpened your technique without the stomach-churning fear of the real thing. I always thought it pretty pointless, as the genuine article was only half an hour's walk away, but I had to admit that those who practiced there usually became better climbers. To my mind, showing off was the object of this particular game, and showing off was what we spotted Jamie doing. As the mist thinned out in the Coire there was Jamie, spread out in a crucifix formation, doing one of the impossible problems. Pretending to have just seen us he leapt to the ground, simultaneously sweeping back his lank cigarette-ash hair.

"Och so, girls, what news from the Smoke?" Jamie was a colorful character, and his usual greeting of "Och so" smiled away our gloom. Even the day was brightening; the dank mist was breaking up into puffy cotton-wool clouds. "You'll be needing a drum up."

"Ta, Jamie," we nodded and established ourselves in the chaos of his tent. Sitting and trying to get comfortable when rock pegs, bits of rope and discarded sandwiches kept lodging into our elbows and backs, we watched in amazement as he put tea leaves into cold water. "We're going to hae a great day."

"Sure!" The tea was declared brewed. The resulting mixture was of a greenish hue, but we drank it all the same. "How dae ye like yer tea?"

"It's grand, Jamie. If we have any more we'll have to rush to the bathroom." We didn't fancy traipsing down to Arrochar all day, there being no "Ladies" on the hill, and we were still too genteel to go al fresco.

The drum up is an important feature in the climber's day. Here plans are made or unmade, and it's usually protracted as long as possible. The reason for this is simple. Involving as it does a move from a position of pleasant comfort to one of acute discomfort, the fearful climber, acutely aware of what his stronger chum has in store for him, resorts to a number of devices to loiter. Among the favorite stalling tactics are appeals to weather signs or the telling of jokes and amusing stories. As a matter of observation, after many years climbing I noticed that the amusing raconteur on these occasions often ended as a protesting haul-bag dragged up the cliff, while his quiet, nondescript friend, whom you hardly noticed crouched in the corner of the tent, became the strong silent leader at the sharp end of the rope.

But we were keen to get going particularly as the weather was brightening. Jamie was very precise in assembling his gear and kept hopping about like a rabbit to another corner of his tented domain making adjustments to all the mysterious bits of equipment that we had never seen before.

"Och so. I am getting my gear ready for the Eiger. But dinna you worry, girls, that's not today."

"What about Ramshead Wall?" Rosie suggested.

"Too easy."

"Well then Ardgartan Wall," I put in.

"That's nae challenge for you. Not worth hiking all the way up here."

"Remember we're still beginners."

"Awa' wi' ye. Dinna be sae modest."

This began to make me nervous, as there is nothing worse for a beginner than being towed up rock way out of your depth.

"We'll go for Bow Crack as a wee warm up, then S crack, and finish up on Dead Man's Grooves."

By now I was completely unnerved. Bow Crack, although only severe, had a ferocious reputation, while the last climb made me wonder if we might end up in the Arrochar cemetery.

Rosie was thumbing through his dog-eared guide book. "How about Punster's Crack? The graded list says it's a good severe."

We all agreed on Punster's as a compromise, which would stretch our talents but not unduly.

"Aye. It'll be a good warm up for us all. We can go on tae Cupid's Groove and maybe Gladiator's." I knew the last two were way beyond us, but was relieved knowing that I could sufficiently protract our activities on Punster's to leave no time for the rest.

Amongst white thinning mist, the sun's reflection sparkling in each droplet, we walked steeply up the path to the foot of the north peak, finally breaking through the cloud into impossible warm sunshine, the sky an immaculate cerulean sheet, while below our feet the clouds lay in a ruffled, puffy sheet. We were totally detached from Mother Earth beneath us; Glasgow, Arrochar, dark depressing streets no longer existed. Here and there across the horizon peaks such as Ben Lomond lay like longships becalmed in the sky. Above us brilliant, painful white snow-capped the summit. Most unusually, the rocks were totally snow-free and invitingly warm in the sun.

The crazy leaning tower of the north peak now revealed itself as a complex mass of gullies, slabs, and steep prows of rock. Everywhere there were possibilities for climbers.

"I bet there are hundreds of routes here!"

"Just twenty-five to keep us busy." Jamie spoke with the assured voice of authority leading us to the foot of the climb. His tone was severe, as if telling us he was the maestro, but I wondered and then dismissed the fleeting thought that there was a tremor of anxiety in his voice.

"Rosie," he announced, "you're going to lead the first pitch."

"Great, Jamie."

"Aye, that's the hard part."

"Do you think I'll manage that?" Rosie queried. Up till now she had been giving our leader her usual look of unquestioning admiration, but confronted by the mass of steep rock she had to lead without any protection, her expression changed to one of questioning plus slightly less adoration.

"Nae bother." He was more confident than we were about our ability.

"Moira's got the last wall, the exciting pitch."

Why wasn't he doing any leading?

"Because I want to see you both in action." Fair enough. We took our sacs off and roped up in an excited hurry.

Like a conjuror with a rabbit, Rosie drew out of her sac a brand new pair of Robert Laurie rock boots. Looking like

52

red-and-black baseball boots stuck together with bits of bald tire, they were as sensitive as ballet shoes. Wearing them after big bendy boots was like handling a racing car after driving lorries. With the exception of P.A.'s, they were in their day the ultimate weapons. Quickly tying on she said, "Just watch that rope, Jamie," and twinkled up the rock in minutes. "How'm I doing?"

"Just keep going," Jamie shouted and then muttered to me through clenched teeth, "Wait till she gets tae the hard bit; that'll slow her doon." He seemed tense, not quite so confident of our ability as he said.

From down below the crux, a committing step across a gap between two walls of rock looked evil. Her climbing became slower and more considered as she approached it. She stopped and, looping a sling over a flake of rock, attached it to her rope as a safeguard. We could feel the tension vibrating along the rope. Knowing that once properly embarked on this traverse there was no turning back, she teetered a bit, made a few speculative attempts to start, then retreated. Her breath was pumping like a squeezebox. She gasped, "Watch me really carefully," before launching herself decisively on the move. It was hard, but she danced over neatly, making it look all too easy. Once across she laughed in that annoying way of hers, curls bobbing like springs on her forehead, then padded up easily to the belay.

"Come on up," she cried.

"Was it dodgy?" Jamie called.

"No swinging," she grinned, giving us the thumbs up,

the calling card of a long defunct comedian.

When Jamie got to the tricky bit, it was obvious that he found it hard going. Muttering "Och so" he made some dithering attempts. Several times he half made the crucial move, but his toe only tentatively tickled the key hold before leaping back as if scalded. Finally he leapt across the gulf shaking out his great mane of hair, his "Och so" ringing like a conjuror's "Hey presto."

It was now my turn to take my first steps on Cobbler Rock. I trod warily, not having experienced anything like it before, but with the safety of the rope above I was soon able to relax and take in my surroundings. From the greens, purples and blues of grass and heather I moved into a mono-chromed desert of stone. The color, predominantly grey, is far from dull as it sparkles in the sun with the crystalline admixture interwoven into its fabric. Smooth to the touch, yet the friction—like that of the roughest of rocks—bonds your feet to its surface. The walls and slabs undulated with ripples and folds as if a breeze-stirred duck pond was set on end. Every now and then, huge chunks of quartz crystals popped up to provide accommodating sharp holds, like the blocks of sparkling rocks that jewelers drape watches and diamond fripperies on. Otherwise there are few jug-handles to clutch onto, and so the climbing provides delicate balance work set at a sharp angle. The combination of elegance and danger is a heady brew, and I was tingling, charged with life as I moved upwards. If there are rocks in heaven may they be like the Cobbler.

A heave and shuffle got me up the difficult bit silently muttering, "Thank God for the rope."

When I reached the belay stance, Rosie chuckled, "Look what's in store for you."

I tilted my head backwards to see a fiercely steep wall with no visible holds, capped by a fringe of snow. I gave Jamie a doubting look.

"Nae bother, Lassie, nae bother at a'. Just haugh yer hands at the top and mantleshelf up."

Well, easier said than climbed, but he seemed to have confidence, so I would have to pretend I did.

Checking the rope paid out freely, I pushed the bowline knot round to the back and with heart in throat stepped unsteadily upwards. At each move snug little holds materialized so that although my heavy boots made me feel like a clodhopper, I rapidly gained in confidence as I distanced myself from the pair on the stance and began to relish the drop beneath my feet. Here I was first on the rope, going well and in that state of mild fright that is akin to euphoria.

For no reason I kept saying, "Holds and more holds." Turning around to let them in on the secret I shouted down, "Great climbing."

Rosie cheered but Jamie nodded tightly like an anxious parent. I was now at head height to the snow fringe, the cornice that jutted over a foot out from the top of the cliff. If I went up to chest height I would be pushed out way back. For the only time in my life I wished I was a boy—but only for a wee while. The situation was serious. I could not get over the top without an ice axe. Going down the way I had come was far beyond my ability, but I was not worried; my exhilaration was not going to be crushed by any little problem. Standing well in balance and on good holds with my face just over the top I was able to enjoy the summit view and sunshine.

A well-equipped walking party was scrunching their way up the snow to the summit cairn. Help was at hand. I shouted, "Give us a loan of your axe," with no breath wasted on please or thank you. They seemed to be taking a long time looking around the apparently deserted summit table.

"Your voice has gone funny, Ernie."

"I didnae say a word."

"Coo-eeh," I trilled.

"It's no haunted is it Jake?"

"Jings!" They spotted my head peeping over the cornice, grinning like a monkey.

"Your axe, please." I remembered my manners.

"I thought it was a speaking cairn," said Jake as he handed over his axe. "Och, you're a lassie," continued the observant fellow. Now I hacked away with vim to make a V-shaped groove in the snow. The snow went hurtling down the crag in great lumps.

"Watch it!" and "Mind where you're dropping that stuff!" came up from below.

"Can't help it," said I, and plunged the axe right up to its hilt in the snow, ready to lever myself up on it. My arms and elbows were in position over the axe head, dynamite plunger. I was on tiptoes ready to spring. I sprang—sort of, hesitating half through. If the axe didn't hold, it would be curtains. A flash of fear shook my insides, my feet stuck in mid-air like the rest of me, totally frozen. Luckily the axe-giver, seeing my plight, stepped forward and held on to my elbows as I wriggled over the snow till I landed.

"Phew!" I gasped. "Thanks a million." I flashed him a winning smile and went on to use his axe as a crude belay, taking the rope in tight down to Rosie.

"Climb when you are ready!" I shouted down and promptly started singing "The Road to the Isles," the first thing that came into my head. The walkers grinned at me singing tunelessly while sitting with my bottom wet in the snow.

I am sure they knew the exultation of leading a difficult climb on a beautiful day for one of them said, "Punster's a good lead." From these quietly spoken men that was eulogy enough; there was no nonsense about "for a lassie."

Heaped on to the pleasure of this bouquet was the somewhat malevolent satisfaction I got in watching Rosie struggle up the pitch. "Watch the rope!" she shouted, ascending in a series of scuttles and scuffles. A few seconds later: "Keep it really tight!" This came out in a noticeably higher pitch. This sort of pleasure at your mate's poor performance everyone feels but no one admits, unless I am meaner than the average, which I doubt. So I fairly glowed with pride when her head appeared in my V in the snow and she said, "Well led, now just pull me over the top." She looked like a target in a fairground shooting booth. For a moment I was tempted to keep the rope slack until she said "please," but my better half tugged at the rope, whereupon she rolled neatly onto the summit. The walkers let out a cheer. Quickly recovering her poise, Rosie gave them a mock curtsey.

I let Rosie bring Jamie up, untied from the rope and walked farther round the edge. From my new position I was able to watch Jamie make his ascent unseen. The unseasonable sun on my back was so hot that I could feel my breeches steaming dry while I watched our leader making an awful hash of things, his feet skating all over the place, holding on far too tight and even making the beginner's mistake of hugging the rock. At one point his cheek was against the rock giving it a cuddle. He was cursing and looking yearningly at the rope. I could tell that he was about to grab it, so I coughed. He looked round and spotted me.

"Look Moira, tell Rosie it's getting late. She'll never catch that bus if we don't get a move on." So saying he grabbed the rope and shouted, "Och, haul away," so that there was no doubt up top. Rosie had scarcely time to take the extra strain as Jamie pulled himself up like Burt Lancaster scaling the tyrant's castle. I had totally forgotten that Rosie had to catch the Saturday bus. It was lucky that we had such a responsible leader.

As we coiled the ropes, our faces were bright, warmed by the evening sun that was tinting the great mass of candy-floss clouds beneath our feet a delicate pink. I felt so proud and warm inside. What a great day; what a great climber I was. Only later did I realize that the great chunks of snow that I had knocked down had melted, soaking the rocks, and Cobbler rock, extremely trustworthy in the dry, is like soap when wet.

Leaving the summit dropping into the clouds in the corrie we re-entered dark, dank November reality. Nothing seemed to have changed when we saw Rosie onto the bus. It was still dull and dreichit; discarded cans of lager and broken screwtops strewn about the shelter gave the place an air of abandonment, and the bus was as dirty as ever. Nor was our pal the conductor at a loss for words of welcome.

"Aye, see, they've sent the gooseberry home," was his jocular greeting. As we returned up the hill I heard in the breeze, "I bet yir mither disnae ken aboot this."

I should really have gone home with Rosie, but the promise of another great day tempted me back to the tent. There was no danger of any hanky-panky with Jamie, unlike the Irish Bluebeard at the party—definitely someone your mother would warn you against. Funny how thinking of him made me shiver as if someone had walked over my grave. Jamie, on the other hand, was too full of climbing the Eiger and other such fantasies to be bothered with carnal thoughts. Or so I thought. Ah, foolish virgin that I was—I had to learn the hard way.

Jamie was a chef by trade. "No, it is my art, not my trade," he pronounced, sprawling at the back of the tent. Certainly he did not wish to demean his gift by heating up the mess of stew, beans and tinned potatoes that was tea. Although he was not much taller than me and slim to boot, there would be too many cooks at the tent-door, so I was quite happy to indulge his sensitivity. Besides, I wanted to show him my gratitude for taking us climbing without being called upon to pay the price later in the night.

I was still full of the glow of the day's climb, and the hot sloppy food carried that heat right up to my toes and fingers, making them all of a tingle. There was no lack of things to talk about as we sat cuddling our brews in the dark. I was happy listening while Jamie poured forth his wide experience of mountaineering, in winter and summer, but always in Scotland. Why? For Scotland was a mountaineer's Valhalla, with more treasures than I in my wildest dreams could imagine. This to me was a novel creed. "But what about the Alps?" I questioned. "Scotland in winter—far better. Aye, better by far." The Manchester group of climbers, who at that time dominated the climbing world, were pooh-poohed contemptuously for cavorting on the mere boulder problems that passed for serious ascents south of the Tweed.

"They're just a bunch of plumbers whae cheat their way up climbs wi' nuts 'n bolts." The proof of this was that they could only climb up cracks where they could insert their cheating aids. They lacked the craft and elegance to climb slabs and walls, unlike the more dexterous Scottish climber, while their extremely severe climbs in the Llanberis Pass couldn't hold a candle to the easiest moderate in Glencoe. I listened to this unadulterated balls, drinking it all in with my usual credulity. This amazingly chauvinistic viewpoint of the superiority of all things Scottish was held by not a few in those early days. We talked far into the night, moving from climbing to his interests in the arts. He considered himself a beatnik, a stance he maintained by wearing a beret on Princes Street.

"Moira, I'm a neurotic—an artistic neurotic," he said. I was meant to infer from this that beneath his seemingly stolid exterior there breathed the passions and creativity of a Scottish Picasso. Cubism was the school he favored. Holding out a rusty piton he placed two sugar cubes thereupon, slowly dipping them into the greenish brew. Movingly he spoke of the apocalyptic moment when he could feel the cubes melting.

"See, Moira, them melting into...nothing. Gotterdaemmerung!" he whispered in the flickering half-light of the candle-lit tent. It was just beginning to strike me that I might be camping with a nutter when he laughed and threw back his lock of hair, cackling, "Och so," with an air of finality.

The new subject to entertain us was the weather, something you can't avoid in a tent. The rosy Alpenglow of our sunset with pink clouds lazily scudding past was gone. Inside was damper and colder; clamminess seeped into the tent as we tried to stop shivering in our sleeping bags. Pitter-patter on the roof came the first droplets of rain.

"Could have to come down a grade or two, Moira. This rock's hellish when it's wet."

"Hm," I muttered sleepily, not really relishing climbing in the rain.

"Och, it's all good training for the Eiger," said the master, turning his face to the tent wall for a good belch. The comparison made me even less keen, the north face of the Eiger being a by-word for mountaineering suicide. In passing I noted that the Eiger in Switzerland was the only exception to his embargo on all matters non-Scottish.

The rain outside was now lashing down. Not realizing that tent fabric gave a loudspeaker effect, I panicked. The sound of drumming rose till it felt as if a thousand machine guns were hitting the tent roof, while the groundsheet underfoot began to bubble and seep ominously from the sodden ground. Being Latin by birth and a Celt by upbringing, I possess an unusually lively imagination. In the background the burn in spate roared as if a dam upstream had exploded. We would be trapped like rats in this tent. I turned in agitation to my partner but he was sleeping the sleep of the just. By the beatific look on his face he must in his dreams have reached the summit of the Eiger.

In my mind's eye I saw the Buttermilk Burn rising and bursting its banks. In the ensuing torrent we would all be swept down—tent, ropes, sleeping bags and us tumbling and rolling down the hillside till we perished in the murky waters of Loch Long. Perhaps it would be weeks before my wraith-like corpse emerged, with my silky black tresses waving about like seaweed thrown up onto dry land by the bus shelter in Arrochar. A shocked crowd would gather round this harrowing scene, and there right in the midst would be the bus conductor. "Aye, I recognize her, officer. She was carrying a Ranger's rope. Ah kennt in ma bones she wid come to a bad end." Yes, he was a Celtic supporter after all.

I shrieked and clung to Jamie for support. He, thinking he had come out double tops—the Eiger and this—responded enthusiastically. Madonna, but they are all alike, I thought as his cold hands started plunging into my sleeping bag.

"The rain," I wailed. "Won't it wash the tent away?"

"No. Whit's a wee bit Highland downpour to men of the mountains, and to women, too," he added somewhat feebly for my benefit.

"Do you mean we'll be all right?"

"Moira, this tent has stood up to the worst weather Ben Nevis could throw at it," he spoke soothingly. "It won't even notice a wee shower down here. I mean, it's the Southern Highlands. We're practically in England."

"Well, okay, if you're sure. In that case would you mind warming your hands in your own sleeping bag?"

"Oh that's where they are! No, sorry, Moira—not at all."

Thus comforted, I went back to the semi-doze that passes for sleeping in a wet tent. I fell away into slumber, but my nightmare tumble down the Buttermilk Burn kept on intruding. I surfaced to find my knickers wet, and my sleeping bag sopping. Grabbing a torch I saw I was lying in an ever-expanding puddle. Above me a constant dribble of rainfall, penetrating the tent-fabric, looked in the torchlight like a liquid stalactite. His side, I noticed, was bone dry. I punched the man of the mountains in the ribs.

"Come on, move over. Let me get some dry." Mamma

mia but he could sleep.

At the second thump: "Whit's up? Moira, pull that rope tight!"

Third time, lucky, he groaned, "What did you wake me up for?"

"What did I wake you up for? How could you go on sleeping when I am soaked through? Feel my sleeping bag. It's sopping. Now be a gentleman and get out of your pit and let me have it."

"But that means I will get soaked and start shivering just like you."

That was true. I had blue and purple blotches all over and my teeth were chattering. My blouse top must be clinging to my body lasciviously from what I could see of the awakening gleam in his eye. My knickers were wringing. I was ready to cry.

"There is a way out."

"Oh, yea."

"Come into my sleeping bag with me. There's room enough for two and we'll baith get warm."

I was so stunned as to be almost speechless, but not for long.

"What do you take me for?"

"A sensible girl. Besides, there's no alternative." He was right. The dry area of the tent could just about be covered by one sleeping bag.

I thought briefly of Miss MacPherson's story of the Spartan boy who stole a pet fox from his neighbor's garden.

He had just managed to stuff it down the front of his toga when he was waylaid by the neighbor, who in all innocence chatted to him about the weather and how you could not rely on the Helots any more. The boy, polite as all Spartans were, responded equably—that is until he fell down dead. The neighbor, opening the boy's toga, discovered that the fox, impatient for his dinner, had eaten the lad's chest away. Full of remorse, the old gossip said that he could have had the fox as a pet if only he had asked him. That was not the point of course and Miss MacPherson, after narrating the fable, urged us to be as tough as Spartans in defending the good name of our school and ourselves.

This all flashed through my mind in an instant. All the while Jamie's eyes were afire with what I used to think was his Ben Nevis look but now recognized as common or garden lust. Not for the last time I realized Esme was a sound philosopher. Jamie saw that I was teetering on the brink of rejecting Miss MacPherson and my upbringing.

"You know, W.D. Mornay says that in situations where survival is in doubt, childish whims and taboos must be thrust aside, and it is your duty to cuddle together as the Spartans did in their winter bivouacs on Mount Hymettos."

Was he a mind reader? As far as mountains went, Mornay was Moses in our circles. It was the first time in my life I had to reconcile a conflict between the mountaineer's philosophy and the lofty values of Lauriston. Sometimes, as the great expeditioneer Liam Bonus once said, it is too cold for ethics.

I climbed into his sleeping bag. Almost immediately his hands were running around like hot ferrets. You may think it is impossible to enjoy the fullness of love's ardour in this position. Well, it's difficult but not impossible, as Jamie set out to demonstrate.

"But remember your training for the Eiger," I pleaded as I felt him maneuvering into a thrusting position.

"Even an Eiger Tiger must unwind sometimes." He had managed to roll my knickers to the thickness of a Hoover elastic band so that they were now just under my bum bone, and sounded as if he were attacking the crux of a more than usually desperate climb.

"C'mon, Moira," he growled. I was in despair. One last snatch would hurtle my undies on their downward path, leaving me naked to frontal assault. "What about some Spartan comforts?"

"No, you will get arthritis in your prodder." I knew it was in vain. In this mood he was not going to worry about the dampness of my clothes. There were three steps before he could execute the coup de sabre. First was the knickers to ankle tug, second the scissors-opening of my thighs, and finally the Open Sesame as he prodded my gates of heaven.

There was a squelching sound followed by a rip as my flimsy panties were torn away. Now I had no defense against the evil moment. "Please, Jamie," I wailed, pleading for mercy. "I am not that kind of girl."

"You will be," he promised determinedly, his knees wriggling and pumping like pneumatic drills as he prized my legs apart.

"But I'm a good Catholic."

"That's okay. My granny was one, once," he gasped, lusty hot breath coming out like a sprinter.

"Oh Mary, Mother of God. Help me! Now!" I prayed, feeling a warm sturdy implement poking me down below. I wondered idly if our priest, Father Doherty, would confess me. Was rape a venal sin for the victim in a single sleeping bag? Had the church met this dilemma before? I could feel a distinct tickling now as it traversed my underside, searching, exploring.

In a token of graceful surrender I put my hands on my head, just about to ask him to go gently with me, when my hands chanced upon the answer to my prayers, the Scottish virgin's last line of defense—a Kirby grip! He drew himself back, priming the homing shot. So, no time to waste. I jabbed the Kirby grip straight into his rump.

"Aagh!" he yelped, even more loudly than my most joyous expectation, his lust-crazed eyes registering acute pain. The sogginess made the sleeping bag's fabric no defense. Once again fortune was on my side. The sharp implement was no longer so hard. I gave him a jab in the other cheek to ram the message home. He sprang backwards as far as the sleeping bag would let him. There was now only a soft little worm lying on my tummy.

"Please stop it, Moira. You know I wouldna try anything wi' a lassie like you." He sounded like a wee laddie caught out by teacher.

"Well, just don't forget. If you try anything—anything at all—you know what you'll get. Now, let me sleep!"

Sleep was of course impossible in this writhing python of a sleeping bag. It took him about two minutes to forget, slightly longer than most men of my acquaintance. His fingers were soon curling round my erogenous zones. Mercilessly and with renewed vigor I recommenced jabbing his rump. So much so that he later complained it looked like a pepper pot. I warned him that I would not cease while his hands were anywhere near the isosceles triangle formed by the aforementioned hot spots. As it was virtually impossible to put his hands anywhere else, he had to take them out of the bag to use as paddles in the ever-growing stream surrounding us. His other more vital organ of assault had its ardour dampened by proximity to my soggy fragment of knicker.

The dawn we eventually did greet was no more than a greyish continuation of the night. The rain was here to stay. I had no appetite and refused his offer of porridge, having heard too many jests about his porridge being specially designed to keep the English invader at bay.

We packed quickly. I hauled a couple of pegs out and watched the once-proud tent that had withstood all that the Ben could throw at it collapse into a miserable heap. It was slung anyhow on top of Jamie's rucksack. As we squelched down the hill to the bus shelter I was dreading what must come next. However, our bus conductor did not even bother to examine our shredded tickets. Almost with pity he said, "Aye, Lassie you're gey drookit," pressed the bell, and we were homeward bound.

When we got off the bus I heard him say to the old dears who sat at the front, "Some lassies never learn, no matter whit their mithers tell them." He must have been older than he looked.

Chapter 7

Getting Off at Haymarket

"Our wild mountain flower has turned into a wet lettuce."

Dad was less than sympathetic the next day when I sniffled my way around the house. Going to work was an impossibility, and I needed to stay away from Meikle, who was now showing unmistakable signs of taking a fancy to me. A day lounging about and then another morning in bed was all it took to make me feel myself again, and so Dad's suggestion that I help out in the restaurant was not unwelcome. The hot and steamy atmosphere would soon sweat the cold out of me; more to the point it would give me an opportunity to have a blether about my adventures to Esme.

I found my friend slapping out the fish suppers into yesterday's Sunday Post. Esme usually had one quip to amuse the regulars. Today it was: "Mind ye eat your supper afore ye read it." In fish and chip terms, supper was a moveable feast eaten at any time of day or night. There was little danger of our stalwarts letting their fish grow cold, as they would have read about Oor Wullie's escapades with his bucket the day before, while the print was still fresh.

While she was handling public relations, I was ladling out heaps of snow-white chips into the boiling fat at the back. It was hot work and I was looking forward to my break. Of course this night had to be very busy, and when we did get our first break, the part-timer Bella was monopolizing Esme so I could only get a brief word in. As this consisted of asking for more milk in my tea, it was hard to conceal my irritation at the unsatisfactory nature of the conversation. They were talking about beehive hairstyles, a fashion all the rage at the Palais. Despite Bella's insistent championship, Esme refused to become a la mode.

"Ahm no pitting lacquer all over my hair. It attracts wasps." This was not a reference to the shape, but to the legend that hair lacquer was a wasp's delicacy. I was glad that she would not budge, as she had fine, shiny black hair tricked up at her shoulders with a fringe over her brow, perennially old-fashioned but always pretty.

At long last we shut up shop. Esme slumped into her chair and said, "Well, I'm glad that's o'er." She lit a cigarette. "Now, and how did your weekend go?" The bit about the climbing I knew would not interest her so I skipped over it. She asked a token question purely out of politeness, but when I was in danger of going on too long with details of the ascent, she said impatiently, "Come on, what aboot this fella?"

When I told her about sharing the tent with him, she shook her head and poked the finger of her smoking hand at me. "It's a waste of time warnin' ye." However, I was brought back into favor when I told her about the Virgin's protection.

"I can see you're no needing any lessons frae me. I like a lassie that can handle hersel'." Esme knew how highly I guarded my honour, and admired the fighting spirit I had shown in its defense. Though there was a thrust. "Getting intae his sleeping bag. If you wasnae the boss's daughter I'd call ye a wee hairy."

But she was in an expansive mood. After plucking a stubbed fag from the top of her ear—placed there earlier in the pursuit of hygiene—she began to tell me several stories of how she herself had outfaced the villains in her neighborhood. I may have given the impression that our conversation was always lighthearted, but this was not so. Some of her tales horrified and appalled me. The life she led was often brutal, and on numerous occasions she had been the object of violence just for the sake of emptying her purse of its pitiful wages. The huge housing estates where she and her kind lived were bleak and squalid, the people's grim lives being punctuated by ill health and the dubious leisure of unemployment. To middle-class Edinburgh they were another country, unknown, to be driven past quickly on the way to refined resorts like Gullane and North Berwick.

She had long ago said farewell to her virginity and

showed no great grief about its departure. The culprit was the local door-to-door purveyor of mineral waters—the "juice-man" as he was called in Craig Milton, her particular purlieu. She was fifteen at the time and had been wooed in a pub, which I found surprising. "He took me oot behind the pub and had me up against the wall in somebody's back green. That's when I had my first fag." That seemed to be of more consequence than losing her maidenhood. "I had one in the pub to stop me shaking when I realized what we were gaun to do. Then one after. That was great. I felt awfy relaxed. It was just like in the pictures."

"What, the—"

"Naw," she laughed, "the fag afterwards."

"Did you ever go out with him again?"

"Naw, his teeth were rotten with all the juice he knocked, and he had a windy belly, but sometimes when I hae a fag I think of him. Course he'll be auld by noo." She looked at her tiny fag end. She smoked them to the last molecule of tobacco. Her eyes glazed over tenderly. "Aye, whit a night that was," she sighed.

You could see the spot from her kitchenette window. It was hardly my idea of a romantic arbor. Broken bedsteads and old pram wheels filched by aspirant guider mechanics strewed the ground, while semi-feral Alsatians roamed the long yellow grass that belied its name of back green, staking out their territory by emptying out their bladder and bowels wherever they decided to place a frontier post.

"But weren't you worried that the pop man might

make your tummy go pop?"

"No, Ahm no sae daft as that. I made sure he got aff at Haymarket."

"Beg your pardon?"

I was not sure of the reference. It was notorious that main line trains from the south always had an irritating stop at the small station of Haymarket before coming to rest at the main terminus, Waverley. But what had that got to do with anything? Esme stopped at my incomprehension. She had the habit of ending every chunk of words spoken with a sharp "Ken!" short for "Ken what I mean?" except that it was not used by her to ensure meaning but for emphasis or punctuation, a verbal full stop.

She said it now: "Ken!" And then, "Ken?" more quietly and with growing realization that I had not the faintest idea of what she was talking about. It had never dawned on her that I would not recognize the colorful Edinburgh metaphor for coitus interruptus—that Moira Fiorelli, the well-groomed and extravagantly educated heiress to a chip shop fortune, knew nothing about life, not even this elementary and somewhat risky method of contraception. With many a "Ken" and not a few "Ken whit I mean"s, Esme patiently took it upon herself to broaden the basis of my education.

As to my ignorance, like every other maiden I suppose I had speculated about the particular nature of this form of interpersonal relationship. Of course the subject was avoided as an embarrassment in all middle-class households, so I didn't have many reliable facts to go upon. I remembered a very uncomfortable moment when I asked Mamma what "conception" meant. The word had been chanced upon in a Reader's Digest article.

"Well, it's when married couples..." Her pinkie did a little dance in the air as a stand-in for her too-embarrassed voice box, and there you have the sum total of my sex education.

Sometime later Rosie and I were giggling together over a bride-to-be's handbook, where we learnt that this supreme moment of love, the explosion of bliss and ecstasy that is called the orgasm, was akin to a sneeze. *In Every Bride's Bottom Drawer*, as the book modestly called itself, described it thus: "Then comes the moment. You have been putting it off for so long. You say no to your body. You can put it off no longer. Now it is building up inside you. Your whole self feels taut with desire. Inside you an ever more wonderful, irresistible force is up against an immovable languor. You look up to the sun for inspiration. Suddenly there comes a great nerve tingling explosion inside you. 'Aah-ti-shoo!' It bursts all around you. Luckily you have your lovely lavender filled lace handkerchief at hand, just for such an occasion."

I looked at Rosie. All that fuss—unbridled passion and so forth—we had been reading adult romances for further clues. "All that just for a snivel?" Rosie said. "Possibly that's why unmarried maids in Tudor times used to wear low-cut dresses." She put a hand like a shelf under her own green apples, as if to show me. "You know, décolletage, so that they could have colds and sneezes." She could be quite clever at times. "And not miss out on the fun."

I was not convinced. There must be more to it than that. Also this getting off at Haymarket did not sound too much of a frolic, a bit like the cake stand being snatched off the table just when your hand is stretched out for a scrumptious Clermiston Pride. I am sure I would be tempted to grab one as they were borne away.

When I got home after my lecture from Esme there was a message to phone Rosie. It was late, but I couldn't wait to tell Rosie my account of the weekend before a more disreputable version made the rounds.

"Okay." I was puzzled. Why was she not asking the obvious question? I was not left long in the dark.

"All Edinburgh knows about the mad virgin of the rocks. Jamie's been off work with blood poisoning of the bum. He's going to sue you for loss of seating power." I was pleased to hear it. "Anyway, enough of that," she continued. "Some of us wondered if you fancied going ice-skating."

"All right, where do I get off the bus?"

She was bewildered by this. There were two ice rinks in Edinburgh, one at Murrayfield and one at Haymarket, but the one at Murrayfield was not for us. "You know. Where do you think? You get off at Haymarket."

She could not understand why I collapsed with laughter. I had to end our chat before she got really angry. Would I be able to tell her in the presence of others? I thought not.

Chapter 8

Pals

"She looks like a French hoor!"

Allow me to introduce brother Freddie, my diametrical opposite (not to put too fine a point on it), a blissfully uncultured ignoramus. Not that it did him much harm, for he applied himself to life, while I dithered around its edges. Together with some of our cousins, he had ventured into the amusement arcade business. They made a bomb. On their days off they used to dress like gangsters out of a bad movie. Thus attired, they were at their happiest splashing money about like big shots. As I was often broke I am proud to say that I was never too humble to reject any largesse that came my way.

"You want to get yourself a boyfriend that's going somewhere instead of these no-hopers you drag home." This standard little big-brother lecture was a small price to pay for his subventions.

Tonight I was going out with a champion no-hoper, Jamie "Och So." I was not living dangerously as might be thought. After the Cobbler weekend Jamie had the mother of all colds. His image as a hard man took a beating when he snuffled in with dewdrops dripping into his beer. Being full of health, I knew I had drawn his sting. Feminists may blanch at my easy acceptance of the events on the Cobbler. From what I had heard from Esme and other sources all men were like that—an opinion I held then and which I have had no cause to alter in the interim. Like all men I was attracted by, he was a multifaceted character. Tonight he was a beatnik and we were going to try one of his cool, cool haunts of midnight jazz.

Freddie's jibe was not too far off the mark. I wore a contour-hugging, midnight-black straight skirt that matched the broad black-and-white stripes of my French Matelote jumper, crowning my outfit with a black beret (set at what I hoped was a seductive angle) and earrings big enough to moor a pirate ship. I did not quite have the nerve to use a cigarette holder, but for the first and last time in my life smoked an untipped Gauloise to complete my act.

The hall that we entered normally functioned as The Deep Sea Mission for Distressed Fisherfolk. Now it was packed full of earnest young men reminding me of nothing less than monks at prayer. The faintly moldy smell of Davy Jones' Locker was drowned by the fragrance of what I surmised were herbal cigarettes. Dimly perceived through a fog of swirling smoke, the stage seemed to hang on an astral plane. Jamie was beside himself muttering, "Och dig it man," as if in an incantation. With all the excitement around I could not help feeling all tingly in my stomach, knowing that something extra nice was about to happen.

The first group came on dressed in the standard gear of the Dixieland swell—straw-boaters, spotted dickeys, striped shirts and zany trousers. An affectionate mixture of catcalls, laughter and applause greeted their entrance, signaling a familiarity and friendship between audience and band that augured well for the evening.

After a quick fanfare and a mild joke by the leader, they dispensed with the introductions and were off into their first number. I find it difficult to describe anything in musical terms, but Jamie assured me it was a "real foot stomper." It had the right blend of high-pitched noises, hoots and hollers thrown together in a discordant melody to qualify as hot jazz. The next item was described as real cool and mellow, and certainly the screeching was pitched at a softer level. At the end of each tune the audience went into ecstasies. The Ben Nevis look came into Jamie's eyes but glowing more softly and dreamily than on that other occasion. Watching the band, who had obviously gone to some trouble to polish their dance routine, was entertaining. At given moments the two right flankers pogoed forward to the front of the stage, raised their instruments in salute to the audience, then pogoed back into line, whereupon the left flankers did likewise. During the virtuoso passages the trumpeters waved their trumpets in the air, playing to the heavens above, while the saxophonist, imitating a guardsman marking time, blew his cheeks out and bent over backwards like a mad limbo dancer. On reaching orgasm the whole band stopped and lifted their boaters to reveal a line of freshly mown flat-tops.

It's always good to have a new cultural experience. Anyway, Jamie's bliss more than made up for my moderate pleasure. On the bus home Jamie put his head in his hands and leant over his knees. I asked him if he was going to be sick as he had celebrated after the concert on several pints of heavy. I had only two half-pints of lager in case you were wondering.

"Och no, Lassie, I was just thinking of yon trombone solo in the second half. Och it was too cool, hot-diggity baby." I can't remember all the technical gibberish he used here, so I just made that up. He went on for some time in the same prayerful posture, attempting to recapture those magical moments. Now I don't mind anyone's enjoyment of harmless pleasure, and it was really good to see Jamie so happy. However, the bus was carrying its usual Saturday night contingent of drunken kielies in celebratory mood, Hibs having at last won a match. Jamie's happy moaning and occasional, "Och, cool, baby, get that bit and that," was beginning to draw their attention.

"Yes, Jamie, it was real cool," I coaxed, vainly hoping to calm him down.

Then, "I never felt so hep since the last Clyde Valley Stompers Concert" was followed by a short and not unmusical trombone impression with an added mime accompaniment. This last gave him the spotlight. For a fraction of a second the whole top deck of the bus went quiet, then the dozy half-baffled looks on the faces of our co-passengers gradually changed into grins. No longer were they listlessly staring at the window or floor. Here was an opportunity for mischief, and with luck a spot of violence might be thrown in for good measure.

It did not take long. A short virtuoso passage on the saxophone emanated from my renaissance-figure boyfriend, and with each riff the Teds brightened as if awakened by some indecorous muse. Their chief was a large and scruffy Ted, who up till now had most of his face in a large bag of chips. I often wondered how they kept their hair so greasy. With a sidelong glance at his mates he bawled out, "Hey, Johnny Ray, gies that bit again." This sally was greeted with roars of laughter. They were so ignorant that they thought Johnny Ray, a now passé figure, a jazzman.

"Come on, you students, let's hear you then!" This was as about as friendly as the Romans calling to the Christians in the Coliseum. Jamie looked at them dumbly, his fingers still and silent over their slide trombone. I knew we were in for trouble. Calling us students was their synonym for a snob. I was not a student and Jamie was certainly no snob, but to their drink-crazed minds we were the class enemy. "C'mon, Jimmy, gies it again!" A very definite edge had crept into their jollity.

"Get on wi'it! Whit are ye waitin' for? Hearts tae score a goal?" This rhetorical question was a threat, no mistake. In reply Jamie just stared, his face agape like a rabbit stuck in a car's headlights.

"Listen, woof-woof. Do you want your stuck-up face splattered?"

Nervously Jamie replied, "No thanks." For some reason, his voice left its proletarian home, and took on the air of rectitude of a Morningside madam. It was the proverbial red rag to a bull.

"Watch it, pal," they chorused, waving a phalanx of angry fingers at him; so quickly had it turned ugly.

In a misguided attempt to placate them, Jamie said, "Yeah, okay then, mate."

For some reason this did it, and if you have seen anything more nasty than a Scot with a huge inferiority complex, please tell me. There were about ten of them hurling a chorus of abuse at us. I was now as terrified as my boyfriend.

One of the greasily quiffed Ted lieutenants came up to Jamie, poked him in the chest, and, sticking his face next to him, said, "Listen, pal." It was the word "pal" that made me stiffen, a clear signal that violence is imminent, a time to guard your collar, as head-banging is about to commence.

"You'd be'er no gie that patter when big Tam Gow's here," continued the self-appointed spokesman against the baying background. This indication that they were on first-name terms with Edinburgh's most notorious razor slasher had me, at least, shivering in my seat. Jamie was literally quaking. Up till now I had only seen fear enacted in war films and Westerns. One look at Jamie's face told me that they had been underacting. His normal, healthy pallor was now milk white, while his legs were practically knocking me off the seat. The greasy leader now approached us after ostentatiously punching his chip packet a la shuttlecock down the aisle of the bus.

These were real hoods. One look at their dullard faces showed there was not a scrap of mercy to be found there. They were looking for a fight and a spot of villainy. Cold blocks of ice were being manufactured in my stomach. Looking at these faces full of evil intent, I felt real fear. The greaser (even at this juncture I could not help noticing a particle of chip nestling in his quaff) started fingering my jersey.

"She's quite bonnie for a stuck up snob." Past him one of his henchmen slowly raked his hair with a comb that had a stiletto-sharpened handle in a manner designed to intimidate. I looked at Jamie, pleading. My heart sank even further. There was no help coming from that quarter. Jamie looked as if he was committing urgent business in the toilet. The lout's hand slid down onto my palpitating breasts.

"You're shakin'. Hauld still, while I get a haud of your cans." He was breathing right in my face. Porca Miseria, why do they put pickled onions on their chips? "Ah can tell you're raj for a spot of shaftin' by Pilton Man."

In the background I could hear his cohorts egging him on. "Go on, Tam, gie her it! Gie her it right up tae the tonsils, Tam!"

"Crivens I've got a jake on," exclaimed Tam. "Jings! It's steamin' ma breeks!" I looked, and so it was!

In that long instant of horror I looked into his face. It was that of an animal, pure and rampant. At this the worst moment of my life, my gallant escort was slowly slithering under the seat. There was an odd smell coming from his corner, while fear like a clammy hand clawed at my stomach.

"How dare you!" A voice came from nowhere, or rather from the rear of the bus, where a group of middle-class citizenry was engrossed in studying the darkness outside.

"How dare you! You, you savage!" Every word clear, pure porcelain; Wedgewood to their common clay. "How dare you sully this young lady!" Help was at hand in the ringing clarion call of the manse. Everyone stopped and looked at the back of the bus. No one had noticed the little old lady sitting there, now stirring to her feet. Even the savage paused in mid-grope, his hand resting on the upper slope of my bosom. God knows what she was doing there up on the top deck of the bus at midnight on a drunken Saturday night, and who cares? Probably she had been at a scripture-reading meeting making tea for the minister. She was all of five feet tall, bent with arthritis, frail, her grey coat matching her hair, thick spectacles and a fur hat that you just knew her cat curled up to sleep in at night. The stick that she raised aloft shook, but not with fear. The fire of battle gleamed behind the old grey spectacles. This was the spirit that had held the line at Bannockburn. She was not to be gainsaid.

I will say this for the Teds, they knew defeat when they saw it. She cried, "Get back where you belong! How dare you even look at a nice girl like this?" She was a good judge of character as well, while Pilton Man and his Neanderthal chums started to quail under the lashing tongue of Edinburgh spinsterdom.

"Michty me, we were only haeing a bit of fun wi' the lassie," he whinged. "Listen, Darlin'."

These were the last words he spoke. For this singular piece of impertinence the old lady tottered towards the bow of the bus, holding her cane as if it was the great broadsword of her moss-trooper ancestors, eyes glinting like The Black Douglas. One look at them told you why the English never conquered our indomitable land. The Ted was quick off the mark mind you—down the stairs and off the bus before the piece of stout oak finished its downward trajectory. His pals were fighting each other on the stairs to get away from this true daughter of Old Scotia, while she was laying them on like Wallace Straiks.

All that was left was the most innocuous of the Teds, who had got left behind in the fleeing horde. It was so obviously someone's wee brother, brought along as an apprentice hooligan. He was shrieking as the blows rained down on him. "Michty me! Help! Help ma Boab!"

She was exultant, singing as she whacked, "Lock the door Lauriston." Could this be an old school-tie rescue?

"Dinna leave me like this, Tam! Get my mither please, Tam."

But Tam was far, too far away—haring down Saughtonhall Avenue—to pay any heed to his cries, possibly in training for the District heats.

At long last the conductor came up the stairs, "To see what all the trouble's aboot." He beheld the spanking with a bored and sleepy eye. Life held no further mysteries and excitement for him—he who had seen it all before. He pressed the bell to stop the bus and the bottom-holding novice thug went shrieking off into the night.

I was weeping floods of tears, hardly able to catch my breath for crying. The old lady was holding me in her arms, patting me on the head and shoulder saying, "Never mind, never mind, my puir wee lamb. It's all over now and you were very brave." This coming from one who had the heart of a lioness. "Not like someone else I could point out." She turned and looked at my escort.

This someone else was skulking shamefacedly beside me on the seat. "I was trying to get at them but I was trapped in my seat." This totally unconvincing lie was not even worth sneering at. I could not be bothered with him. All I could think of at that moment was that if folk knew what went on in their buses at night there wouldn't be any need for television sets.

Chapter 9

The Sun Sets on "Och So"

Och So's reign as consort was coming to an end. This he knew, and so was desperately trying to exert himself to keep me amused. Looking back I can never find what I saw in him. But we always say that, don't we? He was not even handsome, so he never had any chance in the sleeping bag. To be frank I retained him because there was no one else in the offing. Whenever I looked at him he could see his fate in my eyes, and got nothing more than a brief peck on the cheek as a tip at the end of the evening. Attempted rape topped by arrant cowardice was no high recommendation for a suitor.

In the end I agreed to go to Traprain Law that Sunday with him. On Saturday it was all hands to the fish fryers. There was a big box-office attraction at the pictures, and Dad expected queues right round the Billiard Hall next door. In the end it was elbows on the counter waiting for the lonely drunk on the horizon to stagger up for his fish supper.

"Lots o' pickled onion and vinegar, hen. That aye fools the wife. Ta, darlin', you're smashin'."

His wife would have to be gey daft to be fooled by that, I thought as he keeled over at the doorstep, the lovingly pre-pared fish supper splattered all over the pavement. No doubt the dogs would enjoy it.

Inexplicably it had been one of those quiet spells that even the best-managed business ventures have to ride out every once in a while. No one that night had any stomach for battered cod and drooling mince pies. Even Esme had little solace for me to make up for the evening's failure.

"Ye should hae given up yon puir laddie, yonks ago. Yer just ta'en a len o'him. Him paying for all those Beetho-ven and Jimmy Shand concerts. You're nothin' but a gold digger, Moira Fiorelli." To the last, Esme failed to distin-guish between the classical and jazz musical genres.

"Well, it's the same type of folk goes to them." She was right again though, but what was worse in her opinion was that I didn't even fancy him.

"It's just like chucking aff auld claes tae ye. See's how you like it when it happens tae ye." I did and I didn't, but more of that later. And then, her valedictory envoi: "Get yer-sel' a real man that'll drag ye roon by the hair—a Rock Hud-son, no this Jerry Lewis."

Well, it was to be Jamie's last outing.

With time on my hands I fell to musing about our ven-ue for tomorrow, Traprain Law, that flawed gem of a hillock about thirty miles east of the city, whose south face held impeccable climbing on sharply planed, rectangular planks of rock. There were two cliffs about a hundred yards apart. Both of them were subdued—merging with, not standing out from, the hillside—as if they realized they were well-bred Edinburgh cliffs. Here there were no brash excrescences, no spiky, extravert flakes, and no treacherous gullies to trap those unwary in descent. The holds were tiny flakes that required you to edge up the slab, so minute that after a while your clinging fingertips began to burn and sting, giving rise to a complaint known to the cognoscenti as Traprain fingers.

Buried treasure had been found on the summit—magnificent silverware hidden there—filched from the embers of the dying Roman Empire. The hill was the tribal capital of the Votadini, who allied themselves to Rome after the battle of Mons Graupius. I wondered if, long ago in that pre-Scottish past, there had been a legionary Fiorelli who had come to this spot to parley with the local Celtic chieftain.

In a field adjacent to the crag, there was an old standing stone. I had often passed it without giving it any attention, until I discovered a magazine article about the megalith. It was named the Loth Stone after the king, who was founder of the concept called Lothian way back in the Dark Ages. A tribal youth was having hanky-panky with Loth's daughter, with the inevitable result in those days before scientific contraception. "Mildly embarrassing" was how the author described the ensuing bulge. How would you guess it was written by a man? Anyway, to avoid Loth finding out about the mild pickle, the youth shot him with an arrow on the spot where the stone now stands, a testament to embarrassment averted; a bit radical perhaps, but there you are. I tend to take history's lessons personally, and resolved never to give Cupid opportunity to draw back that particular bow.

One final pleasure: sitting on a stance and taking up the rope of your partner on the crag, you can look away to the distant, hazy, rolling hills that lay across the plain to the south where once warbled Lucia Di Lammermuir. If the sun was shining as it often was, and if your partner was slow as he often was, you could sing to yourself the whole of the mad scene with little fear of embarrassment, mild or otherwise.

I opened the curtains to another fine day. Downstairs I could hear Dad singing. Today was to be his twenty-fifth ascent of Tinto, a little pudding of a hill about twenty miles south of Edinburgh, which he had made his personal Everest. A wee celebration was planned on the summit with a larger one later. I hurriedly readied myself, as Jamie would be calling soon. Dad asked me to join him in the duet from The Pearl Fishers, but I could only give him five minutes, as outside Jamie's motorbike was already throbbing and ba-rooming.

I shoveled some food down, and in what seemed minutes we were leaving the city behind and heading for the plain of East Lothian. I love this fresh open countryside with its black earth. Like southern England, I used to think. But where in crowded Kent or Sussex do you have the same cold, sharp breath off the sea amongst lovely rich farmland. Now we were passing through the neat and pretty village, which once again had won the competition for the best-kept village of East Lothian. So I could safely say, "Sweet Haddington, loveliest village of the Lothian Plain." And moments later we were hurtling through the deceptively sharp-cornered country lanes beyond the village. Soon Traprain Law, my best-loved crag in miniature, emerged in the May sunshine. I wondered if the historical symbolism of Celt meeting Latin had any message in store for me. Would I, the undoubted descendent of the Roman legionaries, be confronted with a rude Celt and have my treasure stolen?

We parked and passed by the Loth Stone with its awful warning of lovers' follies. From a distance the crag seemed to be carrying more than its normal complement of climbers. Arriving at the base of the cliff, we could see that it was awash with Glaswegians far away from their normal hunting grounds. We moved from the east to the west crag, but even here there was a brace of them hopping up and down the crag, all jabbering away in their incomprehensible lingo. The only phrase that I could make out of their Doric was the continual "Hauf-covered, hauf-covered, gies a hauf-covered."

Several climbers were shouting this at once. As they were all occupied on the cliff, I assumed it must be some new-fangled piece of climbing gear that had passed me by. That is until I saw their seconds reach into their sacs, break open a packet of chocolate biscuits and throw one up the cliff to be smartly caught by the peckish leader. Half-covered, that's a neat description, I thought, a bit envious. You see, in one small but strange way it was we who had an inferiority complex towards the west-coasters. That was because the Sunday Post—our arbiter of culture, a vox pop Scottish Castiglione—reflected the tastes, habits and vocabulary of the city on the Clyde, and not the capital. The envy survived only a minute, when I realized that I had never seen a whole chocolate-covered digestive. Have you?

Wandering about amongst them was a tall slim figure strangely dressed in a Teddy Boy drape jacket and winkle-picker shoes. The abundant quiff that completed his D.A. hairstyle bounced with vitality. Teds were well-dated by now, but this man did not look the type to be left behind in wake of fashion. He carried himself with a stamp of authority that seemed to say that his style was style itself, and no heed taken of the whims of ephemeral fads. At this point he turned around, and I recognized the lecher Mick of Eddie's party.

He looked at me as if he was about to scratch his head quizzically but couldn't quite be bothered. I saved him the trouble by stepping up to him and said, "Party, Glasgow."

"Ah yea, I was thinking you might be one of my exes." For just a second it looked again as if his hand would travel headwards.

"Eddie McCann's place. I'm his cousin."

"Yes, Eddie née Enzo Cannelotti, the ice cream baron. 'The cream that you Cann taste.'" This must have been one of Eddie's more recent excursions into literary inspiration. Of course this leftover Ted hadn't remembered me from Eve. I felt it was about time to pull him down a peg or two. He seemed to be so sure of his right to be here.

"My name's Moira—what's yours?"

"Dermot."

"Well, Dermot, I think you passed the Palais thirty miles back."

"Oh whit a shame. No, I'm partial to a bittie fresh air and exercise; clear the tubes, ye ken. I brought the boys here. They hoped I might fancy a new hobby." This was a fiction. He was a superb climber and would remain so until...

"I see, and how did you bring that coach party of yours?" He pointed to a dingy vehicle that up till now I had assumed had been abandoned. This abiding uninterest in cars was another affectation of his.

We drifted away from each other quite casually as one often does at the foot of crags, and I roped up with the Eiger-taming Jamie, who led off up a quite modest climb, upon which he was soon thrashing and frutching about in a horribly shaming manner. Some of the Glaswegians were beginning to smirk. I had no doubt that within about a minute they would be exercising their wit on my mountain Picasso.

Just a few feet away, Dermot launched himself at the rock. It took just a moment to realize that he lived in a different league. In my cloistered and somewhat traditional climbing environment I had never seen anyone climb with such grace or elan. The others were good, but his simian friends could never match him with their pulling and swinging style of ascent. As he padded up the slab as lithe and soft as a dancing panther, all eyes were on him. This spellbinding action lasted only a minute; he moved so swiftly up the slab to a niche under the crucial overhang. Attention now returned to my partner, whose legs at that moment were going like a manic windmill.

"Get your fingers out of your ears." This not very helpful piece of advice was laughed up the crag to Jamie, who had elbows, knees, chin, every possible and impossible protuberance of his body in desperate contact with the rock.

Noticing the attention was being taken away from himself, Dermot turned to his followers and said, "I see I must take up this climbing game." It took him just that fraction of a second to forget that his winkle-pickers were not an adhesive rock boot. He slipped down from his niche, banged his shoulder against the slab and landed with a heavy thump. He fell all of twenty feet, and I am ashamed to say I laughed, seeing Humpty fall to the ground.

Immediately his associates were around him. Holding his right shoulder awkwardly, he was obviously in pain and, equally obvious, his code wouldn't allow it to show. His lips must have been bleeding trying to hide it.

"Listen lads, you carry on climbing. I'm awa for a wee donner roond the hill."

He walked away, just far enough so he could suffer the pain in peace, and sat down on a boulder. From the way he was hunched, it was evident how much pain he was in.

There was a scuffling and sliding noise behind me as Jamie effected a retreat. Taking off my rope in disgust, I told him to coil it himself. I was going to have my lunch.

Before opening my haversack I looked over to the boulder where Dermot was swaying back and forward in agony. He ought to see a doctor, I thought, but perhaps in the meantime some hot sweet tea would do him good.

"Jamie, I'm going to see if that bloke's all right."

I took the flask out of our sac and walked the short distance over the sheep's path to where the Irishman was sitting. At times I am quite soft-hearted. I approached him and said gently, "You okay?"

Taken by surprise by my soft footfall, he had no time to assume a better countenance and turned towards me with a face full of misery. He looked totally vulnerable, a lost lamb. Pity moves to love, and with his mask and his guard down I couldn't help but be drawn to him. I stood there quite unable to move or speak. My heart, tripping out arpeggios in that brief captured moment, was doing all those things that the romantic novelists said it would do. The sinking rays of the sun had just caught the dark colored tips of his hair, giving an illusion of bright fire around burnished copper. There was a noise behind me. It was Jamie following me like a lost puppy. I turned to him standing beside me. Poor Jamie; he looked at Dermot mystified, unable to share our magical meeting. "Och So" had met his successor. I could only compare it to that moment in Ancient Rome when the aging dictator, Sulla, met the new generalissimo Pompeius Magnus.

"Destiny," said Pompey, "looks to the rising, not the setting sun."

Chapter 10

Unwelcome Advice

I hope I haven't given the impression that my relation-ship with Dermot Mulvaney was consummated on the spot. Nothing really clicked till an incident seven months later (despite the fact that we mingled together in the same social scene), for while his arm was in a sling he had decided to move to Edinburgh. "Escaping bookies with flat noses and cauliflower ears," he said. I could never tell if this was true, since fact and fiction tended to run together with him as in a three-legged race.

On some occasions we even shared a climbing rope. "Make sure you tie a bowline, not a lover's knot—it's safer," shouted that wee besom Rosie. She could make me scarlet at times, but really I was above all that, for during this time I was walking on a pink cloud of expectation, waiting for my life to burgeon and blossom.

Esme was, as usual, sharp and to the point about these

matters. I went round to see her on Monday evening, post-poning my visit till her savage hound—called Elvis for some obscure reason—had had his tea. On a fashion note, I had decided to discard skirt and stockings, as they tended to get ripped when her pet was in a playful mood. It was, I think, the first time I wore slacks when not climbing. I realize that for us feminists this is an important milestone, which I have a duty to record, but racking my brains, I can't remember what year it was.

Esme was at the sink; the usual fag-end slumped from her lips. Wound around her head was a scarf knotted above her forehead, an indication she was engaged in domestic du-ties. Once I asked why she wore this distinctly old-fashioned housewifely cap of office.

"I dae it tae warn ma man to stay oot the kitchen."

Her husband, a formidable toper, was inclined to wax sentimental in his cups and to follow her about the house. His, "Ah luv ye, Ah luv ye, hen, e'en wi' yer elbaes in the sink," got on her nerves. It had needed a sharp blow with the rolling pin early in the marriage to stop this practice. Now the housewifely uniform warned that the kitchen was out of bounds, and marital harmony was ensured. I had to admire Esme. Everything she did had a precise logic.

The kitchen overlooked the back green that had played such an important part in Esme's story, for it was here that the pop man had got off at Haymarket. I wanted to ask her whereabouts in this unkempt greenery the unpetalling had taken place, but forebore to mention it, as too much interest would seem prurient.

"Fancy Pants. Trust you to fa' for someone like that. Don't deny it. I can see it in your face. You look quite pretty wi' the light of love in your een."

Esme was a sterner critic of my looks than I usually allowed, nor had I denied my infatuation, which I had just been pouring out to her.

"And that name, Dermot Mulvaney, that sounds Irish tae me. You'd better watch oot. He's probably a Pape. Oh, sorry, ah forgot the noo."

I did not mind. Anti-Catholicism was a standard part of the Scottish equipment of racism and bigotry that was paid lip service to, and with friends mattered not a jot. Like these Flodden mourning Scots who go to Blackpool for their holidays and find that their transient drinking chums are English and "actually okay." She was perceptive enough though; my short description was sufficient for her to deliver a damning indictment.

"Ah ken the type. Flooers and presies all the way tae yer bed. Then before ye ken whit's happenin' yer in the dustbin like an auld suit o' claes, ken. Moira, listen. That yin's gaen tae break yer heart. I can see it just the way you're talking about him. Ye cannae keep yer hands still." Her tone changed from urgency to resignation. "But it's got tae happen. Yer all the better efter it....So they say." That last phrase was spoken so wistfully that I felt there was a part of Esme's story that even I was not allowed to know. Of course she didn't understand what I saw in Dermot. How I was so drawn to him that nobody else mattered. No one did. They only saw the blemishes. I wasn't blind to these. They were there, but as filler in the background, like wintry hills far beyond the summer strand. Every little good thing he did I magnified, and thereby turned him round, so out of the sinner I could only discern a saint. Well, not quite.

She roused herself and began to bustle. "But I'm no' goin' to tell ye that, ye'll no listen."

But why did she tell me then? Maybe Esme was just a mite jealous. There she was standing at the sink unwrapping a huge bag of washing from the steamy. Perhaps just looking at her own romantic trysting spot, and hearing my tale, pregnant with love unborn, was just too much. That is what I thought then, but now I know she was doing me the service of a kind friend. Dermot—high, wide and handsome, the generous friend, the brave climber, the amusing and witty companion, a man never cowed by officious functionaries such as headwaiters and bus conductors—was to the last a consummate swine. And most of you ladies wise in the ways of the world need read no more of my history. For you know already what is written here. As for Sulla, sometimes I think he got a better deal. He retired and spent his pension going fishing, while the Great Pompey ended his days as unburied driftwood on an Egyptian beach, slain by a renegade Roman; his gift-wrapped head was sent to Julius Caesar, who cried when he got it.

Chapter 11

A Toast to Friendship Over the Water

While I was waiting to emerge from my chrysalis, great events were taking place in our family. For years now, Dad had been raking in a mini fortune from the chip shop. Respected and liked in the Italian food community, he had his own circle of hill-walking friends, and had just made inroads in a local amateur operatic society. Now he was expanding the business.

Our priest, a frequent and popular visitor, was at the house today. ("Chatting to our people is thirsty business, I'm thinking.") He downed a hot mouthful from his own special mug, encrusted and revered with age, inscribed "Manchester United F.A. Cup Champions 195—"? Once again, my memory, so faithful on points of detail, lets me down with numbers and dates. As my mother used to say, "Just make sure you turn up on your wedding day, Moira." This mug had been specially bought for him by our Manchester friends, knowing Father Doherty's fondness for the Busby Babes. The day when the news of the Munich air crash came over our radio was the only time I remember seeing his jovial countenance shaken in public.

Today his usual two pints of thick tea were enlivened by a juicy heavy fruitcake. "You know you will be causing me car a breakdown with the extra weight, Mrs. Fiorelli."

The father's broken down car was a standing joke in our community, but his trust in God had got him round. Personally I am a member of the Scottish Automobile Association.

"Now, Claudio—" (Dad had refused to Scottify his name.)

"You want to have me blessing for your new restaurant."

Father Doherty was to ceremonially open our new restaurant sited in a prime West End spot (to be called The Napoli—what else?). I hoped fervently Father Doherty would turn up in two shoes. He had an amiably absent-minded manner, and had been known to conduct mass wearing one shoe and one slipper.

The great day began with Dad solemnly handing over the keys of the chip shop to a family from Pakistan, the forerunners of a new wave of asylum seekers on our Scottish shores. The ceremony itself was invested with meaning. The keys bore a large label, which said, "Our chip shop in Corstorphine. Scene of many happy years. Auguri. Addio." I raised my eyebrows at this, the first use of the words "chip shop." Truly, we must be moving up in the world.

With the staff behind him and the new owners facing him, Dad became noticeably emotional. In the end, afraid that English would desert him, he burst out into a surge of Neapolitan—the only time I had heard him use it in years. There was a ragged cheer from a little crowd of our loyal patrons, and the moment of embarrassment passed. As we drove away Dad never looked back. I could hear faintly one of our staunchest customers saying, "And ye had better make sure yer pies are as hot and juicy as them ities'." The word "pies" being understood, I think.

Months later I did one of those foolish things that one is warned against. I went back. The windows were steamed up, but that was all that remained the same. The very name, Fiorelli's Fish Restaurant, had been recently excised, and now, shamelessly emblazoned in its place was "The Bombay Chipper." The shock of seeing it was as traumatic as when a favorite landmark suffers the scourge of development.

Nerving myself I went inside. The faded mural of the Bay of Naples with Vesuvius in the background that I used to dream about was gone, replaced by garish representations of the Taj Mahal and other less familiar Indian palaces. The square Formica tables were no more, replaced by a softer wood grown in the Orient. On the wall above each alcove, almond-eyed houris beckoned each diner to table. Some of the veiled ladies were surmounted on elephants whose trunks seemed to be dipping into the customers' fish supper, so real was this illusion of the East. Everywhere was crowded, and there, large as life, was that customer nominated our most loyal supporter, joking away happily, immersed in his food. He caught my eye, but quickly looked away shamefaced.

Even Esme looked happy. "Hyah, Moira, fancy a curried chicken?"

It was still early days for Indian restaurants. Few people at that stage knew the difference between a Korma and a Vindaloo, and the fodder on offer was bland compared to the bum burners of years to come.

I rejected Esme's open-hearted greeting. "No thanks," I said rather churlishly. I was a bit miffed that she was so happy with her new bosses, causing the only shadow in our relationship, but in the end it was she who brought me out of it.

"You ought to be ashamed o' yersel'. Life goes on even if you're no longer Lady Muck in the kitchen. There are times when you need to grow up." She was right I suppose, although I was hurt that she always thought of me as the boss's daughter.

Over at the West End, there was much going on. Dad, who could be a smart operator at times, had persuaded the bandsmen playing in Princes Street Gardens to do a selection of Neapolitan airs. The Calvinistic bandmaster refused to give us a direct endorsement. Dad hinted that he might say something to the effect that those who had enjoyed this musical walk in the sun could prolong their pleasure by eating pizza and chips at Mr. Fiorelli's new restaurant. "Mr. Fiorelli, I enjoy your Eyetalian music. I don't need a bottle of malt whisky to make me play it."

Dad got round this refusal to do commercials by making Freddie and me hold up a banner at each side of the bandstand inscribed "Don't wait till you die till you eat at the Napoli." Fortunately it was during the festival and there were enough cultured people around to catch the rhyme and spot the admittedly feeble allusion.

A zealous constable put a stop to Dad's advertising initiative, making us put down our placards. I was glad as my arms were getting tired, and anyway I was fed up being the object of attention of American tourists. "Gee honey, is that not just a cute wee Scotch lassie. Say, is that 'Napoli' a wee bittie o' the bonnie Garlic lingo?"

The bobby gave us a little lecture on the sharp consequences of any breach of the city ordinances. He was getting a bit carried away in claiming that we were breaching the peace of the citizenry. Fred was a touch worried, but I knew it was all my eye. I was smiling at him and at the same time giving him that intrinsically female once over, mixing both promises and potential for nastiness in equal but confusing parts. He was beginning to blush under my friendly but silent challenge to his authority, his face becoming as mottled as his chequered cap. Obviously new to the beat, he even accepted my hand-out—a further invitation to dine at the Napoli, etc. We then fled, our placards making useful paddles in gaining a passage through the thronging sea of humanity on Princes Street.

We were on time to see most of the opening ceremony. It was well worth the effort. Father Doherty, both feet shod for the special occasion, was on a very dizzy height of eloquence. His gestures of almost papal benediction were offered to a large crowd containing the usual Edinburgh mixture of indifference and zealots crowding the grey pavement. He was rhapsodizing about the long years and stout bond of Scottish-Italian friendship—a new one to me—"finally sealed by the opening of this new restaurant of Mr. Antonio Claudio Fiorelli, a Scot by adoption, who has often trod the hills where your Covenanting ancestors fought and died." This reference to the slaughter at Rullion Green on the south slope of the Pentlands in the Killing Time was largely lost on the crowd, but they gave a mild cheer anyway.

Now he spoke in symbolic terms of our kitchen, shared by both haggis and pizza. "Aye but nae by whisky and Chianti," shouted a grizzled veteran of the Sicilian campaign, but it hardly interrupted our priest's flow.

Now Mary Queen of Scot's secretary, Rizzio, was mentioned as adding lustre to our historical bond. The fact that he solidified the bond by rogering the queen passed unmentioned, as did the fact that he was stabbed to death by the unappreciative Scottish nobility. The apogee of this alliance had been the visit of Bonnie Prince Charlie to our capital city. There was a cheer at this point. The Young Chevalier is an evergreen favorite. We were told how he had enchanted the citizenry of our town, the ladies especially, who fell collectively in love with him. "All the town turned out on the High Street to welcome him, all wearing the white cockade.

At the ball in Holyrood Palace the lassies fell for his charms, indeed fought to get on the dance floor with him. Aye, many a dress was ripped in the scrum round his princely person." This unlikely tale of sexual zeal by Edinburgh's maiden ancestors was taken at face value by the now very excited street party.

"He came from Italy, from the very city of our Supreme Pontiff." There were murmurs at this point. It does not do to mention any links with the Roman Church in this fortress of the Reformation. "He was Italian in upbringing, yea even in speech, in gesture. When he said, 'Gentlemen, I throw away the scabbard,' who but an Italian would have been so impulsive to throw away such an expensive piece of silverware?" Even his dress was an import, for the kilt had been invented by the Roman Legionaries. Personally I remain unimpressed by the Bonnie Prince, who in his one solitary, short visit to the Highlands brought nothing but death and misery, and led it to being the great depopulated desert it is today—all just for a few songs, nice though they are.

Nevertheless Father Doherty's speech was a resounding success. The blue riband was duly cut and the door decorated with the cross of St. Andrew, and the Italian tricolor was opened to a floodtide of customers. Some of these were astonished to find, after a speech redolent with tradition, the interior decorated like a spaceship terminal. Father Doherty had obviously not been responsible for the refurbishings. It was reported that a few customers, moved by their newly discovered alliance with Italy, did try pizza and haggis on the same plate. In the background beyond the jangle of tills, the clatter of plates, and the noise of happy feasting couples, the Father and my father toasted the future in the beverages of their three homelands with Grappa, whisky and whiskey.

Freddie, who had gone along with this caper, was more and more taking on the mantle of the "serious" businessman now that he reckoned Dad had abandoned his sanity. "He ought to be buying more chippies instead of going posh. The rich are very choosy about where they get their grub, stingy you might say, and faither's rocket ship décor is not their thing. Mark my words, Moira. He's going to be a fish out of water and soon he'll be floundering." I did mark your words, Freddie. I only wish Dad had listened to his Job of a son.

Freddie's adventures with Eddie McCann were going well. "Very well, ver-ray well," he always said when asked how he prospered, but Freddie was always generous in his estimates with the pessimistic exception of his own father. All of his friends were doing "very well, ver-ray well indeed!" Even those that you knew were enjoying a short recess in Barlinnie. Freddie and Ed were thinking of making a business link with the cousins in Manchester. "Going international, Moira. Think big." I wondered if we would see the celebration of Anglo-Italian comity. I thought not. In business Freddie was totally dry-eyed.

In the home it was different, although Freddie continued to regret my boyfriends—creeps or poets according to him—and thought my climbing weekends a sign of a wasted youth. ("What do you get out of it, wet breeks and a cauld?")

Whereas he could boast the beginning of a mutually benefi-
cial friendship with his bank manager at the expensive golf
club he had recently joined, golf being a game he was trying
hard to enjoy. He would never deny me that little bit of extra
funding I needed to carry on through the week. With money
and other little things I was very careless. Of all the people I
knew, it was Freddie who walked closest to the shady side of
the law, and yet it was he who was the most generous. Funny
old world isn't it just?

Chapter 12

Introducing Algy

That year Rosie and I took a holiday in Skye for which the office had kindly granted me an extra week's leave. Skye in June is another Land of the Midnight Sun, given its imprimatur by none other than W.D. Mornay, who spoke (amongst other delights) of midday bivouacs. He said, "I used to lie in the shimmering sun basking like a lizard on some remote summit. The night was spent in roving and stravaiging ridge, peak and corrie. The only drawback was that me camera wouldn't work properly at midnight."

We were taken there by two of our club's characters, Dunc and Algy, a strange but inseparable twosome. Dunc was about twenty, and looked more at home in the pubs and billiard halls of Fountainbridge. Moderately quiet in comparison with his Falstaffian chum, he was showing signs of being an outstanding climber. Algy was about fifty, and was of the Scots Baronial. He had only recently stopped sporting a monocle, "for the damned thing kept getting in the way of me goggles in a blizzard." Algy had one great advantage over other climbers. He owned a car.

Like many other extraverts, Algy was an obsessive. The guise of the patriotic Scot was his idée fixe. Recrossing the border after a weekend in the Lakes, he would sigh, "Ah, how sweet the air is now after yon southern miasma." This was something, I must say, I hadn't noticed up till now. Why, I asked him, hadn't he worn our national garb when tramping the Lakeland Fells? Surely an ambassador had a duty to wear the kilt when abroad? "What, and give away a national secret? Moira, those English breezes are like the folk down there: not to be trusted. One minute they're all smiles and 'Ello matie,' and the next they have their hand in me sporran."

We stayed at the youth hostel in Glen Brittle. Climbers didn't usually find hostels sympathetic, hostels being full of muscular cyclists exuding heartiness, pushing your pan off the stove so that they could put their syrup tin on for a "wee drum up." In the toilets there was invariably the notice "Kilroy's missus was here." Hostels meant sing-songs ("Ye canna push your grannie off the bus") and early morning chores. They were not for us. Glen Brittle, tucked away in a corner of the Cuillin was an exception; it was designed for climbers.

For once W.D. was wrong. The weather, particularly at the week, was awful. We never even saw the famed broken-toothed ridge that adorns the sleeve of many an LP of

Scottish patriotic songs, often paired with a gargantuan thistle leaping out of the depths of Loch Coruisk—twin images
guaranteed to bring tears to the eyes of many a whisky drinker down in the depths of the Cowcaddens.

At last the weather cleared. A ridge of high pressure
was moving southeast from Iceland, and Algy announced
that we were to do the entire Skye Ridge. Not for nothing is
the traverse of all the summits of the Cuillin Ridge called the
finest day's mountaineering in the British Isles. In the event,
the finest day's mountaineering took us two days. We scrambled and climbed in the midst of the most sublime scenery.
To our right was the whale back of Bidean Druim nan Ramh
looking like a monstrous Viking longboat upturned. We lost
a cache of food and drink, took too long on the easier sec-
tions, and insisted on roping up when we should have scrambled unharnessed. In the gathering dusk we realised we were
only half way round. No one spoke of retreat. Algy simply
refused even to contemplate it. "Let's bivouac here," he said,
pointing to a pile of stones. We made ourselves comfortable
on the spiky rocks and waited, shivering. Duncan offered me
his jersey.

Rosie, through chattering teeth, said, "Would Dermot
be so gallant?"

"Perhaps," I wondered aloud, taking the jumper. A
noble refusal would have stung Dunc more than any cold
he would suffer through his self-sacrifice. At the time I felt
none of the aforementioned pompous bilge. I was freezing.
He offered me his jersey, ergo he felt the cold less than I did.

Five minutes on I was shivering just as violently, thinking what codswallop were these folk songs extolling the joys of sleeping in cold barn sheds with straw for a pillow. They were probably all written in overheated Victorian lounges. Cold equals misery. On a cold mountaintop you can only sit and suffer in silence.

In the grey hour before dawn we decided to move on, stumbling over easy ground with ropes for reassurance rather than security. Dawn came without announcement. The clammy mists splintered, parted and then vanished. In no time at all, jerseys, anoraks and all the other cold-weather clobber felt uncomfortable and itchy. The sun, our former absent friend, now began his work in earnest. Our limbs moved from goose pimples to sunburn without the intervening stage of bodily comfort. I was almost deranged by dehydration with multicolored dragonflies buzzing soundlessly in front of my eyes, and needed a drink to get rid of these lepidopteral mirages. We had no water with us and could not find our cache. But I had a rather desperate idea.

On the peak ahead I spotted a trig point, so I put on a little spurt. Sure enough my hunch was right. There was water in the three tiny sinkholes in which the retaining lugs were buried, three miniscule dewdrops left behind by the morning mist. I sucked it out with a quick greedy gurgle, before the others cottoned on and fought it out for the two remaining waterholes. In the end it was Dunc who held back, Sir Philip Sydney at Zutphen once again.

My other clear memory is of the ridge going on and

on, its terminus always hopelessly distant; the sea and Loch Coruisk both green, both shimmering tantalizingly under a blue sky and a relentless sun. Rocks, loose ones and lots of them, (Who had told me that Cuillin rock was as solid as marble?) were dislodged by our party. Detonated by our clumsy boots, they crashed and banged like cannons leaving a reek of burning sulphur hanging in the air.

At long last we stood on the top of the last peak, Sgurr nan Gillean, the Peak of the Young Men—named presumably after some prehistoric manhood ritual. To the north lay the wet, peaty flatlands of Skye; behind us in place and time lay the great Cuillin peaks linked by that shattered sinuous chain that had given our untrained bodies their first serious lesson in mountaineering. As a viewpoint, looking straight in the eye of the westering sun dipping over the Atlantic, it was peerless. What effect did this splendid concatenation of triumph and scenic grandeur have on my thoughts? None whatever. Tired, all but exhausted, I split our last two Spangles into four portions as refreshment for our stumble downwards on the last lap.

Of my two friends, only Algy plays a more than peripheral role in my story, so I will give you a brief account of their future before saying farewell. Dunc, without any apparent provocation, suddenly became one of our most brilliantly gifted ice climbers. On a Thursday in the pub we were entertained with his thrilling exploits: bivouacs in icy grottoes, climbs lit by moonlight, summits swept by storm. Some climbs were done in hazardous circumstances, viz. the time when Dunc lightly tapped the ice with his axe to reveal a spout of water. The mountain was melting like an overdone baked Alaska. Soon he went on to make a stunning series of Alpine routes. The north faces of the Eiger, Grandes Jorasses, and Matterhorn were ascended in stormy weather in quick succession. The guides shook their heads and prepared their rescue bills, but they were never needed. Dunc surmounted all these difficulties with effortless ease, only complaining of soggy boots.

Then all of a sudden it all ended. Duncan, mercurial by temperament, simply lost interest in climbing, and his gear mouldered in a cupboard. Business interests took up his time. He moved down south, becoming a partner in business ventures sponsored by a group of South London entrepreneurs, where the daring and speed of his driving were much appreciated. He has now retired, living a life of considerable style in the southeastern corner of Spain.

Algy, left behind partnerless by Duncan's dazzling exploits, did not repine. It was not in his nature. He soon found his métier striding over ridge and corrie seeking the shining summits, not spending the day fiddling away on some obscure little rocky outpost. "The Grand Design, Moira, the Grand Design. I can better reflect the wanderings of the King who might have been (this was his ornate way of describing Bonnie Prince Charlie) roaming the Mamores than clawing my way up a teeny rock problem on Arthur's Seat." I understood, and saw how a fifty-year-old Scottish public schoolman might feel somewhat embarrassed being given an ear-bending like a wee laddie by an officious parkie.

Algy went on to become well-known. His arrival in remote Highland Taverns was always awaited with affection, for his stories were entertaining and he stood his round. He published several popular books, which combined the love of Scottish history with his current obsession of record-breaking ascents. "From the Palace of Holyrood to the summit of Arthur's Seat allow no more than fifteen minutes. Only if you take your wife is a longer time allowed." He stopped and looked at me. "In your case, Moira, if you take your granny." In case you are interested his most popular titles are *With My Dog in My Pack Round the Hills* and the much loved minor classic *No Ice-Cream Vans on Lochnagar*.

When I got home after these high adventures, I found the tedium of the insurance office hard to bear. It was time to leave. Fortunately I saw an ad looking for a thrusting young executive in a bakery specializing in Scottish quasi-home baking, which sounded like heaven to me. I applied for the post, masquerading as a quality-control officer on the basis of frequent tasting of their products. When I told the office I was about to leave they were most disappointed, and I even had some correspondence with one of the managers urging me to stay on. When I left, my colleagues banded together to buy me an unnecessarily expensive farewell.

Chapter 13

Letters To and From an Employer

Dear Miss Fiorelli,

The Staff Department, in preparation for its annual report, has had occasion to note the large number of absences that you have incurred this year, the majority of which have fallen on Monday, Tuesday or Friday. It seems that on Wednesday and Thursday the Midlothian Mutual is guaranteed the stimulation of your presence and the inestimable contribution you make to our company by checking the dates on the death certificates of our posthumous clients.

On further research, the staff department records show that this year you have mourned the demise of no less than eight grandparents. Allow me to congratulate you on your plethora of ancestors. The Fiorelli family must indeed be a proud one. Mr. Meikle and your other colleagues were united in their admiration for the stoicism with which you have borne your grief. It is a new phenomenon to see one of so obviously Latin temperament in her dealings with her fellow workers behaving with such Spartan fortitude. We also had no idea that the usual mourning garb for Neapolitans consists of boots and breeches. You were observed thus attired heading for the Maybury, a favorite stop on the Glencoe road, I believe. Is there a cemetery or crematorium in the vicinity? The large sack on your back—did it contain the picnic by the family mausoleum for the bereaved relatives?

Those absences on Mondays and Tuesdays usually caused by "sniffles," "coughs," and "colds" are always brushed aside by Wednesday with that strength of character often noticed by those working in the same room as yourself.

The letters sent in by your mother after longer absences—that week in June, for instance, (Do you have a sunlamp in your bedroom?) when you were too weak to lift a pen—is in a noticeably similar hand to these very literate memoranda composed by yourself on the subjects of premiums cancelled, paid-up policies, and surrender values. It must be said that the style is different. For example: "My puir wee bambina struggled to her feet and croaked, 'I must get in to help Mr. Meikle. He's fair snowed under today.' It needed all a mother's strength to force her back to bed." A heart rending picture, which finds no echo in your office prose containing those entertaining and edifying classical allusions whose relevance to the subject of life insurance is not always immediately obvious to some of us.

I look forward to reading your explanation of your

somewhat fractured year.

Signed Reginald Mudlow - Staff Manager

....

Dear Mr. Mudlow,

Did I say eight grandparents? I must have been confused in my grief. If you will allow me to sidetrack for a moment, I will explain. The word parentes in Italian means one's relatives, not one's direct antecedents (parents or grandparents). Sometimes I think in Italian and speak in English, so particulars may get muddled in translation. This usually happens when I am upset. I was, of course, grieving for my dear uncles and aunts, who were not up to the challenges of the Scottish winter.

As for my post-weekend absences, it surely has been noticed by my very observant colleagues that I also suffer during our arduous winters. I had never realised they were so concerned about my well-being. I am quite touched; I thought them so cold to me. But perhaps you could ask Mr. Meikle, when he next comes to report to you on the state of my health, if he has noticed the long woolen drawers I wear to keep out winter's chills. When discussing my work he always endeavors to maneuver himself so that he has direct visual access to the secrets of my underwear. In fact he can be quite intent about it. I have observed beads of sweat appearing on his brow after a prolonged study of my memoranda. This cannot be good for his health, and I think it is my duty to report it to you. I do not know what we would do in this office if he went sick for a prolonged period. Does his wife know about the way he worries about his work?

I also believe most strongly that employees working for a life assurance company have a duty to appear for work only when in the best of health. If anyone turned up at the office while obviously under the weather, what would our customers think when served by such a sniffling specter? Such intimation of mortality might put them off paying their endowment premiums.

I hope the above explanations will satisfy our staff department.

Yours, M. Fiorelli.

....

Dear Miss F,

While being touched by your conspicuous devotion to your departmental head and your loyalty to the company philosophy, I do not find your account entirely carries conviction that your absences have been totally legitimate. I also require an explanation for your latest outburst; this time directed at your Mr. Meikle. I will not tolerate one of my managers being referred to as a "lecherous, gloating, sneakit, glaecit, lying, old bastard." I expect an explanation of your conduct together with an apology—today.

Signed Mudlow - Staff Manager

No reply.

....

Dear Miss Fiorelli,

We think it is now time for you to choose between your hobby of mountaineering, which takes you away from the office so often, or your career with Midlothian Mutual. If you decide to remain with us, we shall expect an undertaking from you with regard to your behavior with colleagues and your relations with your team manager.

Signed pp. Mudlow

....

In return, a short letter from myself, offering my resignation and stating how much I enjoyed the view of the Forth from the office window.

....

Dear Moira,

Thank you for the letter of 16th inst enclosing your

decision to leave us. We are all sorry to see such a color-ful personality go, but needs must. I believe your colleagues bought you quite a large box of chocolates. Mrs. Mudlow joins me in wishing you well in the future. She will miss the stories of your escapades that have enlivened many an otherwise stodgy Ravelston Dykes dinner party.

Reginald M. - Staff Manager

Chapter 14
W.D. as Best Man

Where was I? There was a long line of people to be surmounted before reaching the room that was to be the main
arena of the event. But what was the function that was bringing this assortment of people together? My fixation with my
own personal narrative clouded any extraneous factors. A
Scottish Mountaineering Club Dinner? No, that was impossible—the patriarchs of that august body made the monks of
Mount Athos look like satyromaniacs by comparison, and
here women were present, as I am the living witness.

But there amongst the celebrities, the heads to be nodded to and a few words to be spoken before drifting on down
the reception line, was W.D. Mornay himself. Might it have
been a rival function such as a whisky distiller's annual dinner dance? Could it have been a wedding? W.D.'s presence
does not exclude that as a possibility, for he was a romantic
in his quieter moments. As I recall we were sitting at long

tables where some mediocre food was dished and eaten as quickly as possible before the male contingent got down to the serious business of soaking the effects of the food from their insides. The menu proclaimed this to be the Mons Graupius Hotel—odd to name a place of good cheer after a field of slaughter—but being a standard Carte de Jour not even tarted up for the occasion it gave no further clue. In my daft daydreaming way I saw Dermot as Calgacus, leader of the Celts, the first in a long line of those dedicated to a lost cause.

W.D. banged his spoon against his port glass. The sound rang clear and true to the furthest corner of the room. With nothing else bar a belligerent grunt he commanded our entire attention. "Because," he surveyed the whole room, "it's there." He articulated slowly, his eyes finally resting on the bride, whose pink blushes contrasted nicely with her immaculate white confection of satin and lace. What was the challenge? Was it to be a mass assault on the as yet unshafted bride, or on the icy slopes of the cake behind whose peak-like form the chaste-but-chastened maid was trying to hide.

The whole setting and the speech that followed seemed so wrong that I suspect my memory, usually so faithful, was engaged in mixing and matching wishful thoughts. I must check the back numbers of the Edinburgh Tatler for likely wedding snaps. "Mallory's words have given generations of climbers an excuse not to reason why. How often have we answered critics by saying, 'Why play cricket?' (a game which is the Saxon answer to the mysteries of the universe).

What lies behind the Delphic utterance of the first conqueror of Everest is the challenge, like seeing a sign saying "Keep Out" on a private estate. Even if the gamie is armed to the teeth, you know you just have to go in. But it's only part of the answer. Each must make his or her own response."

The use of the feminine personal adjective was unheard of in the vocabulary of the Scottish Mountaineering Club misogynists. Was its arrival today due to my presence? W.D. bowed in my direction.

"It's your mountains and valley he wants to explore." This came from the leering lips of Archie Stewart, sitting next to me, sniffing into my bosoms. For some explicable reason I had been placed next to the most moronic mountaineer in Scotland, which if nothing else intensified my bafflement at the whys and wherefores of this assembly.

"Some of us may claim that the urge to climb is instinctive, starting when we try to clamber out of the cradle. The urge is an atavistic harking-back to the carefree days when the ape men used to swing through the trees in the search for their daily banana."

Stewart was now, I swear, slavering over my breasts, which were quivering with embarrassment. "Twa lovely dumplings," he smirked. This one had definitely arrived at his climbing via the gibbon route.

"Civilization wipes out this instinct for most of our colleagues, so really it is we who are normal." This was met by a small outburst of concurring applause. The Edinburgh citizenry at large looked upon climbers as oddities, like the many colorful tramps who wandered the streets of the New Town accosting those less indigent to "Gie's a tanner!"

"Gies some custard so's I can pour it o'er these for my puddin'," pointing at my breasts for the benefit of the waitress. This lecherous bastard was steamboats, of course, the alcohol adding fuel to his impudence. If the custard did arrive, I would pour it over his head and have it as plum duff. But it never did, as the waitress had run away in tears. Poor thing, she was not a mountaineer accustomed to storms, verbal or those provoked by Mother Nature.

Meanwhile W.D.'s discourse was moving towards its crux. With fingers spread out over the snowy linen he thrust his jaw out pugnaciously. "I can't stand bananas. So what am I doing here?" he thundered. "I asked myself this same question when I stood on top of the Fruity Pillars of the Be— the Blanc. I almost said Ben Nevis—I often confuse the Ben with the Blanc. Most of you know about this, the greatest epic of my career. Quite apart from having to suffer the frightful Englishman tied on to my rope, my reactions were too mixed to provide any answer. Storm, dizzy slopes of ice and snow, brown rock that to climb was to caress, incomparable scenery, moonlit bivouacs and the desire to belay my axe in that fathead's skull, and finally the finest summit in Europe—outside of Scotland that is. Months later when I had calmed down I knew the answer. Every so often I will sit and nurse my pet dram and relive these peerless days. You have all climbed your own Fruity Pillar."

He pointed into the audience, unmistakably at me.

"You all know your own reason why." There was a crescendo of applause. "You feel it immediately when you stand atop Lladhar Bheinn, in sunshine or storm, and see hill and loch stretching infinitely away; when you top the second crux pitch of Centurion or when you break through the cornice on Tower Ridge! These are the great days. There you have lived, have tasted the infinite joys of the hill and can only pity the poor valley dwellers whose only horizon is the top of their three-piece suits." At this point the clapping was like a cloudburst. W.D. had touched an echo in each of us.

"But,"—his quieter tone commanded a hush— "to go almost to the opposite extreme from elation," he spoke almost chattily, "some of you will have climbed or walked in the English Peak District." There was a semi-ashamed murmur from areas of the audience.

"Take a day out when it's degging down, as our Mancunian friends call it." This was received in sympathy for Mancunians, ritually despised as Englishmen, were generally liked and respected for their friendliness and toughness—both assets to a climber. "Then go up to Bleaklow—a mountain they say. I call it a mongrel, somewhere between moor and mudheap. You march along, but there's nothing to be seen in the fog and drizzle, bar the dew dropping off the end of your nose, until you slide down into a Grough—or is it a Clough—which is their name for those slimy horizontal gullies that are everywhere on this hill. Drag yourself out the sucking mud, and somewhere in the heather- and heath-wracked landscape you realise you're lost. So you sit down to eat your sopping piece, or butties as they call them. When you have finally decided to call it a day you have nothing to show for it beyond muddy clothes and the threat of a cold. Yet there is something there, which makes you know you will go back again. I think the answer is as individual as our personalities. For these few short hours I have been transported to a new realm, an altogether different plane to the quotidian. Even on Bleaklow, my choice as the nadir of mountain experience, there is this pleasure—remote, intangible, minute, but most definitely there."

"I would like to be there!" With that we dropped straight from the clouds into the stye. This broke the no-man's land of silence between tumultuous applause and the outset of conversation. Archie Stewart's eyes were bulging, fixed on the starting point of the softly flowing ruches of my dress. For a moment I thought he was going to vomit into my lap.

"For heaven's sake, Dermot, do something about this vulgarian."

"Whit, that paddy useless climber?" Stewart's body and neck made an arch across my frontage, fingers splayed like a pantomime witch, pointing angrily at my escort. "You used a peg on Centurion." How the tapping of steel on steel in a lonely glen could cause such ire amazed me, when road improvements were daily tearing up the landscape. But no doubt about it, a fight was on hand.

Dermot reddened and spluttered, "I didn't put it there. My hand just slipped onto it."

"Yer a useless, useless climber." This was rich coming from Stewart, the four-letter-word haul-bag.

"Watch it, pal!"

Is it only in Scotland that a jolly occasion turns so quickly to nastiness? Both drunks on either side of me pushed back their chairs and stumbled into each other.

"Dermot, thank you. I would love to dance." I turned on my instant charm and melted silkily into his arms, sparing everyone an unedifying brawl.

We danced. We pirouetted round the circumference of the room. Then the lights dimmed one by one, leaving only a sprinkling of tenebrous glow-worms. Softer and slower the music sang, enveloping us in a world made for two, Dermot whispering, "Och, when you came in, the music stopped. You know that light...?"

"When? Where?"

"...That was playing above your head. You looked—what's the word. You looked beatific—at Eddie McCann's remember."

"Oh, Dermot." I looked up dreamily, swallowing it all romantically, drunkenly I suppose, even though I knew it was all my eye and the Blarney Stone. The music had never stopped. I had to shout to be heard and he, when he did notice me, was more interested in my blouse than any halo.

But tonight was the night—no doubt about it. There was more, much more, of the confettied nonsense that lovers talk. He gazed at me with what I surmised was rapture, and I had to prod him back to life by asking coquettishly, "Why beatific, my love?"

That stumped him, for he mumbled on about how I was his Mountain Madonna and Angelic Delight, and then kissed me lightly on the forehead. It seemed to be the thing to call me a pudding that night, but I minded not a whit. I stopped in my tracks, slumped into his arms as I had seen film stars on the silver screen, and offered my mouth to him. He bent forward and held me tighter, lifting me ever so lightly, so I was standing on tiptoe. Even while his tongue was exploring, the kiss was sending surges of electricity fluttering back and forth through my body so that even my toes were prickling with excitement, while my heart was flooded with honeyed sweetness.

The music stopped—had stopped for a while—leaving us alone on the floor. The whole gathering burst into good-humoured applause. With the bridal pair gone, we were filling the void in the party I suppose. Why did Dermot not take me away now? Surely something momentous would happen between us.

As we clutched and stumbled our way back to the table, Dermot stopped by the group clustering round W.D., talking climbing. Clearly the hangers-on disliked him butting in, particularly when he started to monopolize W.D. by drunkenly insisting on telling him what a great climb Centurion was. W.D., to whom this was no news at all, was tolerant of the intrusion.

"You should know. You pegged your way up it." This came from Stewart, burning with resentment that his hero was actually in conclave with the Irish outsider. Dermot did not even break stride in his monologue.

"You talk like a potato and you climb like a coo!" was bawled into my Dermot's ear. Enraged at being supplanted, Archie began gibbering and jumping up and down in imitation of the hunchback of Notre Dame, intermittently alternating his pantomime to slaver like a dog on Dermot's sleeve. "You useless, useless climber," he snarled like Quasimodo, an unwise choice of mimicry, uncomfortably close to the truth, except the original had a certain nobility of character lacking in his epigone.

"I saw you at Traprain fallin' aff a dead-easy climb. Then her feelin' sorry for you, ye saft pudden, and rinnin' up wi' a hanky tae stap yer greetin'!"

"Is that so? Well..." The light gradually dawned on Dermot. I was his! "Well, she's mine. keep yer hauns aff my woman!" This was news to me. Good news, I think.

Archie turned to me, "Why are ye wastin' time wi' yon tosser?"

Dermot turned round and punched him in the face. Stewart's expression registered astonishment and stupidity before the mass of red spurted from his nose. All this storm in a teacup over flesh touching metal... Oh, silly me! It wasn't climbing rock they were embroiled over. The doggy show was over, and Stewart returned the punch with a wild haymaker that knocked the glass out of W.D.'s hand.

"I say, what the—!" W.D.'s words went unheard. They were both brawling like Saturday-night rowdies, rolling round the edge of the dance floor—both so mortal that few of their punches connected.

On the floor people were taking their partners for the Dashing White Sergeant. Two kilted gentlemen came up and asked, would I favor them with a dance?

"Why not?" My escort was otherwise engaged. I did a quick pas de deux over the miniature Trojan War underfoot, then on with the motley. Out of the corner of my eye, as I was being birled around, I saw Stewart pick up a chair and take aim. Dermot saw it and nimbly rolled out of range, unfortunately straying into the flight path of a leaping Highlander who was upended, revealing Scotland's great secret. Being a lady I covered my eyes. Well, curiosity killed the cat they say, so I couldn't help having a wee keek. Imagine—he was wearing an auld pair of hockey knickers.

Meanwhile everyone was doing their war whoops and sets of three, dancing gingerly round the embattled pair. "Why does nobody stop them?" Perhaps this is what they mean by the spirit of the Blitz—business as usual while fighting is going on all around. Archie's face was now a spectacular rosette. Dermot surged forward for a final lunge then stopped quite suddenly, his punch aborted. His face went white; his lunge now a lurch. "Moira," he wailed, remembering whom he had come with, "take me to the lavvy."

Of course they are all the same, little boys really. I took my brave wounded soldier and held his head over the toilet. "Moira darlin', stay here with me," he gurgled, ejecting an eye-catching stream of rainbow-hued vomit. "I love you, Moira. Stay with me while I die." An odd situation, I thought, for a romantically minded girl to hear a long await-ed declaration in the midst of the miasma of honk, which soon put out of mind these strange words.

"There now, darling, you'll feel better after this." I patted his back as each lurid retch traced a Jackson Pollock across the toilet bowl.

"But I never used a piton on Centurion," he wailed.

"No, of course not, Sweetheart."

Three doors away his bested opponent was honking in harmony.

So my daydream had come true. The curiously named hotel had had its replay.[1] But Archie Stewart as Agricola? From his stall came a roaring sound, as of a bullfrog, fol-lowed by a violent up-thrust as the contents of stomach were voided. I thought not. In a flash of prescience I saw that it was me who was the enemy. I had won the first campaign, but guerrilla war would prevail. As well as put a deer to the plough as domesticate Dermot. The lost cause was us—both as doomed as Jacobites.

Somehow we got away from the vomitorium and I took my treasure home. Ben the hoose were Rosie and an-other girl called Kirstie. Both had been at the do, but left

---

[1] A word about the name of the hotel. "Mons Graupius" was the name of a battle amounting to a Kultur Kampf in AD 83 between the "civilizing" Romans and the reluctant to lose their freedom Caledonians. The Romans won the battle but soon gave up colonizing the Scottish Highlands as not worth the trouble, an early victory for the weather and the midges.

when the hooligan element took over. Now they were sitting on the sofa, intently watching the simulacrum of culture booming forth from the telly. Dermot propped himself on the top of the sofa, then rolled down its slope, forcing the girls to take refuge on the other chairs. Rosie, knowing him, was only faintly irritated, but the other girl, seething at the loutish behavior, muttered, "Thank you, kind sir," staring at the box as if the most important message in her life lay therein.

"What about a nice cup of tea?" I said to break the unease.

Two mumbled yes's came back plus a "yes, please" squeezed through Kirstie's gritted teeth. Mamma in the kitchen kept asking who my young man was. "I am sure he could be very nice," suggested something else. I explained that he had fallen ill at the do. "Oh, in that case give him a slice of my Caddiston cake and a nice cup of tea. Your pappa takes it if he is ill and it always sets him right." I doubted the efficacy of her remedy in this case, but, always willing to experiment, popped a large slice on the plate and an extra spoonful in his cuppa.

Rosie was sitting alone, chin resting on elbow, gazing at the screen in a telling manner. On the sofa the other two were writhing like Laocoön; both pairs of hands were undulating back and forth on each other's backs, occasionally wriggling in and out of the ports of entry of their clothing.

Fortunately, perhaps, the cup did not hit any of the increasingly exposed parts of their bodies, but was hot enough to put a stop to any further activities. They yelped in unison, and the Kirstie girl turned on me. "You dirty wee scrag! You've ruined my new dress. I'll never get it clean."

"You've got a cheek. You came to my house. Get off with my boyfriend. Can't you get one of your own?"

"Your boyfriend since when? Gey possessive aren't you? You better pay for this to be cleaned, you wee wop."

"I am not!"

"You are so and you had better pay up or I'll get my dad round!"

"Are they all like you in Comely Bank?"

Even after stealing my boyfriend in my own house all she could think of was her stupid dress. I turned round to the other guilty party. "And what have you got to say then?"

To my surprise Dermot turned to Kirstie and said, "Here, have this ten bob note. Take the dress to Fullers of Perth. They'll clean it as good as new, nae bother at all."

"Aw Dermot, your awfy nice and that. Are you okay?" By this time I was fleeing upstairs, but had enough nous to leave the doors open for further revelations.

"Sure, but I'm burning."

"Oh dear, what'll we do?"

"Burning for you."

"Aye, ye're a lad 'n a half, aw richt."

She giggled, the sullied party frock forgotten, while upstairs I was thumping the pillow. I could hear their footsteps to the door and Rosie saying faintly, "I think it's better you go." I, as the poet said, wept myself to sleep, borne to slumber in a torrent of tears.

Next day I was more than noticeably moody. "On clouds of love, I see," said Dad as another door was slammed. The doorbell rang.

"It's your Irish friend that was ill last night," Mamma shouted up to me, immured in my bedroom.

"What a lovely tin of biscuits, McConichies, Moira's favourite." This was stage whispered, but the trap was not baited so easily.

"Tell him to leave the biscuits, then go," I shouted downstairs to Mother. I could hear her translating diplomatically.

"She's thrilled with the biscuits. But my puir wee lamb has got a bit of a headache, foreby late nights don't agree with her." There was a sloppy card inside the tin, inscribed in Mulvaney's hand with the following:

> Don't tear us apart not now or ever.
> Hot was your tea; hot was my tear
> May we lie together with the snow forever
> As our winding sheet, and bier.

It was so odd, so awful I decided it must be original and perhaps even drunkenly sincere.

The first three times he phoned I was not at home to him. But on the fourth occasion I reckoned even his persistence must have limits, so I let him to speak to me. I was not immediately forthcoming when I answered, "Okay, I've eaten the biscuits; what with that and the laundry bill you had an expensive evening."

"What is mere silver besides you?"

"All right, so when are you seeing that tart again?"

"Oh come on, Moira, give us a break; I was drunk. I didn't know what I was doing."

"What about earlier? Didn't you know what you were saying?"

"No, that was *in vino veritas*. I meant it. I do mean it. Give me another chance, please!"

I did.

Chapter 15

Cloudless, Unspotted Days

Years later I met a Mexican quasi-alpinist at the Biolay refuge in Chamonix, who was trying to lure me to take him up Mont Blanc by the voie normale. He introduced his girlfriend to me. "This is Beatrice."

"Oh, Beatrice," I said. "Then you must be Dante."

"No, my name is Ernesto," says he, looking bemused and indeed rather as his name suggested. That's how we were in those days, Dermot and Moira as inseparably linked as Dante and Beatrice, Pyramus and Thisbe, Paris and Helen, Romeo and Juliet; and alas, it ended under the same ill star as all those other tragic twosomes.

The first few months were cloudless, the good times the very stuff of heaven. In that year of perpetual summer we held hands strolling along Princes Street. My parents commented on my sunny behavior. "See your face—is no sae dark now you are smiling." Apparently I took to singing on waking every delicious morning.

At my new job, my workmates enjoyed having such a friendly colleague, one of whom, a master baker with many years of cake-making under his belt, said, "Every time you pass our oven, Moira, the yeast rises perfectly. Your smile sweetens my cakes." The auld flatterer. I would have to make sure his yeast didn't rise if I was left alone with him in the cake store.

Returning home from work, nights: "There's a boy on the phone for you." Mother's voice did a swift run through—a verbal kaleidoscope from vaguely censoriously prim, through coy, finally settling on muted excitement as she relayed the news to me. I rushed to the phone to find Archie Stewart of all people wanting to ask me out.

"Hi, Moira, hoos aboot a date?" The direct approach was always fine with me. So on the volley.

"Not till I've gone out with the pug ape from the zoo." There's no way a conversation can go on the upswing after that.

Pause.

"Oh!"

Sounds of anxious breathing.

"Sorry to hae bothered ye. Sorry. Sorry." And Uriah Heep backed off the line. I had let him run on enough to preen myself in front of the mirror. What girl, after all, does not like being courted? Then I settled down anxiously for the call from Dermot.

In our actual rendezvous we went to quiet alcoves

where lovers could talk. And could he talk? Me, used to the plain speech of Lallans, was borne away in the bilge of Liffey water, awash in a floodtide of compliments, churned out by this practiced Blarney Stoner. "When I first saw you, I knew my life was going to change. You were my road to Damascus, my fate, my Helen of Troy, my Dido, my..." He hesitated uncharacteristically.

"...Francesca da Rimini?" I supplied, breaking the spell of his rhetoric and unfortunate choices of archetypes. But more often than not I drank it all in, so little did I know then. And you know, even now I believe some of it sometimes. What else did we talk about? Now, I can't rightly remember. It is easier to recall that we did not talk about laying down the deposit on a house or wall-to-wall carpets. Dermot's chat consisted of hilarious anecdotes where he was the man destined for the custard pie, but ducked at the last moment as guess-who got splattered—Archie Stewart now featuring frequently as the Laurel to his Hardy, or was it the other way round? I can never remember. He had the habit of leaning over his pint as though it was a microphone, and splaying his fingers like frogs' legs on top of the froth, a signal that the punchline was on its way.

One serious chat does come to mind. He had flipped his head back quite a la "Och So," so that his hair slowly recoiled strand by strand over his eyes rather scrumptiously.

"W.D. didn't really explain anything, did he?" Dermot posed the question.

"About why we climb? Well, come to think of it, I suppose not." My role as a cheerleader was not to add too much when the oracle was speaking.

"No, he didn't answer it at all, he just provided the aesthetic furnishings. The desire is within. You either have it or you don't. No explanation possible." He had a way of being dogmatic that made any rejection of his dogma appear contemptible, if not laughable.

"Oh! I see."

But now his eyes started wandering along the bar. The serious conversation was over. Judgment had been given.

Other nights we would sit alongside drinks that ebbed as slowly as the tide on Joppa's beach. We always held hands. He liked holding hands, and I liked him for it. To break the silence our lips might touch in a kiss that was not quite a kiss. Weekends, far from the cattle market of the Carousel and the Palais, we danced the night away, swirling around in our dance of dreams, lost in each other's smiling eyes. Only when the music stopped did we touch down again. Of course afterwards, kissing farewell on my doorstep, the war of attrition with my clothing would start again. Slowly, very slowly over months, his hands moved forwards in their remorseless advance, but bridgeheads consolidated over weeks could be wiped out by my hand pushing his away in a manner that brooked no discussion.

"No! I mean it! Now!" At these times I was at my most schoolmarmish, but when I went indoors I needed to spend a long time on my own, gasping and panting as I caught my moral breath back again. These were times when my knees would weaken, my thighs melted and juices began their march to the sticking point.

During these moments of trial by ardour I would concentrate on the manufacture of Poor House Perkins, a seasonal favorite, popular amongst expatriates in the U.S.A. Most evenings I got no further than pouring ingredients down the mixing tube before I cried, "Halt." But that night when Dermot did his legerdemain with my bra straps, I watched helplessly as the indeterminate gungy mass slid into the ovens. His fingers were swirling round my taut tummy, nearing the forbidden zone. The biscuits were all but packaged and boxed. What now? What could I think of next to maintain my objectivity?

"No! Nothing!" I said to myself aloud. Dermot stopped. The danger passed. Dermot was rigid and strained with passion. Quite soon he realized he was sitting in the rhododendron bush, and I was wishing him a pleasant trip home from inside my doorstep.

Dermot had the odd twinge of culture, which usually occurred on rainy afternoons when, out of pocket, we went to the National Gallery at the foot of the Mound. There was one painting there that I could never take my eyes off nor get out of my mind, *The Traitor's Gate* by David Scott, depicting a boat entering a medieval watery dungeon. The black, hunched shoulders of the jailors radiated a terrifying aura of menace, but it was the prisoner's eyes stark with terror that held me spellbound, staring at me in my worst nightmares.

Dermot galloped past most of the paintings, only braking to a halt beside a few favorites, such as the aforementioned Francesca da Rimini, unlucky in love. "Too much is a surfeit, Moira. The paintings become indigestible." He was like that about climbing. On any one crag he would only do a couple of routes, on even the dinkiest outcrops. Partly this was laziness. But as he said, "See those guys who burn off the crag in a day. They've no reason to return, and all they're doing is cutting down the number of places to visit. Mark my words: they're the first to give up climbing."

....

The crags and mountains were the stage on which we acted out our romance. Like memories of seasons past, the conditions we enjoyed were nigh on perfect, like this day in Glencoe.

"Come outside. It's beautiful!" Dermot was standing in the entrance to the Lagangarbh Hut at the entrance to Glencoe. I clumped out and gasped thick white steam in cold astonishment. In front of us the vast moor of Rannoch was ablaze in a glory of gold and purple. A few tiny, limpid clouds lingered like smoke on the flat plain. All the rest of the sky was a bright, steely blue. On our right, the rocks of the Buchaille were light pink smothered in white lace. A few patches of mint green were the telltale signs of ice—wonderful, reassuringly climbable ice.

From this angle the Buchaille was not the perfect melodious triangle seen from the road over the moor, but rather an imposing lump, almost self-satisfied, as if saying, "I know I am not perfect from all angles, but I am quite happy the way I am." Or as if the divine sculptor had created a masterpiece from one angle and then nodded off.

That day we climbed Arch Gully on Stob Coire nam Beith in Lower Glencoe under ideal conditions, with snow like icing on a Christmas cake. The first ice pitch, a frozen drainpipe of ice steeper than a church steeple, glinted hard and unyielding as adamant. Below Dermot's feet, the slope tilted dizzily down to me. Hardly a breath of wind disturbed the cold-sheeted ice, although an occasional snow devil spun crazily around the burnished red retaining walls. Neatly and confidently he cut precise incut ice holds to the snow above, the immaculate white of the slope punctuated by a tear line of mottled dashes of sea-blue where his steps had punctured the ice. Going up I wondered if I would ever climb ice or would always be a passenger. The eponymous arch was completely blotted out by a great fan of tilted ice. It was my lead, and for once I accomplished it without tremors or impatience from my companion. From there we trooped up, coils in hand, to the summit. Stob Coire nam Beith is really only a lower limb of Bidean Nam Bian, yet even here, under a relentlessly azure sky, we were granted a magnificent vista of snowy peaks and blue lochs shimmering away to the sea and the isles of the west. Dermot stopped, his breath coming out in white clouds, and pointed with his ice axe at our surroundings. "This is the answer, Moira, when anyone says, 'Why climb.'"

It was getting on, but we still had time to walk along the ridge to our parent peak Bidean Nam Bian. Once there we sat by the summit cairn, drinking in the landscape. In the west the sun was sinking in a gossamer scarf of pale fire. An English lady came up the ridge and—taking in the stupendous view of all Glencoe and Lochaber, where glens, ridges and bens stretched into infinity in a glorious jumble of chiaroscuro colours stolen from the unrestored masters of the Renaissance—exclaimed to her companion, "Ooh! It's just like Switzerland!" I was too immersed in my companion to share her ecstasy. But I remembered her words, and took note of the scenery. Years later when I had the opportunity to compare, I knew she was wrong. The high dry air of expensive Switzerland was beautiful, but nothing could equal the grandeur of dusk seen from the summit of a mountain in the Scottish Highlands in deep midwinter.

Chapter 16

Dropping in on Friends

Towards the end of January we were tramping across the vast plateau of the Cairngorms. The snow was deep and it was late in the day, when out of nowhere the mist came down. With no rocks poking through the snow to focus on, it became impossible to distinguish ground from sky—both merged into one grey blur. We kept stumbling into snow-drifts, but after the first few times no longer laughed at finding ourselves chest-deep in snow. Even though the snow was too cold for us to get wet, we became increasingly tired and frustrated. A few minutes later I looked in front of me and saw footprints. "Dermot, look—we're okay. They'll lead us home."

He looked at them, then me, his eyebrows white-whiskered with rime. "Moira, these are ours. We've been walking round in circles." He sounded so calm that I didn't feel frightened, not just then. A rising breeze flicked snow pellets into our eyes, making them smart. We dug the map and compass out of frozen pockets to plot a way through the whiteout, which was pretty useless as we didn't know where we were, and there were no landmarks to home in on and fix our position. But we had to try something, so one of us moved forward in little leap-frogs while the other steered with the compass, shouting instructions whipped away by the increasing gale. It was slow work, the wind pushing us off our line of travel.

I was out front and shouted, "There're some boulders ahead. I'll use them for markers." I stepped forward. Instantly, the mist swirled away; the "boulders" were huge cliffs hundreds of feet below. I was on the rim of a cornice. Another step! It didn't bear thinking about. I moved back quickly, and then leant on my axe, shaking. At the edge of the precipice, spumes of snow higher than a ship's mast hurled themselves upward before being flung away in flat, horizontal, white-jet streamers.

"I think we should rope up, don't you, Dermot?" He nodded, already uncoiling the rope. After that we traveled tied together through the white murk, pirouetting in our traces torn hither and thither by the gale. Angry flumes of wind-driven snow stung our faces, thus we walked with one hand shielding that little area of exposed skin.

Darkness was now setting in, but we still refused to believe we wouldn't get down before nightfall. My man was grimly silent. I was on the verge of tears but refused to give in to that wasteful indulgence.

"Hold me!" Suddenly Dermot shrieked and plunged out of sight. The rope snaked along the snow, slashing corrugations into its surface. I rammed my axe down, whipped the rope around and threw myself over it. The rope went tight and held. I drew breath. There had been no time for fear.

There was a great howl and then a chorus of curses. The pressure on the rope eased and I wondered if the mist and wind had deceived me, but then this was the haunt of the Grey Man.

"Dermot, you all right?"

Granite City curses rent the night air. I walked to the edge and, peeking over, saw Dermot looking up in astonishment. He was sitting almost cozily between two climbers from Aberdeen, who were picking snow off their clothes like fastidious diners clearing crumbs from their suits. The conversation was heated. Dermot's Santa-like dropping-in on their snow cave had demolished it. Thinking, oh well, the damage is done anyway, I slid down and landed smack on the lap of one of the cave dwellers. He was screaming blue murder, not appreciative at all. Then I remembered I was still wearing crampons.

Long before us, our companions accepted that they were not going to get down that night and had dug out a snug snow cave in the lee of the slope. Our unexpected visitation meant they would have to start all over again. Luckily we were out of the wind, whose biting, heat-sapping blast was the most serious danger we faced. In the half-light above us, wisps of snow and ice from the broken cornice kept flying into our gully. The Aberdonians went to work with a will, taking turns at excavating a new cave. In the school for survival you need to be a quick learner, so I set to work carving the entrance, while Dermot stood around waving his axe futilely, as if it was a fairy wand.

The men from the Granite City let me have a spell inside. "Wheech lassie, dae a shift doon the pit. You'll be a'richt in thon colliery, mun, nae doot."

I lay flat on my back, my head torch reflecting on the dull green ice, howking out great blocks of ice to carve out our bedroom. It was warm work, so much better than standing like a snowman out there. So why was my hero so useless, standing like Venus on a rock-bun? The two Dons came in, putting an end to my reveries, comparing their places of abode to tonight's digs.

"Aye, better than Donnie's hoose tho'."

"Aye, nae hauf, whit a scunner!" They both laughed. I never asked them the joke, just prayed never to be invited to tea by Donnie. "Nae doot about it, hame's best. Ye weet, mon?" At last they had noticed me, dripping with snow and sweat. I decided to get into the spirit.

"Aye, mon, I'm steaming and aw'." They both laughed again.

"Yer a grand lass. I'll buy you a pint o'heavy."

"Nae doot," I replied with what seemed their catch phrase, and for no reason all three of us began laughing. Dermot slithered in, and at once they became sober sides. The Aberdonians unwrapped their sleeping bags from sacks, neatly lined with waterproof poly-bags, while we sat watching, shivering. Everything they did was impressively organized—piling up neat little packages, putting their poly-bags down as groundsheets, laying out their sleeping bags, then finally tucking themselves in bag and rucksack. Besides them we looked like miserable ne'er-do-wells. The one called Jock looked at Dermot and said, "I bet you two hav'nae sleeping bags." He was right. Dermot's impetuous approach to mountaineering did not allow proper preparation. "Well you'd better hae mine."

It was a truly noble gesture, although a bit spoilt by his throwing it at Dermot. His pal, Dandy, was fairly reluctant to share his sleeping bag, but it was a matter of survival and he grunted his acceptance as the two of them wriggled together for the double sack race. They were not amused, although it was difficult to tell, blinded as I was by the glare of their head torches.

Then Donnie, I think it was, said it. It was the sort of unpleasantry we usually shrug off, but this one refused to be budged. "You twa are a calamity on the hill. Ye got awa wi' it the day. I widna bank on it again." He leant over and whispered in my ear like a stage villain. "I'd get rid o' thon chancer, if I were you. He's as reliable as the weather."

Here was a classic W.D. Mornay situation: two couples locked together in the Spartan embrace, necessary for survival in the Hindu Kush. To break the ice, metaphorically speaking, I suggested we pass the time telling jokes. Jock, who I think was quite a wit when unwanted visitors were not bursting into his home, started the ball rolling. He had a few new jokes, which, delivered with his pawky Aberdonian wit, made us laugh and forget our discomfort for a wee while. Encouraged, he launched into one of those anti-papistical jokes that are one of the staples of Scots low humour. We laughed politely. Then, possibly noticing the formal note in our chuckles, he realized he was with new friends and asked if any of us were Catholics. When we both said yes, I am afraid that ended our new found hilarity. It certainly put a dampener on the party. Jock just said, "Oh," while Dandy gave a malicious snigger.

For a while we just lay there in the darkness feeling the odd icy drip splashing onto our faces. Our body heat had raised the temperature to just that annoying degree above freezing. There was no action replay of my Cobbler wrestling match, Dermot showing no interest in conquering where "Och So" had failed. Our damp, steamy bodies in close proximity just added to the general discomfort. My Kirby grip went unused.

Jock, who was emerging as the more chatty of our squashed hosts, asked if we had any food, theirs being destroyed when we made our entrance. We had the usual packets of McConnichies half-morsels. Jock suggested a game: if anyone sang a song or told a non-partisan joke, they would be rewarded with one biscuit. This little contest raised our spirits as we dredged our memories for howlers from the past. Funny, clever, in poor taste, or just plain flat, it made not the slightest difference: to all of them we responded with the same hollow laugh. I suppose that was because we were all concentrating on our bon mots to win the prized digestive biscuit—or were we too miserable for a proper chortle? I quite outshone them with my repertoire of song. Could it be the first time "O Sole Mio" was sung within the hearing of the Grey Man of Ben MacDhui?

With all this excitement, the four of us were dozing quite comfortably when the sun's early rays turned the dull grey ice into bottle green. The steam climbing up from our moist bags having an almost hypnotic effect, we had simply dropped off in our damp world.

Hours later I awoke with a start. Were the mountain winds playing tricks? There seemed to be voices outside and eerie, whining, bumping thuds, signaling the onset of another Arctic storm. I woke Dermot up. "What time is it?"

"Crivvens, it's noon. We had better make tracks afore we're caught oot another night."

The Aberdonians woke from their slumber to see Dermot again vandalizing their home. With his axe he smashed down the wall in front. Outside, the sun was shining on a happy holiday scene. Staring at us were a dozen brightly colored novices of the ski slope, and all around were happy shrieks as fashionably clad skiers cavorted, slalomed and bounced off moguls in joyful abandonment. We had bivouacked bang in the middle of the White Lady, Aviemore's most popular ski-slope. Above and below us were the gates for the McConnichies' Rassles Grand Slalom cup, with the biscuit shaped flag flaunting its sponsorship. Our cave was exactly in the middle of the course.

A child halfway down the line of pupils was the first to recover. "Maw, see those twae bummers cuddlin' up with each other!" The mother slapped the child but she was evidently incorrigible. "Whit about the wee chappie in wi' thon big gowk? Jings it's a lassie. Her maw must be gey strict if she has to go this far for a nicht oot wi' her boyfriend." Her mother hushed the precocious brat with a short slap from her ski-stick. The look she gave me told me all I wanted to know about my situation. The student, who was about to snow plough straight into our living room, braked goggle-eyed, collapsing in a heap just in front of our sleeping bags. No one laughed.

Shamefacedly we packed and trudged down the slope. All the way down, elegant skiers wheeled in and out of our tattered line. Everyone seemed to know about our escapade. Indeed you couldn't miss the black hole gouged out of the piste. I dared not look up at the restaurant at the bottom of the slope to see the lines of grinning faces. My cheeks were burning, but not with the fresh air.

Just as we were about to make our escape, an authoritarian figure stem-christied to a skidding stop in front of us, spraying us with snow. He was in a fury, screaming and waving his poles in an alarming manner. "You're banned, banned frae this corrie for the rest of your living lives." A novel concept but not one to argue with at this moment. He was in a proper Gaelic tremor. "I'll hae the sheriff on you lot. You've ruined the U.K. Championship this afternoon!"

Our wet dispirited group made no attempt to challenge the lone Highlander. We got into our cars and drove away quickly. I tried to make a joke to lift our shame. "Are you driving so fast in case the sheriff sends a posse after us?"

"Aye, with a few more like him Culloden might have been a different story." Dermot skidded the car neatly round the bend, just missing the ice floes emerging on the melting Loch Morlich. I only felt safe when my customary blush came on as we drove past the amorous tree of Lynwilg.

Chapter 17

French Lessons

"You English, you live like pigs," were the gendarme's words of welcome, casting a disdainful eye over the horrors of le camping anglais, with all its appearance of a medieval plague village. Dermot and I had pitched our tents in a forest clearing on the edge of Chamonix. After listening to this homily we took a wander around the Alpine Blackpool, a curious mixture of high chic tourism and down-at-heel climbers, the British noticeably the scruffiest. There seemed to be a ban on razor blades, and as a further identifying mark some of the British went about with crusty loaves filling the back pocket of their breeches like holstered revolvers. There was little love lost between them and the dapper French mountaineers elegantly sauntering along the rues and boulevards sniffing disdainfully if they happened on a malodorous rosbif. No doubt the French were arrogant. This hurt the British, who disliked getting a taste of the medicine they had been dishing out to the world at large for so long, and as a result lawlessness prevailed.

Avoidance of camp dues was only the most minor offence. By some strange quirk of nature the collector's visit often coincided with the entire British contingent's migration to the malodorous woods beyond the camp boundary. There were no furnished toilets in the encampment. It was au naturel or nothing. Gaily colored parasols shading neat white tables, affording Chamonix cafe society a modish Parisian air, found their way to the British encampment. People— who at home would be mowing tidy lawns, the apple of the bank manager's eye—stole food from supermarkets, raided ice-cream fridges and filched beer mugs. Small wonder that the Gendarmerie clamped down hard on any offender inept enough to be caught, raiding the campsite at well-spaced intervals for the return of stolen property, or to close it down for reasons of hygiene.

At the time we noticed only that the town was cheerfully colored and alive; the mountains dominating the valley seemed immense and remote as if they wanted nothing to do with the cosmopolitan gaiety. Our campsite was in a small grove well set back from the squalor. In a frosty dawn we awoke to the chirping of the crickets as regular as an alarm clock, the tent a jeweled tabard of morning frost. Yawning, we sniffed at an evocative fragrance of woods and flowers, which even now, together with the smell of Gauloise cigarettes and glacier cream, brings me back to the French Alps.

That first morning we were totally unprepared for the

heat, and spent the next couple of days skulking under ever-diminishing patches of shade. At least we had more sense than our sun-worshipping neighbors, who spent their days broiling in the open, and then all night groaning in their tent.

Rosie and Rab's arrival shook us out of our sun-avoiding reverie. Within an hour of greeting each other and catching up with stories, we moved from total indolence to frantic haste. Rosie was grinning from ear to ear relating her adventures in Paris and their "night of passion" in a pension near the Gare du Lyon.

"Oh," said I, raising my eyebrows.

"Tell you later," she smirked. We were bustling to pack our gear quickly to catch the last teleferique up to the Albert Premier Hut. Swinging back and forth in the seat of the cable car I let Rosie tell me her story.

"We bought a cheese, a big round one like a guider wheel, and stuck it on the sideboard."

"In the bedroom?"

"Yes. Oh! Dinnae fash yerself. We slept head to toe. I warned him to lay off the funny business. My ice axe was at hand."

"Well, any amorous thoughts were soon drowned by the smell. Both of us thought the other hadn't washed their feet. Then I saw the sweaty cheese, the real culprit."

"Where's the cheese now?" I asked suspiciously.

"It's in my sack. We'll eat it tonight."

I wondered about Rab, the innocent in the big bad city, his jersey still firmly clamped inside his breeches. He seemed completely docile, ready to fall in with every sexual prohibition or permission of Rosie, or whim of Dermot whose dynamism tended to put everyone else in the shade. While our leader outlined the plans for tomorrow like a troop commander, Rab was packing his rucksack with essentials like chocolate and sardine tins, seemingly accepting his role as beast of burden. On the path these thoughts kept returning as Rab's rucksack, bobbing in front, blocked out any other views of the landscape. The going was steep, although the path itself was easier to follow than any of our Scottish ones. Had Dermot not been just a little bit over-ambitious in choosing the Forbes Arete of the Aiguille du Chardonnet for our first route, at over 12,000 feet? Here at only 7,000 feet I was feeling the effects of the altitude. When the peak first came into sight with a wreath of cloud round its summit, it looked remote and unattainable, like an icy empress. To be on its top tomorrow morning was unbelievable. My progress along the path was dismally slow. The difference in altitude gave me a thumping headache. The hut, just a blot amongst the boulders at the foot of the glacier, got no bigger, even after I had avoided looking at it for quite a while. However, even all bad things come to an end, and there I was looking up at a bronzed Adonis lolling about on the terrace, regarding our tortured progress with annoying indifference.

The hut was an old-fashioned wooden building with ropes and ice axes draped around the walls. It was quiet at first, but other toilers were coming up the path; the continuing good weather would mean that it would be busy tonight.

"Why not book the beds now, Dermot, before it gets too crowded?"

Dermot had passed Higher French, and had on occasion been taken for a Parisian, he said. I stood back in anticipated adoration as he approached the hut guardien, tapping him on the shoulder, whereupon the guardien spun round with a look of mild astonishment. Dermot put his two hands together in prayer, then rested them on his shoulders like a little boy going bye-byes. Just three words accompanied this mime. "Eh, monsieur, sleep."

The monsieur regarded us wearily, then turned to an Oxford chappie who was on matey terms with the guardien and on tap for such an emergency. A few deft phrases sorted things out, and the little chink in Dermot's armor was duly noted.

"Rosie and I would like a ladies room with a nice view of,"—I waved my arms towards the Chardonnet— "that mountain, si vous plait." The Englishman looked puzzled, then laughed and walked away. I was somewhat taken aback at being ignored, but more so on discovering our "bedroom" consisted of a plank at head-height stretching round the room with a few blankets laid out anyhow. No niceties, everyone just packed together willy-nilly in a mixed dormitory.

We plonked our stuff down on the middle of the communal shelf, then went downstairs to prepare ourselves for tomorrow. On returning, the shelf was crammed tight with bodies. In the half-light filtering through the small window we saw our gear thrown right to the back of the shelf. It was our first time abroad. Even so I suspected an unsavory atmosphere and lack of welcome as we scrambled over the slumbering bodies towards our possessions.

A quartet of Frenchmen was forced to sit up while we claimed our previous bed-space. One of them muttered bilingually and oddly, "Bloody Anglais," as he lopped off a hunk of salami with a rather menacing clasp knife.

"Ahm no, je suis ecossais," Rosie said bravely, but it carried no conviction. A torch was flashed into our faces.

"Jolly filly," I heard whistled in amazement. The salami slicer was looking at Rosie as if she were a particularly fine piece of rock to be assailed. The air was taut with hardly bridled lechery. "Ha, the nice English girl ventures abroad," said one, quoting from Henry James, I think. The little laugh they gave was not reassuring. Our mothers had warned us about lascivious Frenchmen, and here we were in a seething hotbed of them, all staring at us with unmistakable intentions. That knife looked as if it could be positively nifty in slicing through clothing.

The best thing to do would be to ask to borrow the knife to slice into the cheese Rosie bought in Calais, and take our minds off them. I nudged Rosie to get the cheese. It emerged from the sac hot, sweaty and cheesy after its journey by train and cable car across France.

"Phew," I said. "Not much on romance if Rab's feet smell like this."

"No," she giggled, "it's a hummer! That's how these continentals like it though, don't they?"

I turned to the man with the knife. His face was screwed up in disgust and horror. "Cow of un vache," he gurgled in his lingual mélange before rolling away from us.

On the other side, his friend who had just been sizing up my blouse buttons muttered through his sleeping bag, "Fromage de une vache morte." The sound came indistinctly as if he was suffocating. Soon we had plenty of room to sleep.

I gave a hunk of cheese to Rosie, who only took a wee nibble. "Really pongy."

I agreed, "Disgusting froggy stuff." We lay for a bit under our blanket fully clothed except for boots, listening to the whistling, snoring and other night airs.

Before I passed into dreamless sleep, I heard mumbled something that Dermot told me later was, "What pongy anatomies these English women have." But later Rab admitted it was, "So this is how the damoiselles Anglaises maintain their invincible honour!"

I was fast in dreamland with my heartthrob on a sandbank in Warwickshire. "Deux heure!" a voice roared. The door banged open. What a dreadful awakening! Blankets were thrown back. Headlamps flashed in my face. Muffled French oaths were our pre-dawn chorus. By the light of our head-torches we breakfasted. Dry French cake, sickly chocolate and over-sweetened coffee was gulped down, almost scalding our throats. I shivered in the night frost, my steamy breath mingling with the vapor of the tightly clutched, piping-hot coffee mug. But my shakes were a mixture of fearful anticipation and excitement. I have never met anyone who relishes these Alpine starts, and didn't know that by simply getting out of bed I was over the worst bit.

Almost immediately after leaving the hut we roped up and donned crampons. In the dark you could see their steel tips sparking off the boulders fringing the glacier. Dermot had it in his head to be first in the large queue tramping the glacier. Of course I was to blame for holding everyone up.

"Come on, Moira, hurry it up! It's not makeup. You're not going to a party; just slap it on."

This was the glacier cream, which was supposed to be plastered on anyhow, as if appearances didn't matter. Well, I don't think it does any harm to look your best whatever the circumstances. David's drawing of Marie Antoinette going to the guillotine makes her look so shabby, it's distressing. I was going so slowly across the glacier that the French parties kept leap-frogging in front of us, brushing past with a brusque excusez moi. Dermot should try harder at his French; it seemed quite an easy language to learn. Ahead were the Oxford Anglais, helpfully shouting out "Hole!" whenever we passed a crevasse. It was just like a game of hopscotch with, instead of chalk marks on the pavement, black holes in the snow.

In the pitch dark we could see strung out along the glacier and up the first slopes of the mountain a line of bobbing headlamps, and hear the Frenchies cursing and bemerding each other, reducing the great adventure to the level of queuing for an overdue bus.

"With all these people here we can't come to much harm, can we?" I was still uneasy.

"Mm, well maybe," he replied. Dermot had enough sense not to tell me that the reverse was true. A guide shot past, hauling his client as if he were a reluctant dog going walkies. Somehow my spiked feet got in the way of his rope. I learnt more French: "M'selle—La corde regardez."

The darkness drifted away in a blue-tinged pallor. There were shouts of "Attention!" in a French accent as we mounted the first slopes of the mountain. Bits of rubble kept falling off the shattered crag on our left. Above and to the left, pink tints touched the top of the mountains, and minutes later, standing in a grumbling queue of climbing commuters, I saw the Alpine dawn in all its full glory and beauty, as peak after peak blushing in their early morning colors rose up from the silken-sheeted snow. I have been to the Alps many times since, but that first sunrise over the Chardonnet will always remain fixed in my mind as the essence of my Alpine awakening. The mountain itself was a brilliant-white, icy, right-angled triangle whose hypotenuse was the glacier floor, topped by a snow arête spiked with teeth of gold-en-brown rock slanting upwards from left to right, while the ridge dropping steeply from the right was the way down. The whole picture, framed by an incarnadine sky slowly melting into blue, was unmarked by even a puff ball of cloud.

Ahead was the crux, a frighteningly steep bosse of ice. Just looking at it stuck out on that exposed arête gave me the willies. In the event, the whole thing was ludicrous, as rival teams of Frenchies fought it out as to who was to be in front. As if it mattered—the mountain was first climbed a century ago. The Oxford man standing on his ice step above me turned around and winked. "Bloody foreign frogs; no idea of mountain sense." I agreed; these Frenchies had no rights to their own mountains. Up in front the guide, with Fido on a lead, grabbed first place, and the traffic jam moved slowly forward. It was airy and steep, but surely no one could come to harm in this atmosphere that reminded me of Portobello on a sunny day.

Once on the ridge I really started to enjoy myself. Even though we were unbelayed, carrying great straggly coils of rope, I felt safe—more on my home ground. Just as when you were a child playing in the trees in your best party frock, clanking and scratching with crampons over the rock gave that great pleasure of doing something vaguely irregular. The Oxford climber kept encouraging me, telling me where to place my feet and saying, "Splendid! What a splendid Alpinist in the making!" Much preferable to Dermot's constant "Hurry up and don't stand on the rope, stupid!"

What with this and that tremendous exposure as I swung round and about the pinnacles and icy bits on the ridge, I was totally knackered when I reached the summit.

"You look shagged out." This was Dermot's mountain-top greeting. Rosie gave me a funny look. What was she expecting me to say? The English couple croaked a little cheer for me together with a mitt-muffled clap. It was precisely 9 a.m. on a cloudless July morning. All around were the great peaks of the Alps, from Mont Blanc to the Matterhorn faintly sketched in the distance. The top half of the formidable north face of the Grandes Jorasses peeped out from behind a parapet of rock, but today even it looked friendly and beguiling. A flock of cawing ravens swooped around, waiting for crumbs. We held our flasks aloft and toasted our first Alpine climb in warm sugary water. Breakfast was sardines squashed between slabs of dry cake, but I have never eaten with more appetite or pleasure. The English lads who had given Rosie and me such a rousing cheer continued to be fulsome in our praise, making our Alpine debut a jolly party. All around us everything was bright, pure, clean and fresh.

The descent was a different matter: laborious, tedious and dangerous. The sun reflecting off the glacier was exhausting, while the melted snow balled up on our crampons, making us liable to a fatal slip. At every step we had to whack our crampons with our axes to clear the snow.

We returned to the campsite too tired to celebrate; flinging rucksacks aside, we enveloped ourselves in our sleeping bags until the sun turned the tents into an oven the next morning. Then it rained. For three days everything was awash. Our holiday now consisted of nothing more than the struggle to keep dry. Sleeping bags and clothes were piled into the centre of the tent. Hunched like trolls we sat for hours, trying to avoid touching the side of the tent, the flysheet a sagging, overburdened basin softly spraying us as we lay in our clammy bags.

"Holiday fun," I said, watching with fascination a persistent drip disappearing into the blotting fabric of my sack. It was like being thrown into the cold sprays in Portobello Pool without any dry clothes close to hand.

It was in these circumstances that we met our neighbors. By now they had recovered from their sunburn, but seemed determined to continue the punishment of their bodies. A mounting pile of empties outside their tent clocked their restless hours, as each night they sang each other unmelodiously to sleep. Dermot said he would have a word with them if they disturbed his sleep tonight. It was interesting to note how intolerant he was of anyone else's licentiousness, but then—reformed roués make for the sternest puritans.

Rab was outside digging drainage ditches, planning a unitary irrigation scheme for both tents. There was a lull in the storm, with a light drizzle marking time in the interval of the big clouds recharging themselves. One of our neighbors, the type of nosy parker who likes watching others work, surfaced from his tent to chat to Rab. He must have been remarkably thick-skinned for we could hear him droning in a continuous monologue, punctured by pauses for Rab's reply. Apart from the patter of raindrops against the flysheet, these pauses were entirely blank. At length a grunt, an intake of breath—Rab was about to say something portentous.

"Look, I can hear you a' nicht lang, so I dinna need another dose noo. So why don't you just..."

"Okay, message received and understood." Saying which, he waddled off.

"Well put, Rab," said Dermot after Rab came back

into the tent. We sat in the one tent so we could have equal share in the general misery. Rab was not entirely sure. There was always the satisfaction of seeing somebody off when a score is settled, and thus giving our bad temper something to bite on. Our general misanthropy was fortified by headaches from being cooped up in the tents and indigestion from dining in the prone position.

"No wonder the Romans were so cruel and grumpy," I said, apropos of nothing. Nobody questioned this, so stunned were we by dullness. "You know, they all ate lying down on couches, and ate stuffed dormice."

I was having this interesting conversation with myself when Rosie asked, "What's wrong, Rab?"

"I don't know. He didn't seem such a bad bloke. He was just being friendly after all."

That made us feel worse and depression lay like a dull miasma over the tent.

"Perhaps we should make some peace offering."

Nobody agreed or disagreed. Apathy stilled any good intentions. Both couples had other things on their minds, and we split up into different tents.

We were just getting into the heavy-breathing stage when there came a light, insistent tap on the tent door and the sound of a throat being cleared.

"Like a bad penny," said Dermot, pushing me aside and opening the door.

"Do you know your rucksacks are out in the rain and getting soaking wet? Your bread's in them. Could be pretty soggy by now." This came from our nosy neighbor.

Dermot got out cursing.

"Why don't you come in and have a brew?" As you probably guessed, the peace offering was my suggestion. Anyway, by this time everyone was getting fed up with each other, and we were only necking because we had run out of things to talk about.

Our roly-poly neighbor introduced himself as Egremont Basil Kitchener and nudged his way into the tent, knocking down everything standing, and straightaway launched into a long-winded monologue about his adventures. There had been a brush with some guides on the Petit Charmoz, reports of brawls in the Brasserie Alpenstock, etc. I could see he had the potential to be tedious, but there was something engaging about his personality that made him a welcome visitor nonetheless. He was one of those you occasionally meet on the hill, totally out of place, magnificently incompetent, and yet as much a part of the mountain scene as the rocks, ice, and heather.

Basil was an indefatigable visitor to our tents after that. We rarely saw his chum, Davy, who modeled himself on Rip van Winkle, sleeping all day and night with short intermissions for a sing-song and to punish more beer. Every few hours a news bulletin was delivered. The barometer, if tapped firmly, was rising. At the Guides' Bureau they were saying, "Peutetre demain." In Madame's cafe the douche was in operation. The cinema was showing un film James Bond. Well, it was nice of him to keep us in touch with the wide world outside. "It saves us the trouble of getting up," said Dermot, whose indolence was now fast rivaling Davy's. Meanwhile Rab and I went each day into the town for groceries.

"Dermot should'na hae taken you on the Chardonnet for a first climb. It was way too high. In no way were you near acclimatized. No wonder ye were peched oot on the summit. Throwing somebody in the deep end. Yons daft. But then it's aye aboot him. A trophy climb to tick aff in the book, like you." He stopped, his tongue having run away with him, not his thing at all.

The day after this Basil, making his usual early morning visit, asked if anyone fancied going down to the Guide's Rock, a roadside outcrop, "for a spot of cragging." We looked at him in disbelief. Noah's flood was enjoying a major revival. "The Guides' Bureau says it is going to clear up this afternoon."

"Well, in that case,"—Dermot, ever mercurial, threw off the sloth of days in a jiffy— "let's go." Boots, rope and knapsack were soon ready, and he was off without giving us a chance to argue him out of it. Sure enough the weather did begin to improve. When Dermot arrived back he was no longer restless or indolent, but more relaxed and easy to take.

"What was Basil like on the rock?" I asked.

"You'll soon see," he said, emptying his knapsack and sorting out his gear. The displaced orange peel and Mars bars wrappers were left for me to dump in a rubbish bag. I also added his gently humming rock boots. "Okay, okay," he said, picking them up and stuffing them back into the rucksack.

Next day, Basil again. "Boys and girls. How do you fancy the Rebuffat route on the south face of the Aiguille du Midi?" A groan came from the lads' tent. "It's reckoned to be a great bad-weather route."

Still sleepy and bemused, Dermot poked his head out of his sleeping bag. An escaped feather was nestling on his top lip. "A-tishoo," he sneezed on Basil's sandals. "That's better," he said, rubbing a still itchy nose. "A good bad-weather route. No such thing. It will still be plastered with snow."

"Not now with the sun shining so brightly."

"Did you find out if it will be good tomorrow?"

"Beau temps according to the Guides."

"Okay, go tomorrow." He burrowed back inside his pit. As the tent zip was being fastened we heard, "But I won't be coming. With you lot out the way I might catch up on my sleep."

At 5 a.m. the teleferique station was already crowded when the six of us arrived, Dermot included, a testament to Basil's power of persuasion and enthusiasm. Those in front of us had no lack of friends as new arrivals stepped in out of the darkness to shake hands with those they recognized and join them in the queue. There was no end of "Ah Bonjour, Jean, ca va?" and "Ca va bien" while early morning cognac was passed round. "Santé." "Merci santé."

There were brightly colored summer skiers accoutered in all the colors of their designers' spectrum, mingled in with the red jerseys and white caps of the mahogany faced guides. It was all very merry but we, outsiders, found ourselves being gradually pushed back past the door of the booking hall and down the steps.

"If this goes on," said Basil, "we will find ourselves back at the campsite." Being too British and stuffy, we did nothing to counterattack except maintaining stiff upper lips and giving the intruding Frenchmen starchy looks. Evidently these were non-translatable for they had no effect, and even Dermot remained docile, allowing a queue-jumping Frenchman's ice axe to tickle his nostrils.

Eventually the others became separated from us and were carried away in the surging tide into a teleferique cabin. Standing on the platform, we felt like down-and-outs in that exquisite crowd. There were elegantly clad tourists dressed as for a morning trot down the Bois de Boulogne—even the skiers' glacier cream came out of a bottle labeled Pierre Cardin—while the alpinists were like haute couture models roughing it for a shoot in the great outdoors. A chic climber in powder-blue pantaloons disdainfully sniffed at us as he dabbed on his aftershave. We all piled into the next cabin. The crowd ooh-la-la-ed as the cabin jerked suddenly up and then mounted swiftly.

Very soon Chamonix looked small and remote, a tiny toy town with dinky cars in the streets. There were delightful views up and down the valley, spreading out beneath us as the mist spiraled and thinned among the trees. Every time the cabin glided past a supporting pylon it lurched upwards, and the jolly sardined crowd mock-shrieked and laughed gaily, giddily—oh, what fun! Dermot was quieter than usual; he looked sickly and pallid. He had supped too well last night in the Bar National and the heavily aromatic cigar being smoked under his nose was not helping his recovery. I prayed that there would be no eructations in this bubble of humanity with its party atmosphere and hints of all the best brandy, Gauloise, and well-cooked garlic.

Dermot's face was a picture of innocence, like a well-bred monk receiving matins. How did he always look so sweet and seraph just when about to create mischief? Oh, no! At once I tried elbowing my way through the crowd. Now his features were wrapped in concentration. A forest of skis barred my escape. Too late! As we broke through the tree line it started. A long low whistle, shrill and piercing, formed the overture, immediately replaced by a sound of a tent slowly being ripped apart in a fierce gale—a phase that lasted almost thirty seconds. There was a final dull, heavy thump and then silence. Everyone was frozen in embarrassment. Even Gallic insouciance could not cope with this. The sounds lost nothing in translation.

There was a scream. A lady in a Coco Chanel ski-suit clutched her throat, making choking sounds. Pandemonium broke out in the hermetically sealed box. The stench was enormous. It reverberated round the cabin in great fruity waves, echoing the shrieking and gurgling within. Designer ski-suit laid into designer suit, and the mottled faces of the gaily clad tourists nicely complemented their fetching attire.

Lover blamed lover for the miasma. Hands that a few seconds ago had tenderly stroked the adored one's cheeks were now frantically clawing at the other's face to escape the noxious venom. Svelte, elegantly accoutered legs were kicking and thumping against the sides of the great glass pod, which was rocking dangerously to and fro, almost falling off its hinges. All the subtle aromas of a superior Gallic civilization were drowned in the detritus of the Irishman's stomach.

Luckily the station was approaching fast. The doors were flung open to a coughing, screaming mob fighting its way out. The ticket collector was thrown to the side as the well-dressed crowd ran amok, disappearing shrieking into the vast cavern of the terminus. The last one I saw was the modishly dressed climber, frantically splashing eau de cologne over his face. In the distance I could hear shouts of "Merde, merde a lors." Too right, I thought.

Meanwhile, Dermot was staring guilelessly out of the window. "Look, Moira, there are two parties on the Frendo Spur." I looked down. There far below on the perfect snow-white arête were four dots linked by thread-like ropes. I agreed. It looked a great climb. And lo, there were our friends waiting for us at the ice grotto that exits onto the mountain. Rosie rushed up and hugged me.

"We were getting worried about you," said Basil. "There's been a dreadful panic."

Even the taciturn Davy said, "It's great to see you."

I was touched that beneath their tough shells they were really warm hearted.

We emerged from the ice grotto and slithered down the snowy gully to the start of the climb. It must have been standing-room only in the Mont Blanc range that year for there were figures and ropes on every ledge, almost on every hold. There was no question of tackling the climb in our genteel British way. You followed hot on the heels of the climber in front, giving the rock no respite. Dermot was the first to realize that we had to change our ways. He muttered, "When in Rome," then started climbing the first pitch, leaving me to sort out the tangled ropes—all the time avoiding the eyes of our more orderly queuing compatriots, recognizable by their dun colored anoraks and disconsolate expressions. Davy, clearly no slouch when it came to queue jumping, moved with surprising agility into second place. At last it was my turn to touch Chamonix granite in earnest. Here was no gentle introduction; right away the rock put you on your mettle. Every move on this solid granite was a joy, interesting, without any desperate, heart-stopping, out-of-reach lunges. For a while Basil and I were climbing in parallel formation, but I drew ahead as my very impatient leader was trying to drag me up like a sack of potatoes. I landed as if by elevator, gasping for breath. Climbing harnesses were not as yet invented, and the tight rope round my waist was choking me.

"Speed in the Alps is the first essential," nodded Basil approvingly, quoting from some textbook. Then, "Haul away up there."

But Davy, reverting to type—he was lolling on the ledge, the rope a harum-scarum mess round his ankles—just

said, "Climb it properly, man." And Basil, wrestling inele-
gantly with the rock, did his best.

Several pitches later and Basil was still babbling away
cheerily, blissfully unashamed that he was hauling on pegs,
slings and other supplementary excrescences to the cliff,
while I was lost in the pleasure of it, reveling in the contrast of the warm brown rock like oven-fresh biscuits and the
gleaming white surroundings. I started to sing, "I Remember
You-hoo!"

I shouted to Dermot, "Take a photo of me."

"Okay." He fumbled with the camera. "Say fromage."
At least his French was coming back.

Shifting my feet I struck a pose. I looked down so that
I could thrill to the yawning chasm beneath. Just below my
right boot there was a freshly shaved head with a white cap
jauntily perched backwards. It was the Frenchman, obsessed
with personal freshness. A breath of manly perfume wafted
up to me. He was grinning. Then I noticed I was standing
on his right hand. Knowing no Frenchman could resist feminine charm, I smiled, then slowly swiveled my right boot
over his fingers before pivoting upwards for the next move.
I turned my head down again, this time giving him an especially bed-warming look. He doffed his cap at me, quite the
Maurice Chevalier. "Enchante, mademoiselle," he declared.
I could not help noticing an angry ridge along his fingers,
Miss MacPherson's fox-stealing Spartan to the life.

Whatever else he might be, he was a red-hot climber.
No sooner was I on the belay ledge than he was up there

hauling his partner in like a fish. It was getting late, he observed. We looked at our watches. It was afternoon already.
Well, time passes quickly when you want it to go slowly, but
we agreed it was getting rather trop tard. He and his friend
had no bivouac gear; neither had we. So it was better to travel
lightweight. As we were climbing so slowly would we mind
if he passed us? Dermot pointed out that we were climbing so slowly because of the traffic jam ahead. To which the
Frog replied, in that case we would not mind if he passed us.

"Yes, we bloody well would," riposted Dermot.

"Vous manquéz la politesse de la montagne." He gave
Dermot an angry look, smiled, tipped his hat at me, and then
he was off swarming up a much harder crack on the left of
our traffic jam. His partner, an inoffensive fellow but not
quite as agile as his rope-mate, slithered off the rock to make
a wild pendulum, yet managed to give a quick Gallic impre-
cation aimed at Dermot. His leader hauled at the rope and
fished him up.

Soon after this the wall leaned back somewhat and
the climbing got easier. As the smooth blue pantaloons and
white cap disappeared aloft, I reflected that that was the first
time I had seen Dermot so quickly summed up and bested.
My mind was quickly brought back to the present as a spare
coil of rope was dropped onto my shoulders. I looked up angrily. It put me off my handjam. Up above I saw that Gallic
shrug of indifference that says, "So you got in the way of
my rope?"

Dermot looked up. He too was tired of the multicultural problems. Summoning up six years of laboriously acquired linguistic competence he shouted, "Merde a vous!"

Monsieur White-Cap looked astonished, then outraged. Never in these sacred mountains had he heard such barbarous sentiments uttered. Making a sign with both hands he waved them in the air, crying, "And ze same to you." After this well-matched display of fluency both parties kept a safe distance away from each other.

Dermot was now engaged on the crux—a massive open book corner reamed with deadly smears of verglas—climbing as if on tiptoe, clipping into the many pitons hammered into the crack. The Irishman's ascent of this pitch was a superb demonstration of safe and precise climbing. When he reached his belay stance after running out the whole 150-foot rope length, an Alpine guide nodded in approbation. I would rather not dwell on my ascent of this pitch. I was dragged up, feet slithering inefficiently against the icy holds.

Davy, economical with words, simply said, "Throw us a rope down, big boy," and rapidly climbed up on a tight rope.

Up till now Basil had shown no interest in this, the next feature of his ascent, since he was busy expostulating on the tremendous view. "Rab, we are looking at the arena of the world's greatest mountaineering feats." His arm encompassed the Aiguille Verte, the Drus Grand Charmoz, and Grepon. "You see in front of you a hundred years of Alpinism." Now, as he set foot on the pitch, Basil was about to add one minor footnote to his history lecture.

Having no warning from watching the antics of others, Basil's first steps were like a man cycling in too low a gear. From a high point of five feet he slid rapidly back down.

"You didn't tell me it was so icy," he shouted up reprovingly.

"You should have looked instead of giving a bloody lecture."

His partner was lounging nonchalantly against a flake of rock, the rope down to Basil carelessly slack, too idle to give instructions; he was watching the butterfly that had been following us up the climb dancing in the air beside his rope. Basil tried again. This time he lunged at a high handhold, held it for a few precious seconds while his feet were trying to catch a bus. With a slip, a slither, and the noise of ripping wool he crashed onto the deck. Bye-bye bus! But Basil was truly British in his determination, pausing only to catch a few wheezy breaths; he stepped backwards to the edge of the platform then ran up to the rock. Just before colliding with the wall he took a flying leap. He managed to grasp the first handhold and tried to climb the pitch in a series of leaps. Sadly his momentum soon gave out. Davy was deaf to his screams for a tight rope, and poor Basil fell heavily onto the head of a startled Frenchman.

By this time a sizeable crowd was gathered on the platform, all but the dazed Frenchman enjoying the performance. Tired, battered, and winded but still dogged, Basil gave it his all, making progress by hauling himself up the rope and skating on his knees and feet. At every upward pull the crowd clapped and cheered. A Belgian climber, rather good, but a bit of a show-off, was swarming up parallel to Basil's fitful progress. He kept pointing to Basil and then to his own feet— "Technik, technik. How you say it in Anglais?"—while he glided up in a series of precious dainty hops. I began to hope that the arrogant Brussel Sprout might peel off instead of Basil.

And there he went again. His arms, feet, knees all shaking with the strain. "Traitor's Gate" eyes desperately pleading before he dropped like a stone to the balcony beneath. This time he landed amidst the jeering mob, splattering them to the four ends of the ledge.

This time Dermot grabbed the rope. "Come on, man, haul," he shouted at Davy.

Davy responded languidly, "He's going to have to learn to climb sometime."

"Not now. Come on, let's make an effort here! Give it a real good try, Basil," he bawled into the depths of the diedre.

Meanwhile at the bottom, Rab and two Frenchmen had the best idea, and began shoving him up the pitch. Basil's huge arse was prodded and shouldered like a sack of coal. At the top, Dermot, having organized his dozy partner into fixing up a pulley system, shouted down, "Let's put Humpty back on the wall."

Eventually a chastened and dispirited Basil was winched to the top of the pitch, flopping onto the ledge like a beached whale. The two Frenchmen, more sympathetic than the Belgian, patted him on the shoulders, saying, "Trop de frites," and sauntered upwards.

Surprisingly Basil found little difficulty with the rest of the climb. People like him are often quite resilient against the bumps and scars of an unfriendly and unyielding world. At the top he was once again bursting out with joie de vivre saying, "What a great climb! What a great situation. What a story to tell the lads back home."

Soon afterwards we reached the summit of the Midi. The last teleferique but one had gone down. There was going to be a long wait for the last one, which was really for the station workers. Only our little group, the furious Frenchy (he of the cerulean pantaloons and aftershave) and his pirouetting mate were left atop the mountain. It was rather chilly in the open air so the station attendants let us all sit in a rather somber little room surrounded by T.V. screens, showing dull interior shots of the Aiguille du Midi station. We sat miserably, avoiding looking at each other, all six of us ready to fume and be nasty, although it was nobody's fault that we had to wait.

I reached into my rucksack and found the traditional pack of chocolate biscuits unopened, as we had not stopped to eat all day. It was not possible to eat all the packet. I turned my head to Dermot as if to say, "Why not?" then offered the packet to the scowling pair opposite. For a moment I thought they were going to be proud and refuse. The one who gave the Churchillian signals I could see was ready to reject our overtures, but his friend gave a shrug, his way of saying, "Paris is worth a Mass," and took the proffered goodies.

Soon afterwards we offered them a drink from our flasks. They accepted, although it was obvious they found the sugary orange liquid repulsive. They had something better by far in a pocket of their sac. Attendez one moment, and out came a flask of first-rate brandy. Quite soon all of us began to grin rather sheepishly about our previous differences. Both of them could manage a bit of English, which seemed to improve the more we polished off the bottle. They told us about their dreadful journey up. As a result they had been sick in the ice grotto and had to wait for an hour before they felt well enough to undertake their climb. I was beginning to blush, while Dermot assumed once again that look of pure innocence. At this point their English deserted them as they described the cause of their sickness. They kept referring to a famous French soldier, the one who held Verdun in the Great War—Marshal Petain.

That was the last climb we did in the Alps that year. Not a big haul really, but at least it ended on a pleasant note. We went down in the cabin with our erstwhile enemies, singing sea shanties and rocking it from side to side. Once at the station, we shook hands with them before parting. I was dizzy with giddiness and intoxication so I could not follow what they meant when they said to Dermot, "You, my Irish friend, are a real Petain. Tu es un vrai Petain." Was he referring to our battle on the rock and the Marshall's famous motto at Verdun, "Ils ne passeront pas?" Or was it something else that my French was not up to? Let it remain one of mountaineering's little conundrums, not quite in the league of the mystery of the ghost at Ben Alder cottage, or whether Mallory and Irvine reached Everest's peak so long ago.

We saw a lot of Basil Kitchener that holiday. His technique was always appalling. In some ways, with his drunken singsongs and scorching in the sun, he was the typical Englishman abroad. At any moment I expected to see him emerge from his tent with a knotted handkerchief on his head. When people realized how poor a climber he was they shunned him. One evening, dining out on steak, frites et salade at Madame's cafe, I noticed conversation dropping away at other tables. They were all focusing with open-mouthed disbelief at Basil's prandial discourse. It was embarrassing, listening to the sniggers behind beer glasses. We tried to disassociate ourselves from him. Now we were being ridiculous, but climbers are such snobs. I am ashamed to recollect this. We liked him because he was what he was, but in that moment did not have the bottle to proclaim him our friend; a pity, for his bumbling enthusiasm and relish for the traditions assured him entry to the well-stocked pantheon of mountain characters. He was certainly more significant than the ear-ringed jobs who took climbing in their stride till the time came to take up that nice position in the bank promised by Daddy. He was the Ghost of Climbing Past, a memento mori of ancient values, frayed but not entirely subjugated amidst a deluge of self-interested promotion by those making the mountains theatres for their own solipsistic dramas.

Chapter 18

Miss MacPherson at Home

Here I was, twenty-two, and yet the first thing I did when I returned home was to phone Miss MacPherson. Well, not quite the first thing. I had a bath and let myself enjoy Mamma's welcome of the prodigal daughter. As a special treat she had concocted a gargantuan feast with huge dollops of spaghetti, lasagne and tagliatelli. There were other things as well, but the main impression was of a pasta extravaganza washed down with Soave and Lambrusco.

"Mia bambina e troppo magra."

Well, if I was a trifle lean, what I hungered for was simple Scot's fare. I was suffering from digestive overkill, so I asked her to go steady after the third lorry load.

I needed some guidance in the ways of the world. Miss MacPherson, with her Olympian detachment and wisdom, was the right person to turn to. The most important question being, was Dermot a suitable partner for a Lauriston lady?

My starry-eyed romantic outlook was not totally blighted, but I could see troublesome passages ahead, Dermot being dedicated to the proposition of himself being more equal than the rest of us. His sole purpose in life was to flesh out his itinerant court with stock figures such as the handy-man-cum-jester and the solicitous handmaiden. Friends who could tell him where to get off were gey few on the horizon.

"Moira, it's so nice to hear your voice. It's been such a long time. I have told all the other girls who have been to see me in the intervening years that I am sure Moira Fiorelli has not forgotten her declensions."

This nice compliment I was sure had a barb in it, which I would have to work out later. Being busy was just too feeble a defense. I decided not to be cowed.

"Yes, my spare time has been rather taken up by climbing. Regrettably climbers are not the sort of people one meets shopping in George Street."

Miss MacPherson was too sophisticated to feel upbraided by so obvious a retort. She ignored it. "Quite so. Some of my girls have brought their young men to tea. A wee birdie told me that yours is most decorative and amusing"—I wondered where she got that from— "you must bring him along. Shall we say Sunday at three?"

I put the phone down. Sunday. Well, that meant losing a day's climbing, but there could be no disputing her invitation, which still had the force of a command. Why did I go along with it? I think despite my adventurous nature I was still very sheltered, a bit of a lost lamb in need of a Bo-Peep.

I was going to find it difficult to discuss Dermot in front of himself, unless he took a long time to spend a penny. Amusing she had heard. If she was expecting Oscar Wilde she was going to be shaken out of her stola.

Much to my surprise, Dermot was quite taken by the idea. A polite Sunday afternoon tea would be a new experience. He was all for novelty and couldn't wait to see my Roman mistress. I could see a shock coming for both of them, and prayed for no further eructations and that she would not speak Latin for long stretches.

Sunday started off dreich and drab, but by ten o'clock the early morning haar was beginning to thin, the silvery droplets chased away by the faint autumnal sun. We had gone to the Queen's Park for a stroll and could see the red rocks of Salisbury Crags gradually emerge from its diaphanous curtain. It was a beautiful day, with the sky soon completely clear over the whole city, belying its name of Auld Reekie. The church bells were summoning the faithful to worship, and I thought briefly about the world of Sunday-best clothes, with hands clutching hymnbook or missal, saying thank you to minister or priest. It was a world serene, unquestioning, linked to a happy, stable childhood, and I had rejected it. Someday I would regret it. It was something more than having done with pigtails. One of the church bells started to ring out what was obviously going to be a hymn-tune, and that beautiful morning was lifted into sheer enchantment. Slowly, street by street, the whole congregation of all the bells in the city joined in like a great orchestra that stretched from end to end of our astonishing capital. I have heard that hymn many times since, but surprised myself recently by having to brace myself to prevent tears coursing down my cheeks. What for? Regrets for loss of first love, a requiem for wasted youth, possibly. But I think it was simply because it drew out of the cabinet of my memory an old, dusty, forgotten picture of home. For where else should Jerusalem be?

Normally such a splendid setting would make me exult with pleasure, but now I was tense and nervous, although I could not imagine why. I meant to give Dermot a briefing, but he was in one of his flights of fancy, talking of the history and happenings in Holyrood Palace over yonder, linking them with the cragsmen of today training on the rocks we were walking past. Somehow I could not equate George IV's knighting of Sir Walter Scott in the throne room of the palace with us getting chased away from the crags by irate parkies, but I let him ramble on because hearing him in this vein gave me a warm glow. Besides, he was quite likely to accuse me of being boring and practical if I tried to bring him down to earth by asking if we had enough money for bus fares and such like. In his mind's eye such concerns were the function of people like Rab.

I insisted we take the bus. The shame of going to Comely Bank in his deplorable car would have been insupportable. Nor, I think, would Miss MacPherson welcome it. On either side of her house, interested neighbors would be peering through their lace curtains. It would not be long before the jungle telegraph of residential Edinburgh North would know that two tatterdemalions were admitted to her residence, a bungalow painted a soft sunset pink.

I wore a two-piece suit with a rather straight skirt, the slightly pale blue shoes and handbag naturally complementing my suit. After putting on my mother's imitation pearl necklace, I toyed with the idea of wearing a hat. But after trying one on, my mother told me I was wearing it back to front. I realized it was fruitless, as I could never pull off the demure Sunday-school teacher act, not with him sitting next to me.

My eyes took in the garden surrounds. Neat rows of flowerbeds—geraniums, fuchsias and roses—were laid out tastefully in layers of well-bred complementary colors. Along the frontiers of the garden the hedge was high, wide, and clipped in that now extinct art of topiary into shapes roughly recognizable as the eagles of the legion and the wolf of Romulus. The garden could only be seen as an advertisement of her character: neat, colorful and forthright. The doorknocker, a lion's mouth filled with a brass ring, gave a resonant echoing thud, and Miss MacPherson opened the door in person, her companion having the day off. I was going to say she hadn't changed since I last saw her, but that would be a little white lie, since for one thing she looked smaller, and as she could not have shrunk, my memory must have served me wrong in this instance. For the first time I realized that she was a very handsome woman, not at all aged and decrepit as schoolmarms are supposed to be. The boring twin-set and pearls, her school uniform, had been cast aside, replaced by clothes that were striking without any vulgar ostentation. She was wearing a full shirtwaist dress, which had a floral pattern of warm variegated colors and was pouffed out by any number of lacy petticoats—a somewhat passé fashion, but somehow she managed to pull it off. She knew how to dress for effect as a woman of mature years might who is ripe and ready for harvesting. How much had she heard about Dermot? For just a moment I clutched my beloved's arm in panic.

With his suavest smile, he flourished a rather expensive box of chocolates, kept hidden until now. Miss MacPherson was of course delighted, while I thought bitterly of my tin of broken biscuits. We were then ushered into the front room. These best rooms, usually kept for weddings, funerals and other mournful occasions, were usually decorated in a manner fit to depress the corpse, but Miss MacPherson, being an original, had swept out the willow pattern and all the items reminiscent of the grim Edinburgh Sabbath. In their stead were Greek and Roman pots. Handles of crusty amphorae pulled from the deep were set beside black burnished Attic ware and red Samian vases fired in Gallic kilns during the second century AD. The figures on the Athenian pots seemed to be involved in rather curious pastimes. At least that's the only way I can describe it politely. I did not dare go too close to inspect them, as it might upset the delicate party air. Farther along there was a plaster-of-Paris model of the bust of Augustus from the Vatican. Being one of her favorites, his place here was predictable. This was flanked by the heads of other worthies of antiquity, Pericles and Alexander the Great, exemplifying her admiration of all things Hellenic. All of a sudden, at the end of one wall there was a picture of Nero drunkenly leering through his lyre at some Bacchantes, reminding me sharply that not all Rome was sweetness and light. Could this be another side of her personality? If so it was one for which I had no warning.

All three of us were sitting with plates of neatly groomed cucumber sandwiches balanced on our knees. We talked about the weather and the failure of the Corporation to build an opera house, and complained about Edinburgh bus conductors. We were at that dangerous moment when the festivity could fizzle out into an inspection of holiday snaps. Dermot was sitting up stiffly, one hand clutching the Spode tea set and the other holding a partially munched sandwich. It was almost as if he was in a French teleferique cabin.

"Oh no, please not!" I almost shrieked to myself.

Miss MacPherson said, "I think we have had just enough of these," and, picking up the empty plates, went into the kitchen or some other recess of the house.

In a moment she was back with two cake stands laden with assorted home bakery. My heart leapt. The trays were groaning with goodies. In front of my eyes was spread storey upon storey of Abernethy biscuits, Pitcaithly Bannocks, fudge fingers and that splendiferous Mrs. McFadden's coffee cake. On the other stand, nestling on a base of Dundee Cake and Gateau Miserable, was the glory of all glories, an array of honey-buttered Clermiston Prides. I could not contain a teeny squeak of ecstasy. Here truly was my homecoming. The others laughed a little at my childlike pleasure and thereafter the party took wing.

After a while I sat back, replete. Dermot and Miss MacPherson were getting along famously. I looked at the crumbly relics left on the altar of my happiness. It was almost too much, a dreamy situation. My love and my mentor were chatting along merrily at this summit conference. A little tear was gently prodding itself into birth behind my eyes. I needed a relief from too much bliss, so I offered my services to do the washing up, which to my surprise was accepted with alacrity. I stacked the dishes neatly, shoveling all the crumbs onto the top plate. By the bye, Dad told me never to do this when serving in the restaurant, since it makes people feel they are being chivvied. Within minutes I was splashing efficiently and cheerfully in a deep and lavish lather.

From next door I could hear the purr of contented conversation pausing to change gear now and then as the other partner took up the reins of chat. I heard a guffaw; it was Dermot at his least unaware. Surely Miss MacPherson, who we knew underneath was a warm person, was not now revealing herself as a wit. But there was no mistaking it; again the guffaw burst out like gunfire. I caught the words "Moussaka," "guide with moustache," "Aegean," and "dripping with soup."

After a pause filled with applauding laughter it was Dermot's turn. No! I could not believe my ears, for I was hearing "Chamonix," "teleferique cabin," "packed with

French," and "perfume." I looked down. The blush was spreading to my arms and elbows. Over the sink was a mirror. So Miss MacPherson had a touch of vanity like the rest of us mere mortals. I caught sight of my face, drained of blood. My fingertips were throbbing, dilated with the stuff that should be coloring my face. I waited on pins. Soon there would be the inevitable silence and the equally inevitable expulsion. Would my name be erased from the board of honors in Lauriston Academy? It had never been so inscribed, but one's imagination takes flight on these occasions. There was a hearty gale of feminine laughter, if that is not a paradox.

"Oh you are a rogue! What aye one!"

The punchline was totally different. I was so exhausted with relief I clean forgot the story.

When I returned to the best room, it was no longer "Will you be having another cucumber sandwich, Mr. Mulvaney?" but "Oh come on, Dermot, eat up the last slice. It'll give me an excuse to bake some more and invite you back."

"Well I must say it is rather succulent." He drawled on that last word so that it sounded almost lewd. Miss MacPherson's giggle (I noticed for the first time) was rather girlish. Goodness knows how this cake ritual was tickling her spinsterish bosom. As Dermot strode round the room examining her trophies and literature, the eyes that followed him were almost dewy, and at that moment it was I who was the prim schoolmarm.

Dermot was fingering his way along the bookcase. "Ah, Horace." He picked out the volume and thumbed through its pages. "You see on high stands the shivering snow white peak, Soracte." He began to intone his voice, lending perfect weight to its measured stanzas. Every word was enunciated with surprising clarity, dignity and stress. I noticed he didn't favor the new pronunciation preferred by the Church of Scotland, but spoke in that slightly Italianate way beloved of English public schools. I knew this ode and wondered how he would cope with its rather dodgy ending—naughty deeds in dark corners of Rome. Miss MacPherson was sitting entranced, as if Cicero was born again. He shut the book and declaimed from memory. At the words "drawn from a faintly yielding finger," he crooked his index finger and beckoned Miss MacPherson. I gasped at this crudity, and immediately turned shamefully to my old schoolmarm. I could not believe my eyes. She was squirming in ecstasy, her face resembling Bernini's sculpture of St. Theresa (my middle name comes from her by the way), as if a very furry cat were tickling her backside. Even Miss MacPherson, the last of the Romans, was not proof against Dermot's charm.

For a moment it seemed touch and go whether Miss MacPherson was going to rip her clothes off. The air in her best room in one of the more exclusive areas of Comely Bank was pulsating with licentiousness. I felt we had been transported to one of the steamier areas of Alexandria that Miss MacPherson had once referred to askance in one of her little talks on Roman Civilization.

A cough; it was my throat tickling in the charged air. "Would you mind if I made us all a nice cup of tea?"

"Please, please do, Moira. That would be lovely." Once again Miss MacPherson gave her approval with more dispatch than was required. As soon as I closed the door the laughter began anew.

Well, I was blowed if I was going to miss any of this, so I popped my head in and said, "More cakes?" One look told me neither my cakes nor company were required, but at least I could keep the door open, which was of course my aim.

Miss MacPherson launched herself into an anecdote, which I could not help overhearing. Apparently she and a friend of hers were holidaying on the Greek islands. Tantalisingly and rather skillfully she managed to conceal her friend's gender, with a coy sophistry that took me by surprise.

"You know, Dermot, the Aegean is my spiritual home. I wanted to immerse myself in that wine-dark sea."

"To the exclusion of drowning in it, I hope."

"Oh don't interrupt, Dermot, when I am talking." The words were that of the genuine Miss MacPherson, the empress who could freeze hundreds of little Lauriston chatterboxes at a hundred paces, but the tone was that of another, as if a flirtatious leprechaun was haunting her voice box. The surprisingly risqué tale was delivered with all the panache of the professional raconteur, and was well met at least by my companion.

When the laughter had died down I was feeling quite sick. Dermot later ascribed this to the way I had wolfed down all those cakes. He said he felt quite ashamed by my guzzling, and had to cover up by reciting some poetry and otherwise endeavoring to be entertaining.

Worse was to follow. It was quite obvious by the hushed tones of the conversation that Dermot was actually propositioning Miss MacPherson! And (more to the point) she was accepting. I could detect hurried scribbling in her diary that up till now was filled by evenings at the Classical Association and the odd bracing trip to visit the excavation of the Roman Fort at Inchtuthil near Dunkeld. In her more sprightly moments I imagined a night out listening to the Scottish Chamber Orchestra, but the thought that Miss MacPherson could actually enjoy being humped was completely beyond comprehension.

The worst blow came last of all. I had, you may have noticed, not been invited to join in their circle of first-name intimacy. That Miss MacPherson had a Christian name I had long suspected, but I felt that I shouldn't pry into hallowed places and soon lost any desire to discover it. No doubt it would be something with a whiff of Bloomsbury such as Egeria or Hyperion. You can imagine how I literally froze, just after warming the teapot, when I heard Dermot casually dropping "Bella" into one of his little quizzes. I must have misheard. I strained my ears as I plopped in the cubes of sugar with her nice silver tongs. Yes, "Bella" it was, as in: "Bella, could you come here a moment? I can't quite construe this sentence in your Seneca." What a comedown! She might as well have been called Plain Jane. Bella. It wasn't even Classical Latin, just the low medieval variety, meaning "little dear"—or "sweetie!" From the room there came soft swishing sounds, like leaves blown by the breeze sounding suspiciously like the rustling of petticoats being lifted. I barged into the room with the tea tray. At least they had the grace to jump apart.

I gave them two minutes to drink their tea.

"Well, Dermot, I think it's time to go. I don't want to miss Evensong." I gave Miss MacPherson a frosty farewell.

It was lost on her. "How astute of you to choose a young man with the making of a classicist." My hand was already on the front door knob.

I sulked badly on the bus home. There were the usual musical drunks upstairs, but they could neither annoy nor divert me. Were all my childhood idols to crumple in the same way? If I scrabbled about in the loft would I find evidence that dear old Mamma had been a mistress of Mussolini in the thirties? You never know—so many others had been.

Dermot, I suppose, was right. I had refused to accept that even a deity like Miss MacPherson was a person after all. "You should let her get off her pedestal. Teachers have got feelings just like you."

"Why can't they be as they were?"

"It's you that's changed, not her."

"To call her Bella MacPherson: it's so belittling."

"Moira, the problem is you. You've got to grow up."

As he said, and it hurt at the time, I was a female Peter Pan in so many, many ways.

Chapter 19

Hogmanay

I can't say I like Hogmanay. This may come as a shocking confession from one normally so ardently Scottish. But then I don't much like Christmas either, which always feels like imprisonment by television. Perhaps I am just not a festive person.

There is a lot of hard toil involved in the ritual of New Year. You know how it is when you are drinking yourself into the party mood; after the fifth pint, measure or whatever, everything tastes uniformly foul, but this is only a fraction of the priming required to see out the Old Year. Then there is the business of staying up late, your success as a Hogmanayer being rated per festal hour. "Aye, we were still tankin' it at six in the morn" has always seemed to me a pitiful boast, and the only omen propitiated—bad health.

After one thirty-first December when I walked along Rose Street, saw the drunks stretched head to toe in the gutter, and witnessed the bad-tempered fights between friends fuelled by the "fiery creature," I said enough is enough. Now, my idea of a Guid New Year is to put on a nice clean negligee, open a book and box of chocolates, and retire to bed. Unfortunately, when I get up bright and fresh to usher in the New, the whole of Edinburgh lies dead for the next couple of days. The only clues to the existence of life: empty beer cans and smashed whisky bottles interspersed amongst the carpet of vomit. Driving on Ne'erday can be perilous, as there are still a few hardy celebrants weaving an illogical path on and off the pavement. If you are stopped at the lights and one of them comes swaying up to you, it's odds on he will offer you a drink— "Hae a guid New Year, Lassie." To refuse is inviting a bottle through the windscreen. I don't know which is worse, that or the obligatory kiss perfect strangers feel the right to demand. "Gies a wee snog then, ma wee bonnie lassie" is the usual formula. If anyone petitions me for that particular slobbering liberty they are likely to get what they ask for: a smack on the kisser.

I notice that the real fans of this jollification usually spend the first week of January visiting their chums and apologizing for various disgraceful acts in order to patch up disrupted friendships. No, as far as I am concerned the only good thing about New Year is the opportunity to consume that unique confection, Black Bun—that delicious mess of sultanas and flies cemetery—which only graces our bakery shelves once a year. I call it the Brigadoon cake.

All in all it seemed to be a good idea of Rab's to spend

the New Year holidaying on the hill away from it all. How wrong I was. Sometimes it's better to stay in bed with a book and a box of chocolates. It's safer at least if you don't mind the effect on your figure.

I found that I had a lot of time for Rab. In his down to earth way, he had one gift our little circle of high flyers lacked: common sense. Rosie and I had moved to Marchmont, into a little pied a terre where machinery and furnishings were always breaking down. It was the usual range of troubles— no poltergeists or anything interesting. Cisterns would leak, shelves collapse, and record players at a moment's notice would turn Tito Gobbi into Minnie Mouse. Dermot, whose technical ability was limited to opening screw tops and spilling pale ale onto the floor, said the answer was to kick the offending apparatus. Rab, who actually read the manufacturer's handbook, disagreed, and would embark on feats of minor engineering with screwdriver, spanners and other miscellaneous items; then, hey presto, the flood in the sink receded and the record player was restored to euphony. My admiration for him knew no bounds.

To my mind, his greatest achievement was in prolonging the active life of Dermot's clapped-out old banger beyond its allotted span. As well as his interest in cars and other machinery, Rab was also a devotee of that new art form, the T.V. soap opera. His special favorite was Compact, which revolved round a women's magazine office where everybody spent more time necking than typing. This was ousted from top place by Coronation Street, which brought new words into his language. Rosie became "our kid" or "chuck" and was often "mardy." This was after one of those frightening days when Rab had not responded instantly to one of her little whims or fancies. According to Rab it was a slice of real life, and his happiest hours were spent in dissecting the ups and downs of the major characters.

"Rab," I said, "you make it sound like Jane Austen."

"I dunno, ah dinna ken her. Was she in your class at school?"

"No, no, not quite," I replied. What else could I say?

After that our conversation tailed off a bit, and it was only towards the end of the evening—when he had got the hoover sucking up dirt instead of blowing a dust storm back onto the carpet—that he said, "You know, I won't be coming to Torridon with you at New Year." This was a bit of a blow, especially since he had suggested the trip in the first instance. I had a funny feeling that I was going to need a friend, for I had a hunch that battle was about to commence with Dermot, and Rab was my only really solid ally. Rosie's role was at best ambivalent and there was a little worrying nudge on the horizon there.

I pleaded with him as best I could, saying that we needed him in case Lazarus broke down (not really a flattering argument when I thought about it), but he was adamant, which was unusual for him. He straightened up from the floor where he was tinkering and gave me that unwavering look of his. Oh, oh, thinks I, an imaginary Aunt Flossie is about to be conjured into existence, having one of her turns, but he was too honest for that. He was finding Rosie a bit trying, and Dermot's highhanded handling nettled him. "If he assumes just once mair that he is aye goin' to be doing the leading, I'll gie him a Pilton Handshake." A Pilton Handshake? From the violence of his expression I deduced it would be an unpleasant experience. This unexpected flurry of feeling soon passed, which was a relief, for his heartfelt anger shook me so much that for a split second I wondered what my tantrums felt like from the receiving end. Calmer now, he confessed that he really wanted to see the Hibs and Hearts match on New Year's Day, "and not to have 'himself 'ranting on about Rabbie Burns, Hugh McDairmid, and other spare parts."

When we set off on our expedition to the far northwest, Lazarus was filled up with the normal mix of people, food and climbing gear. A mysterious "A.N. Other" made up our quota. All we were told was that he was a Glaswegian, but a Rangers supporter, "if you ken what I mean." Like Rab, he was a man of his hands. It was a safe bet he had been recruited by Dermot solely for his skills as a motor mechanic. I opened the back door to meet this paragon of practicality. It was difficult for him to tell us anything about himself, as he was sitting underneath two rucksacks. We could just about see the top of his head. I moved away a pile of jam pots and climbing bric-a-brac, and there, behold! Off the proscribed list and now implausibly promoted to Dermot's best mucker was Archie Stewart, formerly chief villain and disturber of the peace. Unknown to the rest of us there had been a new tactical realignment—think Nazi-Soviet Pact. The crimes and utter boorishness of which he had formerly been guilty had been wiped away by Dermot's papal absolution. It was up to us to fall into line. All change at Carstairs Junction. The malice formerly darkening his brow all wiped away, leaving a face as innocent as that of a babe in arms. He looked shyly up. I remembered I had only seen him steamboats, so maybe he was a nice guy after all; maybe he had just been trying too hard. I doubted the leopard could be so spotless, but resolved for the sake of the harmony of the trip to give him a grudging second chance. Then I remembered Dermot mentioning him casually, hinting that he could be saved. It was the only time I had heard Dermot using that quasi-religious expression, and realized that he was paving the way. So Archie the yobbo really was Rab's understudy.

Some friends of ours were renovating an old village blacksmith's shop, complete with anvil and bellows, into an Alpine hut set amidst the wild, craggy splendors of the Western Highlands. To make it official they had formed a club and called it the Caledonian Climbing Club. The naming was not the outcome of a moment of patriotic fervor, but because the inaugural meeting took place in the bar of the old Caledonian Hotel. By the time we arrived, people were settling in, laying out their sleeping bags and bagging the best places, and everyone was laughing for no apparent reason—the usual high spirits at the beginning of a promising weekend. The furnace was lit to provide a homely glow, but through long years of disuse the chimney was partially blocked. Well-meaning prodding with ice axes simply increased the general stour in the air. A smoky layer of cumulonimbus clouds rested about a foot above the top bunks. At the end of the weekend we went home with sooty faces, the auld grey heids a lot happier, and all of us coughing intermittently.

As sometimes happens, the thirty-first December turned out to be an extremely beautiful day that can leave you wistfully saying a regretful farewell to what otherwise might have been a mixed or mediocre twelve months. As we tramped across the frozen bog to the foot of the ridge, the day was welcomed by a fiery, lurid dawn of orange and yellow cloud that usually heralds a storm. So far it was like any of a hundred grey days in the hills. Mounting up to the shoulder of the ridge we entered into a thick clammy mist. Another day, another set of wet clothes, I sighed. The wind blew; the wet drizzle spat in my face. I hunched down into my anorak, resigned to another day of dreariness. Sheets of mist billowed down on me in line like a cavalry charge, each one brighter than the last. Then all my petty thoughts disappeared as the mist boiled away and evaporated, and a glorious winter sun took over. Set in front of me were row upon row of pinnacles, crags and battlements glistening like newly baked biscuits under a cloudless sky. The snow, a flawless satin dress, was so bright that even wearing sunglasses we had to turn from the mountains and look to the plain for relief. In contrast with the monochrome heights, the heather, gorse and broom of the lowland provided a patchwork of amethyst, purple and greens fragmented by a myriad of startling blue lochans stretching towards the horizon where it melted into the snow-whitened hills. To the west the Atlantic shimmered, a calm sea broken only by the Summer Isles.

Not even climbing with Stewart could disturb my harmony with the mountain that day. Ahead of us Rosie whooped in exultation, her voice carrying easily in the still air. Even the creak of their crampons and the snap of crisp snow pierced by axes could be heard clearly. No other human sounds disturbed the calm. Brushing snow off the handholds, I was surprised to find that the rock was warm and dry within minutes, the midwinter sun hotter than on many a summer day.

Balancing delicately over spikes, spillikins and gendarmes, I peered up at a neverending series of delights, snow covered bushman's huts and pot kilns all in a line, while some of the towers were like bulbous haystacks out of a painting by Courbet. Sitting on the leaning tower known as Lord Berkeley's Seat, with all around me the lavish splendor of a winter's day in the Highlands—mountain upon mountain varnished with silver, strewn about in prodigal abundance—I thought that, had I a magic carpet, there was nowhere else I would rather be, not even the Karakorum. The little breeze that had sprung up when we started off died away. A century ago, Mummery, atop the Matterhorn, noted the air was so still that cigarette smoke ascended directly heavenwards. None of us smoked to put it to the test, but today would have been such a day.

Perhaps I was enjoying that elusive state: perfect happiness. The philosopher in me started to argue. No, there was no itch in my body, no mote in the eye or blight on the land-scape. Ergo, in the absence of any evidence to the contrary, I was experiencing sheer bliss. For a moment I felt a pang of pity for poor Rab at Easter Road, standing in the drizzle, solitary in the crowd of beer-swilling plainsmen.

My fingers and toes were beginning to nip. Even the thick woolen jersey and anorak that I wore were no longer sufficient to keep out the cold. It was time to go.

Too soon we left behind the last ice-crusted pinnacle and descended to a grand sloping plateau polished into an icy mirror by the wind, its surface changing into burnished gold by the lowering sun, which, dropping behind the ocean, set the Atlantic afire with molten red. On that last long slope down to the Smiddy, the dusk air turned chilly and lifeless, a sudden ominous portent. We hurried down the last steps in the dark, and minutes later were in the hut chattering away over a warming brew and hot soup, the cold forgotten.

I was quite content to linger over the business of cook-ing and changing clothes. For one thing, I wanted to savor the splendor of the day. As each team came in we asked them how they had got on. "Great," they said simply and suffi-ciently. More fulsome praise betrayed the poverty of mere words. One person did say, "Better than a fish supper." Ev-eryone laughed at this corny catch phrase, which I thought bad taste, considering they knew my background.

As is the way of things, everyone forgot about the day and began excitedly preparing for the night ahead. With this crowd around there was no chance to don a nightie, grab a cup of cocoa, slip into my sleeping bag and let the New Year take me unawares. Reluctantly I began preparing myself for the evening's obligatory dipsomania, drawing out each item in my toilette as elaborately as possible. My hair was styled fussily, severely then finally with a frivolous kiss curl adding a question mark to my pageboy style, but the crushing effect of wearing a balaclava for twelve hours ruled out any serious experiment with my coiffure.

We had been invited to join the villagers in bringing in a Gaelic New Year. As they had invited us to join in a community celebration purely out of kindness and old-fashioned Highland hospitality, my reluctance may seem more than usually churlish. The fact that I was going as an unwilling guest made me feel heavy of heart right at the start of the evening's fun. I don't often consider other people's feelings but I could see I was going to add about as much fun to this party as Banquo's ghost.

My delaying tactics had succeeded. Almost everyone had gone on, my boyfriend included, in the first wave. With a bit of luck I could feign sleep, and tomorrow be annoyed nobody had bothered to wake me up. I was trying on a pair of dangly earrings for the third time when I heard an insistent cough, apparently emanating from Stewart's midriff, for his upper body was swallowed up in the smoky murk.

"Are you just about ready, Moira?" Was he taking on the role of escort that night on Dermot's orders, or maybe he still thought he was roped to me?

"Aw don't rush me. They can manage fine without me. Or do they need us to set the party ablaze?"

No answer.

"You're from Glasgow aren't you?" I said. He shuffled his feet and looked down humbly as if confessing to some enormous felony.

"Is that too bad then?"

"Usually." I was determined to extract some fun from my forced date.

There was more bowing and scraping. Sheepishly he replied, "Sorry." And then rallying a bit: "Well, I can't help that. Anyway if we don't go soon we'll miss the party."

"Okay." I snapped my compact case shut. "Let's go."

Outside, the frost on the roof of the Smiddy was a glittering white carapace under a crisp, starry sky. Archie, undeterred by my brusque manner, was trying to take my arm as if he was squiring me to the ball.

"I can manage queat faine," I said all snooty like.

"Awfy sorry. It's just that the road's slippy. Ye might fa' doon and I know I couldn't help blaming mysel'."

"Don't be so bloody pathetic and stop saying sorry. You're getting on my bloody wick!"

"Sorry, Moira. Sorry! I mean sorry. I won't say it again."

By now we had entered the main bar of the hotel, not without a little skip and jump of gallantry as he played the polite lad and opened the door in case I couldn't manage it myself. No one greeted our presence. Lined up in front of the bar was an almost motionless rank of men wearing an assortment of deerstalkers and flat caps, each hat sporting a motley collection of fishing flies, for all the world like a congregation at prayer. There was no hum of conversation, only a few muffled orders breaking through the slurping and clinking. Any Englishman or other outlander happening on this still life would assume this was Scotland at its dourest, but this was not so; this was the build up, the preparation for the ritual ahead. Every man jack of them was busy injecting the required tonnage of booze into his system. The muffled orders gradually distilled themselves. There was "Pint o' heavy an' a hauf, Jimmy," or simply "hauf'n heavy, Jimmy." Jimmy was moving like a whippet from end to end of the bar, dispensing refreshment without pause or interval. All the taps were on, and when one glass was filled, its place was taken by a clean glass with hardly a drop of spillage. And it was a clean glass. There was no malingering of the sort that you sometimes get. ("In the same glass, then?") There was no doubt Jimmy was the hero of the night—the Stakhanov of the bar.

I noticed that the orders had a certain monotonous regularity: invariably a pint and a nip of whisky. Weaknesses such as lager shandy or the effete Dubonnet and lemonade were not allowed. It was just a teeny bit solemn; not quite the priest dispensing the sacraments, more like a masculine version of Sunday afternoon tea in Duddingston. As you probably realize by now, there are times when I just cannot help being naughty. I went up to the bar and asked in my sweetest manner for a lager and blackcurrant, plus a campari and soda. The gasping Jimmy passed a handkerchief over his sweaty brow, then without batting an eyelid handed me a pint of heavy and a nip of whisky. The only concession made to my exotic request was that the dram was Antiquary, not the usual Bells, so I was charged 7/6, not the standard five bob. Realizing my ploy had failed, I said, "Double it," for courtesy required I get my chaperon a drink.

Towards ten, the tempo increased to a frenzy. People were ordering double, treble and even quadruple rounds as the hour of doom approached, when the shutters clanged down on that awful final note. Would we all be flung out and have to celebrate the New Year by the frozen Lochside? This and a number of other uncomfortable questions rose up in my mind, such as: Where is that Irish sod and my supposed "friend" Rosie? All forgotten when our genial host appeared—not Jimmy, he was merely a superior flunky—and announced the three magic words, "Ben the Hoose."

We all trooped through to the party, which was spread out in the various rooms of the living quarters. The men, who just a few moments ago had seemed tireless topers, were now relaxed and welcoming. "Now then, jussht tell me and where do you hail from?" Their speech as pellucid as the sweet, pure waters of the tumbling burns that went to make up the Highlandman's malt.

At least two fights were on the go, a signal that the party was in full swing. A few wildly flung punches petered out into harmless pirouettes. Then the participants stopped suddenly without provocation, as if they simply could not be bothered to carry on. All at once the erstwhile combatants had arms around each other and became maudlin buddies. I couldn't say which was worse, the brawl or the subsequent lachrymose reconciliation. I was tucked up in an armchair out of harm's way, not that that stopped the flow of whisky coming at me from all directions. One timid taste told me I couldn't stand the stuff, but it was no use refusing; they just kept on filling my glass. Maybe I should have said it in Gaelic. Putting my hand over the top of the glass was no good, as they just poured the liquid over my hand. Luckily there was a pot plant nearby. Nobody minded or took much notice when I watered it with 15-year-old malt. Years later, when I became an environmentalist, I felt guilty about that sozzled flower.

Men kept pestering me for a dance, but it was High-land dancing, which (since it consisted of being flung across the room from one drunk to another) had but little appeal. Few seemed offended by my refusal to submit to becoming a human shuttlecock. Anyway, where was Dermot, my protector? I cocked my eyebrows at Stewart, who was busily explaining in great and boring detail the story of our day to an unriveted farmer. Mistaking my signal, he stepped up and took me by the arms.

I pulled away and said, "It's okay. There's no ice on the floor here."

"No, I just wondered if you fancied a dance."

"No thanks! Just take me back to the hut! I'm fed up

with these drunken Teuchters!"

He gasped at me goggle-eyed like a blowfish. I could see he was thinking; could this ingrate be the same etiquette-conscious exquisite he had squired earlier this evening? To his Gorbals grey matter I was an enigma. What he didn't know was that I had returned to my intolerant form of old. Of course he tried to cheer me up on the way back to the cottage. But I was not having any of it. "Listen, I can't stand Highlanders, Irelanders, or people from Glasgow."

"Why not?"

"Oh, look at you and you would know what I mean."

"I'm sorry...I mean. I'm sorry, Moira."

"Just shut up, and shine your torch on the road. That's right, in front of my dainty feminine feet. Your clodhoppers won't have to mind getting wet."

In case he had not got the message earlier I was being fairly discouraging now. His torch beam shook a bit.

I had wondered where my friends were, and now, as we entered the darkened Smiddy, I made a bitter discovery. From the straw pallet in the corner came rhythmic thrashing noises as if a pair of bodies were doing a horizontal St. Vitus two-step. Dimly I saw a huge sausage of a bag getting punched from the inside, as if in perpetual motion. As I observed many years before, it was difficult for two in a single sleeping bag but not impossible—the sort of problem that makes a fascinating challenge for people of spirit such as mountaineers. From the hoggish grunts and squeals not entirely muffled by the downy quilt, I would say that the camel had just passed through the eye of the needle.

At times like these, mere words cannot do justice to the situation. While my Glaswegian friend was helplessly going, "Oh dear, oh dear me!" I was looking round the room for assistance. Sure enough, near the stoves was a large dixie full of water, intended to save a trip to the burn in the morning. A loud groan harmonizing perfectly into a duet came from the pulsating pit after a particularly telling thrust. My blood was boiling so much I was beyond control. I heard the futile one say, "Oh dear! No!" and realized that I had snatched up the bucket, ready for the assault. Too late the deed was done, a small amount of satisfaction to avenge the night's misdeeds. With a great whoosh the water landed on the mounted pair. There were screams all round as tired partygoers were wakened for this last unscheduled round of festivities.

Unfortunately, as a weapon of revenge, a bucket of water is not as selective as a gun. Some unharmed but soaked people on the upper bunk began yelling at me. These were the same miserable ones who later organized a putsch to expel me from their club on the nebulous grounds of conduct unbecoming. A few others cheered my action, one of whom even said, "Well done, Moira, I couldnae sleep with the twae of the baith of thae humpin' bastards ower me."

By now my intended victims had recovered from the initial shock. Shivering in her soaking pit, Rosie began screaming at me in surprisingly fluent foul language. All sorts of imprecations and calumnies shook the night air, tiresome for the reader. Suffice to say Mamma and Pappa were married by a proper priest, and I have never walked the length of Rose Street either professionally or as an enthusiastic amateur, but the remarks passed that night did rather put a blot on our friendship.

I had lost the most important battle. Historians and psychologists will tell you that violent solutions only create more problems. It was of peripheral interest to me that I had lost all the sympathy I would have gained if I had stood weeping by the humping bunk like a wet lettuce. Dermot was now given his excuse on a plate. "You'll catch your death of cold. Get your wet things off and come into mine," says he, unrolling a fresh dry sleeping bag. "It's warm and dry." Of course the coy bitch accepted at once, and they lay there warmly cuddling each other although not actually having it off. I listened carefully to monitor this. But of course, as all the world knows, warm, soft embraces can be even more tender than the most avid rogering. And with that very cold comfort I wept a welcome to the New Year.

It seemed hours later that I awoke. The first light of day was peeking timidly through the slats of the shuttered door, which slowly creaked open. Figures were creeping about in the shaft of dusty light that came from the doorway. I was still slowly drifting downstream with my lover, till we camped in a bay of potted plants. A louder creak brought me round from my sleepy bliss, and soon the dull truth landed with a heavy thud in my stomach—a feeling familiar to any jilted lover.

"A guid New Year tae yin 'n aw!"

Silence.

"Are ye a' deid?"

More of the above.

Three locals, who had missed out on the party, were doing some catching up. Everyone was asleep or dozing half-awake, struggling to return to it. Nobody answered their cheery salutations. One of them soon gave up this thankless task, sat down by the pillar in the middle of the room, and within a moment was fast in the arms of Morpheus. The other two split their forces; one took charge of the top deck, while the other catered to the lower bunk. They offered refreshment from their New Year bottles, shook hands or (in the case of the girls) sealed the moment with a Gaelic snog. As far as I could make out, most people blearily complied, even though the liquor must have tasted quite revolting on their hangover-encrusted tongues. The Highlanders were fairly forceful with their greeting and good cheer. To refuse "to tak a New Year," was asking for trouble. Several slumbering climbers were shaken into the New Year anew, and much whisky gurgled its merry way down reluctant throats. The awoken damosels were quite clearly not enjoying the mauling they were getting, but if their boyfriends were too spineless to intervene, they had better just lie back and think of Scotland, I suppose.

Two along from me on the left, I heard a girl weeping miserably as the drunken giant slobbered all over her. It would be my turn soon. I pulled the draw cord up tight, so that only my nose was poking through like a snorkel. Next to me a rather upright voice was saying, "No, thank you very much. I have had quite enough to drink and now, my good man, if you wouldn't mind letting me go to sleep. We have got a long drive back to Edinburgh. I don't suppose there will be any place of refreshment open this Ne'erday."

"Hey Feargus, jusht listen at this English pfluff. 'No law-de-daw plaice o'ar refreshment open todaih.' Listen, Twala," he roared, "jusht stuff this boattle doon your place o' refreshment or I'll make ye remember Prestonpans." He grabbed the sleeping bag and jackknifed its discourteous inmate up into the sitting position.

"Get a dram of the fiery cratur in yer belly and ye won't need tae stoap for refreshment."

"Oh, well, in that case let me wish you a happy New Year." So saying he poured about a quarter of the bottle down his throat, shook the hairy Highlander's hand and plunged back into his pit. I watched this exhibition transfixed by curiosity and terror. What must it be like waiting for your turn on the guillotine? I crash-dived back under; even my nose was submerged as the immense form rolled on top of me.

"Let's see what we hae here," said he, drawing my toggled cord back. I must have looked like Nefertiti when her tomb was uncovered, for this brute whistled and scratched his head. At length: "Weel now, this lassie wouldna be the waur for a guid shaggin'!" So said the surprisingly literary lout, misquoting Judge Braxfield. Barone maledetto, but his breath must be inflammable. As he began groping feverishly at me, I thanked Our Lady that at least he had shaved. I didn't fancy being raped by a hedgehog. One of his hands was slithering down towards my sportsman's gap, fortunately protected by assorted layers of clothing, but as defenses under his assiduously scrabbling fingers they could only be considered temporary. The overpowering aromas of aftershave and breath stained by tobacco and whisky were clashing inharmoniously! This on top of everything else was too much, so I kicked him straight in his brains—that is between his legs.

He let out a screech, higher-pitched than expected, and pulling back his fist to hit me in the face, shouted, "Ye wee besom!"

I spat at him straight in the bullseye. In the dim light I could see him going cockeyed trying to focus on the gob hanging from a thread on his nose.

I could not hold back any longer. I just burst into tears. No, it wasn't this pathetic Teuchter that frightened me. I would soon claw his eyes out well before he got me out of the sleeping bag, but what he had in mind should have been handed out by one lying practically next to me. For all he cared, I could have been on the other side of the Highland Line, and him all snuggled up in the arms of my betrayer.

My wailing disturbed Feargus who was still in the midst of the lower deck. "Haud on, Donhail. Leave the lassie alone."

"Whit?"

"Go on gie her a break. She doesnae want yer whisky."

"Whit? She just kicked me in the hoolies and gobbed

in ma giek!"

"Well she doesnae fancy you. Some of them dinna'. C'mon doon."

"Whit?"—a favourite word of his. "She'll tak her New Year like the rest."

"No she winnae! Let's awa hame tae oor beds."

"Feargus, awa and bile yer heid!"

"Whit?"—his turn now. "Noone tells me to bile ma heid!"

"Well, go an' bile it wi' a sheep's heid an'a."

"Whit?"

This "whit" made its farewell appearance as, preferring action to words, Feargus took off his jacket and threw it at the third member. "Hector, haud that."

As Hector was fast asleep, the jacket plopped over his head like a grey shroud. Feargus's shirt, I noticed, was immaculately white and well-pressed. He had a good woman tucked up somewhere, waiting for her New Year kiss.

He grabbed Donhail by the feet and dragged him off the bunk. Desperately scratching, Donhail made a frantic grab at me to get some purchase, but I turned away nippily, just rolling back in time to see his face disappearing over the edge. He looked at me imploringly with "Traitor's Gate" eyes lit up by a shaft of morning twilight peeping over the door. I stuck my tongue out at him. I hope he noticed.

Down below there were unsuppressed curses and "Ye'll no tell me to bile ma heid!" followed by three loud, unmistakable cracks. The brawl did not last long. My hero

Feargus was what was known as a bonnie fechter. A few smashing punches soon sorted out the attempted rapist. Besides, Donhail was not allowed to take his jacket off. There was a last sickening thud, a gasping sharp intake of breath and then, surprise-surprise: baby-like sobbing. I peered over the edge. Donhail was blubbering like a kid. His face, awash with rivulets of blood, was not a pretty sight.

"Ma new jaicket ruined!" (It was.) "Ma new shirt ruined!" (It was, too.) "And look at my breeks!" I looked. There was a most gratifying tear in them. "My mither will kill me!" He cried, greeting like a tap. Mamma mia, I didn't fancy meeting this Amazon.

Feargus did not wait to gain my thanks. He just put his arm around the shoulder of his pal and said, "C'mon, let's awa' tae oor beds. I'll tell yer ma ye were jumped on in the dark. But ye fought like a hero to protect your wallet with her picture." I could hear him further elaborating on this fiction as they tottered homewards.

I felt much better after this. All round me I could hear groans as people tried to get back their stolen sleep. I put both my hands up in the air and started singing:

"Hail Caledonia,

Hail Bright New Morn."

I was singing this to the tune of Brahm's Academic Festival Overture. It didn't fit but I was not going to let trifles spoil my euphoria. As I leapt out of bed the groans were reaching chorus level, and I started crashing tin plates together pretending to get breakfast ready, continuing to sing:

"The thighs of Rosie sprawl

  Like Lynwillg known to all.

  Now my true love is betrayed

  By one who abused a maid.

  It was that Irish Swine.

  Mamma mia you'll hear him whine.

  Let he who scorns the Latin Race

  Watch. For Claws may mar his face."

I surprised myself by how easily I could make up this drivel. The people on the benches, unappreciative of Moira's New Year ditty, were now howling for me to shut up. I lifted a pile of mugs, dixies and billies above my head, and saying, "Oops! How terribly careless of me," threw them to the floor.

The loud clatter and echoing shouts of protest at last managed to wake up the third reveler. He was completely taken aback, blindfolded in addition to still being befuddled by drink.

"Whair am I? Turn on the light! Mah e'en, mah e'en!" He was shrieking in panic. "Help! I've been blinded. I've lost mah sight! Oh jings! I should have never hae drunk yon porridge whisky at the bothan!"

He rushed about the Smiddy, and I watched in fascination as he smacked straight into the anvil with a horribly painful crack, then neatly pole-vaulted over it. He looked about him like a lost dog. The jacket-cum-blindfold had fallen onto the floor. Silence. He touched his eyes.

"It's a miracle! It's a New Year miracle! I was blind

and now I can see! See?" He pointed to his eyes in case any-one was interested, and limped out at a run. In the distance I could hear him, "I'm going to the kirk right noo. Whaur is it?" Far away I just caught him practising his New Year res-olution: "I'll never, Meenester. I'll never touch a drop again. So help ma, Boab. No hooch onyway."

Set out neatly along the wall of the Smiddy were ten shining primus stoves, lumps of priming fuel fastidiously crumbled in their saucers. Last night one of the more fus-tian and pernickety ladies had cleaned and filled them with fuel before going to the party. "So's they're ready first thing the morn." I went along the row, tightening up the pressure valve, and then pumped up each one good and hard. I wait-ed a second and then, as the paraffin came squirting out the hole, set a match to each of them. "Whoosh, whoosh, whoosh," and so on and so forth. An explosion of flame al-most hit the rafters. The good ladies from Edinburgh began shrieking anew, fit to take their heads off. With more logic and a lot more tune I started singing,

"Ten Green Bottles up against the Wall,
Ten Green bottles had a great fall."
Whit a Great New Year!

Chapter 20

Moira Alone

Surprisingly, soon afterwards I received a letter from the secretary of the Caledonian Climbing Club encouraging me not to consider thinking of joining. It read, "Your disruptive behavior, followed by attempt at arson, might prejudice the other members against your otherwise stimulating comradeship." Attempt at arson! All I was doing was helping them with breakfast and encouraging them to get up and enjoy the day instead of snoring it away in their pits. And wasn't I justified in my disruptive behavior? But I bit my lip at that. Provocation was no excuse under Scots law, and if I attempted to plead a crime passionnel it would be a lost cause with that jury of worthies. It was a pity in a way, for they had a grand hut, or would have when they got a chimney. The underlying message from his letter was that I was not winning friends and influencing people by my conduct. Perhaps I should be smarmier with folk in the future, but as a New Year's resolution it was a non-starter; I was resigned to that.

There were more pressing problems than currying favor with all and sundry. The flat we shared was in Rosie's name. As a peaceful twosome we were washed up. Trivial arguments as to whose turn it was to wash up had already flared, and I strongly suspected her of making free with my hair shampoo, but refused to stoop to the level of making a Plimsoll line on the bottle. Nevertheless, whenever she had a bath and came in waving her fresh, glistening locks in that show-off way she has, as if she was parading on the cat walk, I always endeavored to get a good sniff at her hair. It was quite easy to do this unobserved while she was busy preening herself. My olfactory organs rarely played me false, and on the occasions when she was hunting big game I didn't need to call in the Yard to tell me that she wasn't using her regular whale oil, but treating herself to my more sophisticated essence.

In short I packed my bags. I still owed her two weeks rent, and for a moment I thought, "Why not make her whistle for it?" But I knew it was no go. Certain things like pouring water over people are all right in their way, and give a certain sweet satisfaction, but to short change or cheat someone is one thing I can't abide. Where money is concerned I am honest—tight (I have been accused of being an adopted Aberdonian) but straight. If I went without paying I would only despise myself in the end and push the moral balance in their direction.

So I cleared out the flat. Latterly it had proxied as a left luggage repository for Dermot's chattels. These made a nice little funeral pyre in the back green. I allowed myself a tear as a fondly remembered pair of unmentionables crisped to ashes. I paid my rent, even leaving extra to cover unaccounted electric bills, and added at the bottom of the note: "Please do not send a receipt signed Miss M. Fiorelli" [sic] to show that our friendship was now glaciated. I suppose I was hoping to gain a slight advantage, making her feel a moment of regret. That was a forlorn hope. Probably she and Dermot would have a good laugh at it that night. It's strange how, as soon as a lover has ceased to charm, they become a rubbed-out Trotsky on photographs, a non-person, discussion of whom is an embarrassment and (if forced into view) a figure of fun. To the outside world they appear ridiculous with their abject clinging to the wreckage of their relationship. That was not my way, but neither was the dignified exit. As far as I was concerned the word dignity had no meaning in this context. I had given them a fighting withdrawal. I wished them well and hoped they both caught arthritis, or at least a cold.

With these benevolent thoughts I left the flat. I am sure I saw Dermot lurking in the darkness of the stairhead. At least there seemed to be a rucksack with a long creepy figure tucked behind, trying to appear invisible. That was awful. My tactful withdrawal had given them an opportunity to set up their sordid little nest.

When I got home, I cut such a sorry figure entering the front door that Dad leapt up, asking in the Italian still there beneath the surface, "Che cosa e successo?"

I told him what had happened in a bowdlerized form fit for parents. In my misery I kept hammering him on the chest. "Voglio morir!"

I didn't want to die, just create a scene. Mamma joined in and soon the whole household was wailing. Freddie was eager to try out a Mafioso-style vendetta. He had some very weird friends with fertile imaginations overstimulated by watching cheap gangster films. I had to stop the tide of tears long enough to dissuade him. My stock, low enough with the stuffier types in Edinburgh climbing circles, would not be enhanced if my ex-lover and his lass were found machine-gunned on their tenement stairs.

To cheer me up, Mamma shoved a huge plate of steaming spaghetti Bolognese under my nose. For once I had no appetite. I just looked at it and went howling to my room. Mamma shouted up, "You no eat, you starve!" Actually, she did not speak this music hall Italo-English, but her words carried the same logic. At ten o'clock I sneaked downstairs. Everyone was watching some horrific variety show on the box. Knowing she hated waste and that the spag bog would still be there just requiring heating, I ate it up and felt a bit better.

I would rather not go over that first week of loneliness. At work and home I was a misery. My father had more to worry about than love-battered daughters. His expedition into the uplands of haute cuisine was failing badly. Despite its sensational send-off, the Napoli had fallen flat. That this was due to ill-timing rather than bad management was no consolation to Dad, struggling to cash his haggis and chips into the means for paying the bills. The reason that it had all gone wrong was that Edinburgh Man, after centuries of having his grub the way Maw put it on the table, had quite suddenly realized that there was culinary life beyond the Pentlands, and foreign food could cross the Forth. Whether this was due to the New Forth Bridge or the International Festival is immaterial, as colorfully outlandish fooderies sprang up all over the unsuspecting city. I ate my first sincerely Indian nosh in a little cafe behind Chambers Street that year, and have been an addict ever since. Paella passed my untrained palate soon afterwards. A Hungarian restaurant, trailing some years after the uprising, opened its doors. Dad's mixture of low-life Scot's fare and Americanized Italian food seemed hackneyed to the new, ever-hungry public. A year before or ten years later and all would have been hunky-dory, but at that moment, with the new cosmopolitan cuisine coming upon our eating horizons, it was a loser. For him life was too serious to spend on time-wasting trips to the hills and the pictures, as he rather innocently imagined the setting for my romantic jaunts. I thought that if he had no time to spare even talking about the hills, I might be wiser to stay out of his way.

To make things worse, an emboldened Archie Stewart took to ringing me up at all hours in a self-assumed role of comforter and applicant for suitor. How this grotesque human being had the nerve boggles the imagination. His bombardment was so insistent, in the end I gave in and listened to him. He saw that I was so attached to Dermot it would take something drastic to pull us apart. Some font of wisdom—probably some wino propping up an end barstool in the depths of the Gorbals—had told him women love a swine. At least it will get you noticed. So, misled, he decided to be one, hence his loutish behavior the night of the dance. Up to a point, his trusty mentor was right, but totally boorish bastards—no thanks. Sometime in the course of the evening he had come to the same conclusion, and as a result had sworn off drink forevermore. Well, that was a start, and he sounded so winsome and pathetic that I was on the verge of giving him a trial run when he spoilt it all by slipping in a few press releases about Dermot's peccadilloes. Talk about jumping in when the blankets are still warm. This guy had the cheek of the devil. Naturally I ignored it. Besides, he was a west coast man, and it was a fair bet he would pass on the news of my grief to Dermot. At times like this you realize that your true friends are quite thin on the ground, the ranks of mine further depleted by the harrowing experiences I put them through when I felt like humoring my bad temper. For the first time in my life I felt the utter emptiness of having all the eggs in my basket broken utterly and irretrievably.

Chapter 21

The Thistle and the Rose

"Well, of course, butter is the most dangerous poison known to man." I watched him swaying by the bar, slowly fumbling to light a cigarette, which he swiftly extinguished when he realized he was being taken seriously. "Heart attacks, hypertension and others"—he churned his hand in the air, the universal sign language for "etcetera" and "lots of other things." I was dumbfounded that such dangers lurked in our cupboards and fridges.

"Even cholera?" I must have looked as if I was born yesterday.

"Yes, butter has been known to contribute—" He saw he had pushed his luck too far and finished limply, "—in some rare strains of the disease."

"What about alcohol?" I looked at him not so credulously. "Car crashes, broken homes, murder, rape, delirium tremens." I held up my fingers, listing the more sensational consequences. I may have sounded more severe than I intended, for the man standing next to me paused in mid gulp and nervously put his glass back on the counter.

"And aren't you doctors amongst the guilty ones?" I added.

"Listen, I can tank up ten pints a night and when my buzzer goes, adrenalin washes out the alcohol and I am steady enough for anything."

"Isn't that when doctors kill patients?"

"Mistakes happen."

"What is your particular specialty?" I asked to change the subject.

"I'm a quim quack."

I looked at him in botheration. Was he going to be so basic the whole evening? And then, for no reason at all, I thought of the time Dermot and I were climbing Piton Route in the Avon Gorge. We were wondering about the cryptic obstetricians' move mentioned in the guide book. It must be doing the splits I thought, when Dermot yelled out to the whole crag, not forgetting the family groups on the Suspension Bridge out for their Sunday stroll, "It's a quim!" He had rammed his fingers in an old borehole filled with water and bird dirt. I had to hide at the back of the belay ledge until my face cooled and the strollers had moved on.

"Sorry! I've shocked you." A faint bittersweet pang of melancholy must have surfaced and registered on my features. I was brought back to the present.

"Can I get you another?"

"Yes please." I was determined to get my money's worth out of this encounter, and pointed my finger along the shelf, where the very expensive ingredients to the cocktails this George Street bar specialized in stood like unfused bombs.

"Just a bit of this, a dash of that, a splash of that, and yes—about a pint of that. No, make it a half. When!"

My date looked at me with admiration not unmixed with discreet calculation. Later I saw him check his wallet when I was supposed to be looking elsewhere. I had graduated from my immature brandy-and-Babycham days, and knew how to drink in a chic fashion. If the mood was right I could offer a provocative exposure of leg on the bar stool, either in a still life pose or in a blinding flash of thigh when crossing and uncrossing my legs. I knew almost to the moment when the eyes busy studying the contents of the glasses in front of them would surreptitiously flick over to the unraveling of my profile. I could deliver a tantalizing come-hither look over the fruit farm at the top of my glass, and then freeze it dead on my features if the mood vanished. No, I had not developed a Jekyll-and-Hyde existence with wild nights on the town that I have hitherto been ashamed to mention. All these tips were picked up from reading the pages of Vogue, The Edinburgh Tatler, and sundry women's magazines designed for the aspirant upper class, whose social wrinkles had been garnered while waiting at the dentist's.

Tonight's rendezvous was one of a series of one-night

stands I was embarking on. The doctor with his daft fads was just doing his best to impress me. He might have done much better if he had not tried so hard, for he was warm, intelligent and quite a dish—all the things that really mattered. But as sure as fate, the result would have been the same. All of you, who have lived as I have, know the feeling. We are all looking for a doppelganger of our first love. Common sense tells us that the expedition is in vain. Each replica we discover is an inexact copy of our inamorato. In my case, I left behind a chain of mildly broken-hearted Glaswegians with Irish connections. Perhaps someone could make a short story out of it, with each successive imitation-Dermot tailing away further from the original model. I might end up being married to a short, stubby Celtic supporter from the Isle of Man, both of us living happily ever after, supping screw-tops in front of a broken-down telly.

This enterprise of mine had come about in a moment of impulse, when I wrote away to a friendship agency. It was rather bonnily named "The Marriage of the Thistle and the Rose," claiming (spuriously, I think) to have been founded in that infamous year, 1707. Its motto, "Broken hearts soonest mended," rather appealed to me. In case my friends found out, I had a cover story. I was going to write an article about my interesting experience in the Cake Mix, our trade paper.

But, when I turned up for my initial appointment to the office in Palmerston Place, a wave of panic almost bore me away. The building had the flavor of the waiting room of an abortion clinic. Father Doherty used to frighten us with stories of those dreadful places to induce us to be good Catholic girls.

"Would you like a cup of tea?" smiled the pleasant receptionist, which helped calm me. I drew a deep breath and took in my surroundings. There, besides all the bric-a-brac designed to make an impression, was a plaque: our school crest. So, the lady director was a Celestinian, a reassuring sign; at least I had placed my future happiness in safe hands.

At last I was ushered into the main office. The lady, sitting behind an imposing walnut desk, looked up at me briefly from behind her pince-nez and then carried on with her knitting. After finishing the row she gave a little sigh and tucked it away in a drawer. She leaned forward on her elbows and stared at me. "Ah, yes. Miss Fiorelli it is."

The imposing display of composure only served to unsettle me again. She opened a drawer (not the one where she kept her knitting) and brought out an already bulging file with my name on it. Perhaps she had got hold of my school reports, for I had no criminal record and the only correspondence that had passed between us had been financial negotiations, which I prefer to get out of the way as quickly as possible, finding these sordid matters inhibiting in such a delicate matter. This was not entirely reassuring. There were some teachers whose assessments of my character were not entirely complimentary.

"All our gels and gentlemen clients come to us strictly with the view to entering upon matrimony." It was a bit of a facer. I was not ready for this gravedigger of romance. I looked round her office. Just behind her there was a full-length portrait of a forbidding matriarch scowling down at me. There was not a hint of frivolity or—dare I mention it—promise of passion in her tone or in the furnishings of the room.

"Naturally," she said to spike the pause, "our gentlemen are all from the top drawer." She patted the drawer containing the knitting as if to back up the metaphor. It was one of those moments when you can hand over your fate to someone else and all to avoid a wee bitty embarrassment. All I was looking for was a wee dalliance, and a large dollop of male admiration. But to say I was not serious? Already the lady was looking at me as if I were a runaway nymphomaniac.

"Of course," I said weakly.

"When the marriage is celebrated we do expect a consideration. You might say we get the collection."

"Or the poor oot."

"Mmm," she replied, looking at me over the top of her eyeglasses. She was a bit of a schoolmarm about interruptions and was clearly thinking that the Alma Mater's producing some frightful gels nowadays.

She continued more briskly, "We require a photograph, head and shoulders only." She cast a glance at my superb figure. "I see that you have already given us a list of your interests. I am afraid that we don't have any Latin-speaking rock-climbers on our books at the moment. But I am sure many of our gentlemen share your enjoyment of Scottish home bakery. We allow our clients six introductions, and then..." Her words drifted away into the air. I got the hint. If six bites of the cherry failed to clinch it, you could be dismissed as one of nature's ordained spinsters.

The doctor with the interesting specialization was my twenty-seventh gentleman. I was beginning to suspect that I was the only lady on Madame's books. All sorts of social misfits were turning up on my doorstep: rich men, poor men, beggar men and, yes, thieves. One fellow could not leave a restaurant or bar without at least picking up an ashtray. I hated to think what his flat must be like. He wasn't even a smoker. Another who cited his interests as classical music turned out to have a liking for T.V. jingles. When I whistled "Una Bella Cosa," he brightened and harmonized, singing, "Just one Cornetto."

Some of my gentlemen, who didn't even know how to assist a lady off the bus, must have sneaked into the top drawer. One of them even turned up sporting a Windsor knot. Meeting all these socially impaired people tended to bring out my not very latent snobbery. Sometimes my sense of mischief went too far, and I ended up hating myself. After one evening, when I had succeeded in humiliating a very pleasant plumber, I ended up in tears. I could see how his face writhed in speechless misery as I outclassed him on all social fronts. Why should he have to suffer for my hatred of mankind? After all, both of us had been gulled by Madame Pimp. After I broke down I let him comfort me just a little. He even got away with making just a little pass. Why not?

He was rather nice looking, and his Gorgie accent was not that strong.

But after this the experiment ended, as did the stillborn article. Still the loonies and desperadoes pestered our front door, driving my family mad. I refused to see visitors and locked myself in my own room like the princess with her spinning wheel.

Wreaking revenge on my escorts did not really make me happy, and I began taking long solitary walks in the hills in that long lonely year, through all the seasons, even to the depths of winter. I would come home after a weekend of not speaking to anyone and be told that Stewart had been making several phone calls. "Oh," said I, and munched silently my Forfar Bridie and chips.

"The amount of stodge you are eating, you'll get fat and ugly," said Mamma, repudiating our family's means of support.

"So what." She was wrong; anyone could see I was pining away despite my apparently huge calorific intake. Walking in the hills on your own was highly recommended by W.D. Mornay as the most pure way of experiencing the high places of Scotland. But being a Lone Ranger was not really my cup of tea, giving too much time to think on what might have been—not really a profitable area for rumination. I was just deliberating on this and sizing up whether to have a slice of Florentine cake or a delicious, figure-threatening fudge finger, when there came a ring at the door. "Tell him I've got smallpox," I said to Freddie, who went out to the lobby to repel the intruder.

But it was not an aspiring suitor with a carnation in his buttonhole and a copy of the Scotsman in his hand, but Basil, about to make a pilgrimage to one of the great shrines of mountaineering, the Scottish Highlands. As usual he looked formidably incompetent. Twelve hours in a fish lorry had not improved his appearance or personal aroma, but for me he was a sight to gladden the heart, and I rushed forward to kiss him, only deterred at the last moment by a whiff of haddock and kippers. He bubbled on about possibilities for winter climbing, and reeled forth a list of the Munroes he hoped to do.

I made him some supper. Dad, with his fondness for the lesser hills, enjoyed his conversation, so I left them having a good natter, while I did some tidying up in the kitchen. Freddie came in and stood fiddling around with the tea towel. "You use that for wiping the dishes with," I said, knowing what was on his mind.

"I'd given up all hope wi' you. But,"—he shook his head then nodded over to the tea table—"whit a lumber." For the first time in his life he put his hand on my shoulder. "Come down to Manchester wi' me next weekend."

"No thanks."

"While I am closing some deals you can go clubbing. You'd meet some real men." I started to hum along as I put the plates back on their shelves. I knew where I was going next weekend.

....

I joined Basil just below the ski slopes of Cairngorm. My line of sight was obscured by Basil's meaty posterior, grinding upwards in tune to his approximate rendition of "Scots Wae Hae." We were traversing below the White Lady, my features muffled by a woolly balaclava in case any avenging ski-instructor was still on the lookout for saboteurs. As usual there were hundreds cavorting on the messy porridge of mud and snow they called the piste. We moved off round the shoulder into the silence of the Coire an t-Sneachda and climbed to the foot of Aladdin's Couloir, a broad gully that breached the cliff in two. Normally one of the easiest climbs in the Cairngorms, it contained that day a long, grey ice pitch set at little more than fifty degrees. While Basil chopped lustily at the ice, I belayed to rocks on its right bank and followed up his erratic highway of holes, scratches, and craters by lengthening and shortening my stride accordingly. He was grinning and singing as he passed the floury rope round his waist. A little downpour of spindrift was piling up behind his rucksack like a spilt sugar bag in the factory.

"Great, eh, Moira?"

"Great," I replied.

The mist was clamped down so thickly that the end of the rope lying down the slope was invisible. Our fingertips and toenails were frozen, while the rest of our bodies were toasting, save when a sly slide of spindrift slithered down our necks. But once again, language was an inadequate tool to describe this form of high living. Great it was, and there was no other place in the world to be.

Using the flat blade of his axe as a battering ram, Basil punched a V-shaped funnel in the cornice. "Great," he shouted again as he hauled himself over the top. "Great," he shouted for the nth time as he took in my rope. On the plateau, the clouds were lifting and drifting, exposing a moon-baked landscape of rock and gravel dusted with snow and here and there with rubbings of glinting ice. As we tramped to the summit of Cairngorm, the clouds were all blown away in one of those magic transfigurations of the landscape that occur so very rarely in even a lifetime of climbing. It was getting late, and the sun's disc was just hanging over the top of the western horizon. The throng of skiers had long gone from the slopes. Apart from us, the mountain, and the sunset, there was nothing.

We sat on the summit cairn, ate our pieces, and generally felt pleased with ourselves. The sunset was gradually building up to a Wagnerian crescendo. Normally I am not a great fan of the Cairngorms. There's something a bit alien and lunar about these lonely plateaus. They are just too big and dangerous. But tonight I felt pleased for Basil. Across to the west, the dark pool of the Lairig Ghru, the slopes and folds of Braeriach and Cairn Toul switched from indigo to gold and then green. Everywhere the smooth curves of the snow-covered hills were ablaze with all the flamboyant colors of the spectrum as the sun's dying rays struck them and then withered. Away to the east in the Spey Valley, the riot of brilliant colors softened as the pink haze on the horizon melted into a placid, pastel green. It was W.D. Mornay country all right. Only he could do justice to the Pre-Raphaelite fervor of the twilight landscape, an old world sinking in a last blaze of glory.

Chapter 22

The White Lady

"Dashed sorry, Moira. 'Fraid it's 'Home, James, and don't spare the cuddies.'"

Basil came off the phone. There was a crisis in the office, and could he get back to Bradford on the morning train? It was most disappointing, especially as there was a wee gully on Braeraich we both fancied tackling. Still we had a good night at the Haggis and Neeps Bar, a ploughboys cottage complete with shanks of plastic venison and ancient targes hanging from the rafters (a tenuous link with a spurious past for the gullible) set in the heart of the concrete eyesore of the Aviemore Centre—of all the Highland Clearances possibly the nastiest. There was a folk group on the rostrum, and I joined in with the rest of the beards and hairy sweaters banging my half-pint glass on the table to "The Braes O' Killiekrankie." Basil clearly didn't know the words, but he joined in the pot-banging as vigorously as anyone. He held my hand during the band's rendition of "Will Ye No Come Back Again." But don't think anything of it. I was greeting like a tap, but not for Bonnie Prince Charlie. Underneath his eccentric exterior—somewhat contrived I sometimes thought—Basil was a caring fellow.

After saying farewell the next day, I set off on my own towards the great pass that splits the Cairngorms, the Lairig Ghru. I felt lonely and blue, but once off the ski road and wandering through the Rothiemurchus Forest, I began to cheer up. In this last remnant of the great Caledonian Forest, the trees had space to grow and flourish unlike the well-drilled rows of battery poles in the dreary Forestry Commission landscapes. The scene would be exactly as enjoyed by Charlie if he had paused to look in his flight from Culloden. That was a reassuring thought, and without noticing it my stride began to lengthen, and I started to whistle jauntily. Quite soon I emerged from the trees and mounted steadily towards the high pass. The wind was soughing gently, hardly above a whisper. Was that Lurcher's Crag up on the left, those ice-splintered rocks standing out spikily like a ruined fortress?

An amiable snow gully sliced the tumbledown castle, surely safe enough for me on my own. Before I knew what I was doing, I was moving upwards. As soon as the snow became hard, I put on my crampons and unstrapped the ice axe. On I went, lightly balancing on my axe while my crampons bit securely into the snow, with that tingling in my stomach when excitement is seasoned with a soupcon of danger.

Maybe the spirit of Hermann Buhl had entered into me. That bold (some say nutty) climber was at least giving me the thumbs up in his rocky Valhalla. Framed by the walls of the gully, cloud-clippers whipped across the blue sky. I turned round to let out a defiant yell to the mountain, and noticed that the bottom of the slope was far away. My yell leapt an octave to a shriek. The spot where I had so casually donned crampons was an insignificant blob surrounded by a nest of sharp rocks. I was easily high enough to kill myself.

Winter climbing gives me the willies, and here I was soloing a climb, I who had always been a vociferous critic of those who went in for this suicidal branch of the sport.

"You fool, Moira," I muttered to myself, instinctively hugging the slope, unsettling my balance. "Paddy isn't going to make you kill yourself."

I cramponed down the slope with exaggerated caution, dragging the spikes against the snow till they slotted into my steps. My arms ached from clinging to the axe.

In that uncanny way it has, the weather clouded over to make my plight seem grimmer. "O Holy Mother of God, I promise I will never again skive off Father Doherty's Sunday Mass." Every protuberance of my body was in contact with the snow to give me the illusion of extra adhesion, but in fact put me into a more precarious position. With hammering heart, I forced myself to climb down properly. A slip from here would tear me to shreds. It was a cowardly descent, but there was no one there to watch so it made no odds. About fifty feet from the bottom, the angle eased considerably. I took off my crampons and glissaded down on my bum. It was exhilarating despite the wet breeches I had for my pains. On the snow-dusted rocks at the bottom, I sat down and had a breather. The sun had shaken off its covering of clouds. Tying my crampons and axe onto the back of my sac, I looked up again at the gully, once again an innocuous, beguiling white pathway.

I decided to spend the night at the Alasdair Sinclair Hut at the top of the pass. I had told my family not to expect me till Monday night, and felt no compunction about wagging off work.

My breeches were steaming by the fire as I settled down for the night. Sitting with a mug of tea warming my hands, feeling my face glow from the spluttering flames of the hut fire, I knew I was happy, or at least content. Outside, a storm had begun to rage, and I enjoyed the contrast with my cosiness in the bothy. I let my mind ramble back to my recent lonely hikes: the sharp Gothic ridges of the Mamores, the vast upland deserts of the Monaidhliath, and the far northwest with lochans set like jewels around the surprising Arizonian Buttes. As a hill explorer I was now able to appreciate the rich diversity of the Highland landscape. For those Munro baggers trying to swallow this feast at one gulp I could only feel pity. I intended to span my climbing of the Munroes till the day I could no longer mount the Mound steps—well, not quite. My last hill would be Ben Hope as a symbol of a life fulfilled, hope to come, and the fact that there are no farther hills to the north.

Even at this juncture, I was aware that there was a less respectable reason for my seeking after solitude. On my own I could wallow in an ecstasy of self-pity with nary an inhibition. Anyone who chanced to meet me on the hills might be astonished to see a darkly attractive girl hurling imprecations at the sky, bewailing Irishmen in general and false friends in particular. Corpo a Baccho, that would be embarrassing! I resolved to end my self-imposed pariahdom forthwith and look the world in the face.

A timid knocking at the door gave me a start. No one should be within a hundred square miles of this place. I plunged into my pit, hoping whoever it was would go away. I wasn't superstitious, I told myself, tightening up the drawstring of my sleeping bag and crossing myself. The slopes above the hut were the haunts of the great Grey Man of Ben MacDui, but that was rubbish, wasn't it—a tale of too much imagination and whisky. It's funny how perspectives are different on a dark and stormy night in a lonely bothy. The knocking went on, still timidly but more insistently. What horror lay behind that door? I lay rigid in my bag with the drawstring so tight that only a lock of hair was left on the surface. If anyone broke the door down, they might think I was a plant. The knocking was now insistent and desperate, not timid at all. I got out of my sleeping bag, picked up my axe and opened the door.

My torch-beam focused on the sack-like object just outside in the white gloom. Although there was a thin layer of snow covering him, I easily recognized Archie Stewart.

Surely he couldn't be that fed up with my ignoring him to have gone to this length to catch me. This ignoble thought was rejected as quickly as it occurred. He was in a desperate plight. He couldn't walk and his clothing was in tatters. His right eye was caked in blood. Looking at me drunkenly, all he could say was "Please, Moira, please"—difficult to hear above the howling wind. The thin layer of snow would fast become a shroud. Already my face and front were covered with flakes of snow.

I grabbed him by the shoulders of his anorak and heaved him in. The top of his rucksack caught the door edge; the snow spattered over everything, freezing my hands, while I struggled to disentangle him. Agitated out of my torpor, I managed to haul him along the floor and lay him down in front of the fire.

His legs were set at an awkward angle, while his whole body was shaking with shock. He stared into the guttering firelight from a face unnaturally pale and blood-streaked. There was no alternative, so I stripped off his soaking wet clothes.

"C'mon my lad, let's be 'avin' you." I tried to impart a no-nonsense Coronation Street jollity. It didn't work. I was frightened. He was almost done for. Blood was splattered everywhere, but that meant it was superficial. Right? So I tried to convince myself. In his rucksack there was a spare jumper, luckily still dry, which I put on him. I managed somehow to get him inside my sleeping bag. Joining him in Spartan comforts was out of the question. His broken limbs put paid to that. What to do? Stick him by the fire and keep him warm, forcing mugs of hot sweet tea and game soup inside him. All through the night I kept pouring hot liquids into him, worried lest he might drop off and die on me.

There was going to be no sleep for me either. Watching him nod and falter and then spill his mug stopped me with terror whenever I threatened to drift away. I deliberately set myself the task of stoking and adding to the fire every so often to pace out the night. As soon as one cuppa was down his neck I added more water to the dixie, which sizzled and hissed when it hit bottom. In his lucid moments he began to complain that with all the liquid inside him he would have to make an epic crawl to wee outside. Quite nobly I said, "If you need it just pee away." My sleeping bag could always be cleaned by the Perth Firm patronized by Dermot. Something in my subconscious told me I must have changed, or things were very serious.

Slowly during that hellish night I managed to knit together his story from his incoherent ramblings. At exactly 10:00 a.m. that morning he had fallen from a high place somewhere between Cairn Toul and Braeriach, the two 4,000-foot mountains that guarded the west flank of the Lairig Ghru. He kept repeating the time so much, I suspected that looking at his watch had caused him to trip over the edge and fall hundreds of feet down an icy slope. He was unconscious for some time before he started dragging himself towards the hut. For nigh on twelve hours he had been limping and crawling. It had taken him an age to move the pack off his shoulder and get a map and compass from the flap pocket, and in the midst of taking his bearings he kept wiping his face with lumps of snow to stop himself falling unconscious again. Even if there was no one inside the hut he would get shelter for the night. If the hut was empty, he was determined to crawl all the way to the roadside at Coylumbridge the next day, a good ten miles away.

Towards three in the morning he started to sink, as if he was going into a fatal coma. I put my arm round him, one hand against his cheek.

"Come on, Archie, you can do it," I pleaded.

He opened his eyes, blinked, and turning to me said, "That's the first time you have called me by my name." That was true. There are some people who drop your name in every sentence, as if they are trying to foist a connection on you. There are others who never use your name, presumably for the opposite reason. I generally steer a middle course, using the person's name to let them know where they stand. It's the emphasis that counts. With Archie, I had deliberately avoided using his name. Now, with his life fast ebbing away, I used it for all it was worth to hold him on this side of the Big Divide.

"You've got to do it for my sake." I gave him that little encouragement knowing I could deny it later. After all he was hallucinating. Mind you he was tough. I could see him summoning up his all. He must have lost a lot of blood by internal hemorrhaging, and who knows what that desperate crawl had cost him.

Dawn found us both asleep. The early morning cold awoke me. The fire, last seen blazing, was now a bed of stony ashes, and a thin scum of brown ice lined the inside of my mug. The full horror of the situation hit me as I heard Archie's rasping breath beside me. I felt totally done in. Reluctantly I got up to see what was outside. The door wouldn't open. Alarmed, I kicked and shoved till slowly it creaked open a fraction, pressed against the snow piled up outside. By shoulder charging the door, I managed to get it wide enough for us to squeeze through, letting in the wind, which automatically turned the hut into a fridge. I shut it hastily.

The wind was screaming against the hut. The tempo hadn't let up. Madonna! What was I to do? Leave him to fetch help? He would die. Take him with me in this blizzard? The same. I wasn't sure I could make it myself even without dragging him along. It was a good distance to the nearest road-head, and odds on that would be deserted and impassable.

It was hellish. Even under my own steam and in fit company I wouldn't go out in such a blizzard willingly. I poked my nose outside. Flecks of snow were whipped up from the drifts. Snow from the sky and slivers snatched from the ground were indistinguishable in this raging grey tornado. I turned back inside the hut, feeling absolutely desperate. To delay facing the inevitable I lit the primus to make a last brew of tea. Bits of broken chocolate biscuit lining my anorak pocket were thrown into the brew. It would taste foul but might enrich the pot. From his rucksack, a few sticky slabs of Kendal Mint Cake were slipped into my pockets. Even with their fluff and dust they would be a godsend later on. I cradled him in my arms, and after looking dopey for a few minutes he seemed to be more alert. Ladling the scalding liquid down his throat, I outlined the options.

"Okay, Archie. One, we make for the road. Near Loch Morlich. It's only three and a bit miles." He looked expectantly. "And the other option…" I had phrased it badly. I let him look at me, following my gaze round the room and left it there.

He was now more self-conscious about my helping him on with his clothes, a good sign perhaps. Dressing him, I felt like a pernickety nurse with a difficult patient. When I looked again at his injuries, the one leg that was twisted horribly seemed definitely broken. The other one, although quite swollen at the ankle, looked otherwise serviceable. By a miracle he still had the ice axe that had been looped to his wrist. I hacked off the straps of his rucksack and tied them round his axe and leg to make a splint. Crude, but it would do the business.

"This," I held out the other axe, "is your walking stick." He nodded. "Right, let's get geared up." We put on gloves, cagoules and balaclavas. He looked at my sleeping bag, rucksack and stove scattered about the floor. "Forget it," I said, without a moment's pang. They had cost me a pretty penny. I didn't feel ennobled by my gesture. Perhaps that would come later.

"If you can support me, Moira, I'll do the map reading." He was shaking and in obvious pain, but resolute.

"Okay, Archie." And with that we stepped out into the storm.

The blizzard hit us like gunfire. We staggered and stumbled, desperately trying to hold our direction as sand-blasted snow stung our cheeks and eyes. Snow pellets the size of cornflakes clogged up our eyes as we steered blindly through the gale. Every gyration throwing us out of kilter, we twisted and turned to avoid the freezing firepower. We had to use map and compass. That was going to be his job. Mamma, but he was some weight. Every so often he passed out and he fell on me.

"Get the compass out. Hold it while I take this bearing." He swayed a bit, held the compass into the teeth of the storm, fumbled and dropped it.

"Oh, I'm sorry, Moira. I mean." He dropped the map as well. It happened so often and so much time was spent scrabbling in the snow, I took on the job of navigating myself. Concentrating on that kept me from contemplating the full horror of our situation.

"Can we take a breather?"

I nodded and we collapsed gasping in the lee of a snowdrift. The eyes registered a faint light, but the face was grey. Our pace was so infinitesimally slow, and the flickering life-light so feeble, that the likelihood of him perishing was extremely probable. Also, I needed these stops as much as him—I was that knackered. At each burst we averaged fifty yards, sometimes more. But the longer hauls cost us, as stopping let the bitter cold bite through our clothing. The snow was piling up, plastering our clothes, and my hands—engaged with map and compass—left my face unprotected against the crystals whipping into us like shrapnel.

I sat with my back into the wind. I knew that if we sat too long our body temperatures would plummet and that would be that. For a moment my feet went out of focus, and I felt lightheaded and drunk. It was not too bad after all. A warning rang in my brain; I snapped back. I was suffering the classic symptoms of exposure.

"Okay, Arch, let's go."

"Just a wee moment?"

"No fear, up we go."

My power of command surprised me. Without a grumble he let me haul him to his feet. Breaking the crust of the snow in the drift was going over the top on the Somme. So much energy was expended sinking and plowing our way through the snow. We clung together as the wind buffeted us all over the place. Direction was sheer guesswork. We were leering drunkenly about so much we gave up using an exact compass bearing and just headed northeast. Fiddling with the compass gave us an excuse to stop.

"Don't sit down, or you'll never get up." I was crying with frustration, trying to hold the map level and read the compass, while he was using the opportunity to sit and skive. I'll swear that tears were coming out frozen onto my cheeks. I felt like screaming with pain whenever I took my mitts off to unpocket the map, and now he was whinging.

"Just a wee moment; a'hm totally shagged!"

"Oh shut up. We're going now!"

It was good having someone to take it out on. But I was wrong; he was not whining, he was in immense pain and battling on heroically. Here I abandoned all pretence at navigation. The gale was a howling northeaster. We put our heads down and steered into the teeth of the gale. His head, encased in a candy-floss-frosted balaclava, was slumped on my shoulder; the hair covering his forehead was matted with snow, and little glacial rivulets trickled from his eyes and nostrils. I wondered if I was carrying a dead man. There was a lull in the screaming frozen inferno. For a moment the visibility lifted. Not more than a hundred yards away lay the Rothiemurchus Forest.

"Come on, Archie. We can make it to the trees." His eyelids flickered. Somehow his legs were still moving. I managed to stave off collapse till we passed the fifth tree. At this stage I was counting every step. Six steps lay between each tree, every object an objective.

"We can do it, Moira," the snowman beside me muttered. It was him encouraging me! That raised my spirits. Perhaps there was some hope. Again we had to have a breather.

"Let's stop a sec."

I let him go. He slumped against the tree and slithered down till the drift he was in formed an armchair around him. Our backs facing the gale, with no rucksacks for protection, were freezing. Like a blood-sucking vampire the banshee wind sucked the heat out of our bodies. The stop had to be brief or we would never get up. I took the battered lumps of Kendal Mint Cake out of my pocket. Without ceremony I shoved some into his mouth and ditto for myself. It was too troublesome to take off my mitts, and so bits of wool and fluff remained stuck to the soggy slabs. Almost instantly I could feel sweet warmth coursing through my body.

Then I had an idea. Hanging on my compass string was a little whistle, which I only carried about because it was expected. More to justify our breather than anything else, I gave it a long beep, then about twenty toot, sod the international distress signal. I couldn't concentrate enough to count the numbers. I felt better after this, even though no one would hear it. The high-pitched whistles were nigh but drowned by the din of the storm. Anyway, who would be out on a day like this?

"Up we get." I helped him up, his stiff clothes creaking like cold canvas. Sitting still had let the snow seep down the back of our necks, the most miserable form of discomfort.

"Okay, Moira." He was still game, but his voice was only a thin echo of a croak.

Another fifty yards. Stop. I gave a perfunctory whistle then off we went. "Twenty-seven, twenty-eight, twenty-nine, thirty. Let's do a couple more to that next tree." This time he slumped down on his knees. "No? Okay, we'll rest here."

More hairy mint cake was pressed into his mouth, like feeding a baby. His eyes were unfocused and dull. Six more toots and off we went, staggering and stumbling in the drifts wrapped around each tree. This time I blew a fortissimo fanfare and waded on. We walked for five more paces and were tripped again by a snowdrift, falling down till we were almost covered. After all we had been through this was not fair.

Somehow I knew we were not going to get up. Archie lay still, his mouth half-open as if asleep. Everything felt peaceful—almost warm. This then was the approach of death. There was a grey cloud in front of me, small at first but steadily obscuring the trees. I never thought of anything but how beautifully the snow covered everything. Around us the wind was rushing and tearing, but it did not matter now.

I looked at Archie again. His face was like wax, and snow was filling his mouth. Should I try to clear it out? There didn't seem much point. He coughed slightly and spluttered it out. "Moira," he croaked. That was all.

Gently I stroked his cheek. "Never mind, Archie, never mind." And then blew the last trumpet.

There were other sounds apart from the wind's rise and fall. Lumps of snow flopped down from overweight branches, and occasionally we heard the sharp crack of a branch breaking. Then, faintly intruding in the background came a regular, relentless swishing, too evenly spaced to be the wind. I shook him, and he coughed again. "Listen."

The sounds seemed to be going away. There was a pause, then it started again, getting louder and stronger.

"There they are, Jock. Just by that birch."

I turned round to see a man faintly outlined by the

swirling snow, pointing a ski stick at our tree. They were two cross-country skiers. They turned in their tracks and poled their way over to us. And at once I recognized my old housewarming chums, Jock and Dandy. Dandy's face was a study. A puzzled look, replaced by a grin swiftly masked by a worried frown.

"It's yon lassie whit smashed oor ice cave. I see ye got shot o' thon loser boyfriend." Then he shook his head. I looked up into their tough, honest faces. "I think this one's had it. We might just save the lassie." My face was being gently rubbed between two frozen mitts.

"Okay, Jock, you ken what to do."

Without a word, Jock dropped his rucksack and shot off into the driving storm like a husky off the leash.

"This is no supposed to do ye ony guid. You'll just hae to be a guinea pig."

About a quarter pint of whisky was poured down my throat. The same must be happening to Archie, for I could hear him coughing and gurgling in protest. The liquid exploded through my body, flooding it with warmth and life as round my head the trees started an eightsome reel. Later on, some doctor criticized this, saying that the enforced drink delayed an urgent operation for several hours. I don't know about that, but of one thing I was sure: it saved Archie's life when it hung on the edge. Dandy pushed us farther out of the wind, piling up the snow with his skis to provide a windbreak. Jock's rucksack was emptied and the extension flap drawn out. Gingerly he put Archie into the bag. I tried stuffing myself in Jock's rucksack, but I was just too weak, and so had to be helped in like an elderly invalid. Carefully he tilted hot coffee down our throats, then looked at his watch and settled in for a vigil.

Every few minutes Dandy blew his whistle, and when he did he grinned at me and tapped my whistle. "You had better frame that when you get hame. We thought we were hearing things until we saw you." He laughed. He had an open, handsome face, but even as he smiled at me I could read into the corner of his eyes. As plain as pie they said, "How long till these two give up the ghost?"

Soon Jock returned with three more skiers who gathered round to shelter us from the wind. The rucksacks crackled like cardboard as they unsheathed us and popped us into sleeping bags. More people arrived, four of them pulling toboggans. Some were on cross-country skis while others plodded along on snowshoes. In no time at all we were gliding along a path to the road at the end of Loch Morlich. I could hear the engines of the mountain rescue vehicles quite far off. Their windscreen wipers were flashing back and forward, with the heater going full blast. It was like entering the tropics when we were put into the vehicle.

I was told later that the journey to the Raigmore Hospital in Inverness over the blizzard-blown roads was every bit as hazardous as our walk from the hut. I don't know. I was asleep for the entire journey. The lurching of the ambulance as we turned the corner into the hospital woke me up. After all, I was only very tired. The doors opened and flash bulbs exploded in our faces. I had enough presence of mind to pretend to be helping Archie out of the ambulance. It was difficult while lying down on a stretcher, but I gave him a feeble push. The dazzling pop of a flash bulb told me it had been entered into the historical record as a gaggle of pressmen let us through into the hospital. After all, Jock, Dandy and the other members of the mountain rescue team were the real heroes. I think it was Dandy who informed them—though goodness knows how he worked that out, as I didn't say a word to him—that the girl had carried the injured climber down from the Lairig Ghru, and he made a little joke about my dropping in on him, which left them all baffled.

I was tucked up in bed by solicitous nurses, a hospital nightshirt was slipped over my head, and a thermometer popped in my mouth so I could tell I was sick. At the other end of my bed a bossy matron was telling all, "Fancy, a young lassie like that out on those hills." I ignored her.

All sorts of activities were going on around Archie's bed. It was around this time that I heard the doctor condemning our rescuers. They fixed splints, saw that he was comfortably asleep, and left. After a while I got fed up with lying in bed with nothing to do, so I got up and started wandering round our little room. From a cardboard box on a side table, I picked up an old copy of People's Friend, a sentimental journal popular amongst maudlin tenement dwellers in Glasgow. Its recipe pages just made me hungry.

Behind me Archie was stirring, so I pulled my chair beside his bed just in case he should do anything peculiar like throw himself on the floor. He smiled, stretched out and took my hand saying, "Thanks, Moira."

I patted his hand. "Don't mention it." It was at this moment that the press gang burst in with me sitting at his bedside like Florence Nightingale. More flashing lights registered the birth of a brief legend.

By now Archie was babbling away, wide-awake and euphoric. "If it hadn't been for this lassie, Moira, here, I'd hae been as deid as Mallory and Irvine." This little slice of mountaineering history may have been lost on the hacks, but they scribbled it down anyway, sensing a good cover story.

"Tell us about it, son."

Archie's story was becoming embarrassing. "She was dragging me like a sledge through the snow drifts." At any moment I expected to be fending off the Grey Man with my ice axe. Off the flash bulbs went again, winking from all angles.

"Can you look as if ye're mopping his brow a wee bit, sweetheart?"

"Ye can gie him a wee kiss if you want."

By now they were seriously giving me the pip, and I asked this particular one rather shirtily which paper he represented. I don't think I'd have done it for the Scotsman. I certainly wasn't going to put myself out for a twopenny ha'penny rag with a circulation restricted to the lower slopes of the Grampians, whose last major scoop was the battle of Mons Graupius. I think they soon twigged that there was more mileage to be gained from Archie than from his less than fulsome friend. My face was getting redder and redder as Archie gabbled on like a drunk.

"She was the heroine of the hour." He was now talking in headlines. Perhaps he was telepathic. "Through the long night vigil she cradled me in her arms. She was my angel of mercy. I was carried on her fragile back through the raging storm" and so on and so forth. Apparently this intoxication is common in people just escaped from deadly danger. I was surprised by how much he was aware of what was going on and by his modesty. His lonely crawl to the hut and tenacity despite his injuries needed far more than mere courage. I wondered unworthily if he was trying to curry favor with me by playing up my part in the misadventure. If you are pondering why a self-centered madam like me should put myself at risk, going out of my way to help someone, the answer is simple. You would do it yourself, even if it was a Glaswegian you were rescuing.

Whatever the pressmen may have thought of me personally, they would get it in the neck from their editors if I was not portrayed as some sort of Grace Darling of the mountains, so they were compelled to persist with their unlikely material.

"Just try to smile, darlin'." This was the umpteenth photo of me mopping the fevered brow. I managed to avert a snarl for the insistent hack. Being a celebrity was becoming a teeny bit vexatious, or was I just too tired for these antics?

"Everybody loves a heroine. You'll see tomorrow morning."

Do they? Personally I couldn't care less. There is too much on my mind to waste time on stifling sobs over some notional fearless fighter against odds, fleetingly produced by the Street of Shame. Some sneaky gentleman of the press managed to inveigle a picture of me in my white first-communion dress from Mamma. I forgave her. After all, I was her only child if you excluded Freddie. The next day I appeared splashed out in the front page, looking sweet, angelic and mysteriously virginal. This was in the cheaper Nationals or at least their Scottish editions. I was dubbed (not very imaginatively) the Saint of the Snows. By the time I reached the Scotsman—on an inside page, I have to say, beside "Record Turnip Harvest in the Mearns"—I was (a little more elegantly) "The White Lady of the Lairig," the consort of the Grey Man of Ben MacDui, I fancy.

This began my time as a celebrity. If any of you have felt some envy for those instant heroes who are plucked from obscurity, you can relax. It is about as enjoyable as a headache. For a week you are pestered by reporters on your doorstep. Day and night, at all hours your phone will ring. You will be summoned to speak to people who believe you owe them something. The carefully weighted prose you give them is so distorted that your friends wonder where you went to school. Heart-wringing speeches you have no recollection of making appear under your byline. Perhaps there was a ventriloquist in the room. Can you imagine for a moment me saying, "I prayed to the Virgin Mary, to spare my wounded lover. For my own life I had not a care. Life without him would be worthless. But if I was allowed to survive, I would do good works amongst the poor in the Grassmarket." Or this, which appeared as an "Exclusive Interview with the Angel of Mercy Amongst the Snows": "I sat in her tastefully decorated drawing room in the family home set in one of the lusher suburbs of Auld Reekie. I put it to her would she do the same thing again. She sighed, 'I would climb the highest mountain, whatever the weather. Love will find a way. If he was bleeding I would use this to bandage his wounds.' She held up an exquisitely delicate fragment of lace, and bravely stifled a tear from her pale yet lovely face." This was entirely fictional. However, I did receive a phone call in my tastefully decorated drawing room, where the same question was put. I replied, "Tell him to call out the mountain rescue," before slamming down the receiver.

Towards the end of the week, the heavies having lost interest in their instant angel, the more obscure sectors of the media moved in. The longest interview I gave was to the Scottish Home Bakery Journal, who were trying to persuade me to claim it was only the sustenance of their products which kept me going. The inducement was a free supply of their cookies for a year. Cookies—what a limit! If it was anything it was Mamma's Clermiston Prides. I always took a bagful with me on the hill. It may be of minor historical interest to note that this was the first known example of sponsorship in mountaineering. At least that was how they disguised their attempted bribery.

Part of the price of fame is that you get people like

Meikle writing in the letter columns of the Scotsman about how proud he was to have me work under him. I examined this singularly ill-phrased eulogy from several angles to see if I could profitably sue him. But an advocate friend advised against it, as it would tarnish the Joan of Arc image I was enjoying in the popular press.

When the nine days are over you are forgotten. People stop staring at you as if you are from another planet (Venus, I hope in my case). Your fate is to end up holding together someone else's fish supper. The history of the world has moved on.

There were two minor postscripts to this experience. The secretary of the Caledonian Climbing Club wrote to me that in view of my obviously reformed character, the committee would feel able to endorse my possible application for membership. I was inclined to write back telling them where to put their possible application forms, but common sense prevailed. They had a nice hut, and a lot of my friends were members. It was going to be difficult carrying on this role as a minor saint for much longer, I could see, so I wrote back accepting their kind offer. Perhaps both of us had to eat humble pie in the end; Father Doherty said a bit of humility is good for us, gives a different perspective—a worm's eye view of life, I suppose.

There must have been a shortage of worthy causes and persons that year, for I found myself nominated as a candidate to be Scotswoman of the Year. In the end I was not chosen. I suspect that my nickname of the "White Lady" had triggered some official's memory of my involvement in the destruction of the ski slope of that name. Or, it could have been that the good readers of the Daily Record, Scotland's largest selling newspaper, had been irritated by my bi-enséance. Inverted snobbery is everywhere. Fewer chips are made of potatoes than otherwise, I fear. You may have noticed yourself how good breeding is now a source of shame. In some shops I have to say, "Gies a haud o' thon" for "May I look at that object, please?" in order to have any chance of being served.

Whatever it was, the detection of an ancient crime or a wave of proletarian feeling, something made me falter at the last hurdle. The award was won by a granny in Drumchapel who rescued her cat out of a tree. She did not, as you might think, do anything rash like climbing the tree and tightrope walking the branch. Whispering, "Who's the pussy that'll hae the cream," she stood at the bottom and inveigled him down. Cunning beats courage any day.

The major upshot was that I felt more drawn to Archie despite—not because of—the efforts of the press, and even took a train to visit him in the Inverness hospital. Perhaps deep down I have some sort of protective maternal instinct. The way he wolfed down the chocolates I brought made me feel quite tender.

"Moira, when I get out of here, I'm going tae gie ye the best meal you've ever had." Some boast! I would make sure he would live up to it.

"For all you did for me." He became quite blubbery,

and I had to dab his eyes with my pressed lilac handkerchief, not however the same one I was supposed to use for
staunching his future wounds. "I want to give you a reward
for everything."

For everything? Well, I suppose I did give him the odd
mug full of soup and some crumbs of Kendal Mint Cake.

Surprisingly enough we got our kit back. Some hero
from the mountain rescue team skied up to the bothy and
filled his rucksack with our gear. I tried to look grateful when
he handed me back the sleeping bag. As soon as he had gone
I dumped it into the hospital incinerator.

Chapter 23

Domus Aurea

The day after Archie came home he rang to say that he had booked a table at the Domus Aurea. I could tell he was nervous by the way he shunted phrases together and then threw them at me in a rush, also by the fact that he kept dropping my name in at the end of every second sentence, as if to check that I had not handed the phone over to someone else. Naturally I started totting up his "Moira"s. I got to thirty-five, I think, when he rang off saying, "Goodbye then." Shouldn't he have said, "Goodbye then, Moira?" I was left vaguely irritated.

Obviously he was going to attempt to cross the Rubicon of personal encounters from mates on the hill to possible beau. I was in a good mood after the phone call, relishing the thought of tonight's performance. Would he get stage fright and chicken out? A lot of men do. Sad to say it's often the nice ones who are most timid, leaving you standing like Venus on a rock bun waiting for the kiss that will never come. The chancers tend to view you as a castle under siege, with themselves in the role of Richard the Lion Heart battering at the gate.

You may accuse me of being fickle, and you would be right, but I have to confess at this point I had done a complete about-turn with reference to Archie, now filling the slot in my heart voluntarily relinquished by you-know-who. Why had this happened? I think my recent experience, our shared experience, had provided what Aristotle called a peripetia, a turning point, while the effect of heroism on the system created a bond between me the heroine and the one plucked from the jaws of death. I can vouch for this quirk of human nature, but cannot explain it.

Now for my campaign outfit I was wearing a new, all-blue outfit in a not too synthetic silky material. The color set off my looks perfectly, and the sensuous satin shimmered with its illusion of allure. Would that daunt him? Well, faint heart wouldn't win this fair lady. I fully intended to be challenging, but would keep the prize within sight if not within reach.

The Domus Aurea was named after Nero's palace on the Palatine Hill in Rome, built a couple of decades before the battle of Mons Graupius. The restaurant boasted, "Have your Roman orgy in the West Port." The menu highlighted pearls poached in vinegar, stuffed dormice, and ostrich tongues, and purported to be what your punter in a toga tucked into after a hard day's blethering in the Forum. It was the end of the line for this deranged cuisine craze. Hopefully there would be a swing of the culinary pendulum back towards good, plain Scots cooking with a particular emphasis on the pie end of the market. It might do Dad's restaurant some good, and by St. Genaro's blood, that needed a little ray of sunshine.

Fortunately for our gastric juices, there was a range of normal food on the menu. The Neronian stuff was there simply to get the trendy show-offs into the place. As I am writing this just after my tea, I am not going to bore you or sicken myself by describing our meal beyond saying it was better than your average fish supper—and from me that's no mean praise. The real meat of the evening was what Archie had in store for me.

The people whose company I normally keep are so voluble that it's a fight getting a foot in the conversational door. Sometimes instead of struggling, I have a relaxing daydream in their company. No one notices. Except when in a hospital bed, Archie was rather a quiet person, and the first two courses were passed in silence, with the only sounds coming from the sloshing of wine in the glass and food being scythed on the plate. We were both too well brought up to make any sounds when eating. The lack of speech had almost reached the embarrassing stage. Coming from Latin stock I tend to consider any silence exceeding two seconds tantamount to a social disaster, but was determined not to launch a conversation, which might make me appear too approachable. Archie was munching cheerfully, totally unaware of any solecism, while I was picking nervously at my steak au poivre. The wine by the way was a very unassuming Lambrusco, not Roman at all. At any moment I might capitulate in this war of no words.

"There's something I want to show you." Archie fished under the table. He straightened up and dropped an envelope into my lap. "Go on, have a look."

I opened it up to find a sheaf of photographs. The top one was of a cat; so was the second, as was the third, which showed a different cat, and so on. These two cats alternated in differing poses of domestic harmony. Possibly the accident had addled his brains. He was deadly serious.

"Aren't they cute? That's Tibby, she's my ma's favorite." A piebald cat lay akimbo on the back of an armchair, where sat enthroned a burly Amazon, arms folded aggressively, a Ranger's scarf like a chain of state coiled proudly round her neck. Porca miseria! I would feel sorry for the Grey Man if he met her on a dark night on the hills.

"That's my maw. Isn't she just great?"

I had great difficulty in knowing what to say to this. I looked at Archie, the proud son and pet owner. The Oedipus complex was something I had never before encountered. He was beaming happily at the snaps and then at me. I couldn't help it, but I just had to pat him on the head. Don't I just get them?

There were further installments of Tibby and her companion Tabby's adventures. Some of the pictures featured a furtive, weasely character, whose thumb and forefinger were curled together at his side as if itching for a fly smoke. I knew without telling that this was Paw, who lived merely on sufferance in the domain of his daunting spouse. Pictures of people's children, pets and sundry beloved quickly bore me, and I was wondering again if his experiences on the hill hadn't been too much for him. This was certainly too much for me.

But wait a minute! Of course. I had been a bit thick. Quite suddenly it dawned on me: he was planting the idea of him being a warm loveable chap, and was presuming that I would react with the usual goos and aahs that we women dissolve into in the presence of kiddies and cuddly cats. He was onto a loser if he was trying to soften me up with this mush. In the presence of these pieces of bait I remain totally immune. But then, quelle seduction!

And then there was Tibby and Tabby together. Tibby, possibly, smugly purring in Maw's lap, while Tabby was draped round her shoulders, a feline scarf. "We call that Hame's best," he whispered proudly. I was about to vomit up the contents of Domus Aurea at this display of maudlin kitsch when he added, "I get such a funny feeling when Tibby tickles my neck and Tabby's purring fair shoogles my stomach. I just love stroking them, their fur so soft and silky. It's braw." This was far more than I had expected from Archie, whose mental horizons were firmly fixed on balance sheets and related items. Suddenly I got it, the riposte to my blue not-quite-satin shimmering at the tremors caused by his audacious stroke—the sensuous hinting at the sensual.

His "I could take you home to show you the real things, if you fancy," would normally have been his farewell speech, but I was interested and intrigued by his tactile tactics.

I would have to be prepared to wade through this non-sense in order to get at his real character; so, playing him along at his own game, I said with as much of a simper as I could manage, "I would love to come and bring a ball of wool with me to play with the Tabbies." He gave me an odd look at my straying so far out of character, and I saw I would have to tread a bit more cannily with him.

The head waiter—or as they called him here, the king of the banquet—sensing that we were about to leave, came over to tempt us with some mulled Falernian. Stand-ing above us, a plastic laurel-wreath dangling over his ears, he recited mechanically, "Just the job for a cold night on Hadrian's Wall." It was obviously company policy, just as more modern establishments force their customers to "have a nice day." We allowed ourselves to be tempted. It was aw-ful! Cardboard Grappa at its nastiest and cheapest. Both of us spluttered it out.

"Satis!" I said; both Archie and Droopy Leaves looked blankly. "'Enough': some Roman soldier wrote it on Hadri-an's Wall."

"Definitely not an advert for the Scottish Tourist Board," said Archie laughing, putting us both in a fit of gig-gles, a relief after all the fencing over the moggie pictures. On the way out I exchanged greetings over the centuries with the Commissionaire disguised as a centurion more Ruritanian than Roman.

"Ave et Vale, Hail and Farewell." I saluted.

"Dinnae try and make a monkey oot o' me, pal!" he riposted wittily. Then it was out into the grey night of the twentieth-century Grassmarket.

I was puzzled by the events of the evening. The fact that he did not make a play for me made him more intriguing, as if he was confident that all he had to do was bide his time and I would fall into his lap. And as for that cat business, it was too contrived, as if his personality was fabricated for my consumption. This picture of him as a soft, furry pet must be a mask to cover a harder reality. Meeting his family would uncover it.

Most people who knew Archie liked and respected him. He was quiet and bought his round. His excesses on the night of the dinner were way out of character. He was completely legless of course, the standard morning-after defense for the Scot. It was a puzzle, which I eventually put down to him playing too hard to get me, a pathetic failure. As his actions were contrary to his nature, he didn't know where the line had to be drawn. All this nonsense about the talking haul bag had been Dermot's sabotage fiction, and my swallowing it showed how much I had been under his sway. For some reason a quiet person is always considered steady and dependable. I could never fathom the reason why; I know plenty of quiet people who have nothing to say or offer. True, Archie had taken over the helm on harder climbs when the acute nervous tension of the flamboyant Irishman had let him down, as on the crux of White Slab on Cloggy. Impartial English observers witnessed the brave boyo going completely to pieces, shrieking for a tight rope, so tight that Dermot was in danger of joining the soprano section in the cathedral choir.

There was no doubt that on a dull November night—that dismal low-point in the climber's year when rock climbing is impossible, filthy weather makes hill-walking uninviting and ice-climbing still a good month away—there was always a little stir and pints were lifted less listlessly when Dermot walked through that door. Even the tone-faced barman raised a smile as he piloted the brown nectar into a pint glass. And the stories. At the turn of a neat phrase, plain days on the hills became Homeric epics—colleagues hanging on by a fingernail, for example. Characters were replaced by caricatures—a dangerous but amusing ploy, for the licensed jester had a cutting edge and at times the less articulate or merely quiet would retire smarting. Even when the witty broguist said, "No offence like," he moved on too fast to see if it had been taken. The steady, softly spoken Archie hurt nobody. Dermot's esteem, high amongst the like-minded exuberant guys, fluctuated with those who liked a quiet, tidy life, and so he made enemies while Archie quietly accrued friends. But there was something slightly unnerving about the fact that, set beside Dermot, he didn't even try to make an impression.

Chapter 24

In the Enemy's Heartland

One very tangible advantage that the Protestant Glaswegian had over the Catholic—in my eyes at least—was that he treated me like a lady, dolloping out consideration and presents by the bucket. For those of you who hold this to be merely an acceptable form of prostitution I make no apology. He got nothing for his gifts bar a smile and my benison. It was better than being dragged along as the unseen part of a Brocken Spectre. Now, with Archie as my squire, I was spoiled. Never would a visit to the pictures go by but there was the rustling of chocolate papers in the back row, normally accompanied by an angry "Shhh" from our surrounding snoggers. Flowers would arrive at the house with a verse or two of homespun poetry. I'm not breaking any intimate confidence if I give you a sample:

"Each time that tree I pass,
  Which by hardy Lynwilg grows

I think on thee my bonnie lass.

Feel a shiver right to my toes.

As these tender boughs entwine

Linking your sweet heart to mine."

You get the picture. But as a wise man once said, "It's the thought that counts."

For the first time one of my beaux got the thumbs up from the family. As she read the above, Mamma shed a little tear. "Bellissima, come Petrarch." Not quite, Mamma, not quite.

Freddie liked him. Archie was "the business," high praise from my fastidious brother. "He's got a career and looks as though he is going somewhere, no' like thon dreamers"—the umbrella term for my past attachments.

Archie listened to Dad's stories of his wanderings on the hills with hardly a tremor of restlessness or butting in, a common Irish fault. Being an accountant, he provided some pointers to stop the foundering of Dad's restaurant empire. All in all they were prepared to overlook his heresy, but if things came on more seriously, Father Doherty would drop in for "just a wee slice of plum cake. Me steering getting wobbly, needs some ballast." You know the sort of "lovely weather we're having" lead-in they use before carrying on the work of the Inquisition.

The sermon on the propagation of the faithful was not even a remote threat when I announced that I was going to visit his family in Glasgow.

"You are going all that way just to see his cats?" Mamma was not concentrating on her baking.

"Well, why not. It's not a diplomatic mission, you know."

There was a suspicious smoldering smell coming from the oven. Cremation was about to commence.

"Last time you went to that city no good came of it." What had happened on my last visit to the great proletarian citadel? My face started burning along with the poor inglorious rock buns. "You were in bed for a week, streaming with a cold." For a moment I thought she had caught wind of my near rape in the soggy sleeping bag!

"Don't worry, Mamma. It's just a jaunt."

"Well, take care anyway." She sounded and looked worried. Mamma knew more about human nature than I gave her credit. I said it was to be a jaunt, and that is how I looked at it. Naturally I was hoping to find more clues to his character when I saw family and furnishings. To my family and friends I pretended I was taking the Oor Wullie annual as my gift. Those who knew me were seriously alarmed. But I had no real intention of doing anything so silly, as they would have them all anyway. Actually I took a tin of Mc-Connichie's Petticoat Tails. In the past I have found them very acceptable. Their toothsome morsels are guaranteed to sweeten even the sourest pusses. After using them to charm a particularly unwinnable character, I sent off the preceding sentence as a possible advertising slogan for the product. I have no idea why it was turned down.

You must excuse me if I do not give precise directions

to Mr. and Mrs. Stewart's doorstep. The fact is that I easily got lost in the teeming streets of our big brother city on the Clyde, and the events inside the pleasantly gardened bunga- low easily displaced any other memories of that day.

Mr. Stewart ushered us into the best room. He was tall- er than I suspected from the feline photograph. "Hey son, you're looking well. So this is Moira. She's not as big as I thought from those photos in the papers. Hiyah, Moira, pleased to meet you." The hand I gave him was firm to show my strong character; his I noticed was browned with the tell- tale nicotine stains I had foreseen—so the camera did not lie, after all.

Sitting in the best chair in the best room in her fad- ed blue pinny, Mrs. Stewart was patting her neatly frizzled perm. Her hair was white with a gentle hint of a blue rinse. I suspected that the curlers were being removed as we ad- vanced from the garden gate. She was deep in conversation with her pal and fellow gossip, Jessie.

"And then I tell't her." They briefly looked up as we came in.

"Jessie Mackay, you never did?"

"I did so."

The air around them was thick with cigarette smoke. It was either my imagination or the early afternoon light that gave this smoke a blueish tint. In fact the decor of the room was predominantly this color, with an occasional touch of white or red to break the monotony. I looked in vain for a patch of green to rest my eyes, but here was none—not even a plant or a lemon. This omission I was very soon to learn was deliberate.

Jessie, sensing this was a formal and perhaps subdued occasion, made the appearance of starting to leave.

"Dinna go," said Archie's mum. "You'll hae to meet Eck's new tart." I recoiled as if I had been shot, then looked around. No one appeared to regard this as exceptional. Jessie retired to her seat again. Archie née Eck smiled encouragingly at me, while Mr. Stewart seemed to be rapidly shrinking to the proportions I remembered from the picture. Tibby and Tabby—my raison d'etre for being here—were sleeping on the back of the sofa.

The new tart handed over the shortbread biscuits to Mrs. Stewart, who prised open the tin saying, "Nae bad, nae bad at a'", and passed them round after scooping out a generous handful. "She can come again." She nodded approvingly at her son. Her acts confirming what up to now I had merely surmised—that this was a matriarchal household.

Apparently it was up to me to open the conversation.

"Have you lived here for a long time, Mrs. Stewart?"

"Aye! Why no? Whit aboot it?"

"I'm sorry. I didn't mean to..." I stopped. I did not know what I was meant not to imply.

She looked as if she was about to poke me in the bosom with her finger, but tucked into a little shortbread cartwheel instead. "Ahm frae Brigton and prood o'it." This came out in a bristling half-bellow, which passed for her conversational tone. Bridgetown. So that's where we were. As there was nothing I could think of to say to this I lapsed into silence.

Archie's dad must have felt sorry for me for he asked if I was "biding a wee while for a nice cuppa."

"That would be very nice, Mr. Stewart."

"Auch awa wi' you, call me Sandy."

"Mair like Rusty," cackled his spouse. "Ye should see him in the mornin'. He needs an oil can on his joints tae get him stairted." I hoped this passing metaphor was not a snide reference to their love life.

"Aw, you mustna mind Maw. She's in a good mood today. She's gawn tae the Bingo the night wi' Jessie." The idea that her moods had to be catered for made her give the man of the house a look that could have frozen Vesuvius. It was such a face that might launch a thousand Rangers fans onto the pitch at Parkhead. What a mother-in-law she would make!

"I had better go and see to your tea," said Sandy, re-treating into the kitchen. My sympathies went out to him. I wondered briefly about their courting days, or "wenching" as it would have been called. I could never imagine her as a wench, but thought maybe a winch wouldn't be out of place as an aid to their courtship. The story of their romance would make for a very interesting series in People's Friend.

In the interval between Sandy's return with the tea, I had a good look round the room. On the wall above milady was a fine portrait of the queen by Karsh of Ottawa, and re-flected that in the Protestant sector the worship of Monarchy was the only religion left. On the wall directly opposite me was a portrait of a predecessor (but non-ancestor), William III, at the battle of the Boyne, surrounded by luminaries of the current Rangers Eleven.

At last I was beginning to get the message about the color scheme and the absence of plant life. I was in the heartland of the enemy! Meanwhile, Archie was doing nothing about keeping the conversation flowing. I couldn't blame the Cairngorms for this; it was more likely that his mother's dominant personality had accustomed the rest of the family to keep mum. Indeed, just then Mum looked at her handsome, accomplished son and sighed, "My braw lad, my bonnie Jo. Aye, Jessie, mind when he was jist a bairn!" The two beldams looked at Archie dewy-eyed.

"Aye, Eck was cock o' the walk, king o' the street. Mind when yon pape gang tried to work him over. He gae them a' a guid hammering."

"Aye," Jessie interposed.

"And just efter he went up and doon yon wynds shoutin', 'Nae papes in oor street.'" They both chuckled at this fond memory. I turned to stare at Archie when Sandy pushed through the door with the tea and some delicious looking soda scones. It was lucky he came in now, for I had had just about enough of their prejudices, and was about to say so— or so I told myself.

The surface of the scones had all but disappeared under a preliminary coating of butter and a final gloss of blueberry jam, so I tucked in with a will. The food altered my mood, and I reconciled myself thinking there is a time for speaking out and a time for saying nothing. Even if the cock crowed three times I would keep my own counsel. I justified this cowardly policy by convincing myself I was merely testing out the ground.

She now went on about her Ranger's religion at some length. I wondered why she was so bent on expounding it. Jessie must have heard it umpteen times before, and as for me, I was a complete stranger. Surely you would not reveal yourself to be a gross bigot to someone you had just met? Surely not? But then I am not a fanatic about anything, though my friends tell me I am not as perfect as I think.

Her detestation of everything papistical was so great she would not allow a bottle of limeade in the house, the color green being forever tainted with its wearing by Celtic. She had even petitioned the corporation to have the grass painted blue. I know. I didn't believe it either when she told me. Why hadn't she changed her name by deed poll? I wondered. Surely the connection with the Catholic Jacobites must have been anathema to her. Had Sandy put his foot down there? I looked at her husband and rejected the idea. It did pass through my mind to point out the interesting historical point that a large number of her hero's army at the Battle of The Boyne were Catholics, and William had been sent on his way with a papal blessing, but I chickened out as a more serious danger appeared on the horizon.

Handing round the Caddiston Cake, Jessie gave a sly look. "Whit would you dae if Eck brought hame a pape girlfriend?" I almost choked on my slice.

"I would take an ex and split her skull," bawled my benign hostess, "and I would gie him sich a skelpin." She slapped his arm playfully to show he was forgiven already.

How I managed to swallow the cake and keep a steady countenance I can't remember, but I was measuring the distance from the coal shed, wherein lay the Orangewoman's murder weapon. That evil Jessie—did she have a real suspicion or was she just a mischief-maker? She looked innocuous enough now, scratching her blouse under her right armpit.

"Aw, Jessie, I bet you are feeling a right tit the noo!" guffawed Maw. I knew then that I was a million miles from Morningside, and my right pinkie sprang out involuntarily from under my teacup handle as I sat up sniffily.

My little pointer towards etiquette brought some sobriety to the party, for Mrs. Stewart inquired, "Florally, Firefly, how do you say it? Is that a Welsh name, Dearie?"

"To be sure,"—was that Welsh or Irish?— "I enjoy a welcome on the hillside," says I, doing a shaky imitation of Harry Secombe, the only Welshman I had ever heard of. "Bach," I croaked as an afterthought.

The silence was broken by the pet budgie adorned in its ritual orange with a blue splodge near its beak. He gave three chirps, supposedly "The Sash My Father Wore." It didn't sound like that, nor was it the cock call before dawn, but whatever it was he had got my number all right.

I was almost on the point of collapse when Archie drove us back home to Edinburgh and safety.

"You did very well," he said. "Most girls are feared of my maw." So it was a test.

"So where do I stand now?"

"Well, Paw liked you and Maw, well—you know mothers. No one is good enough for their son." This deflated me a bit.

"But I think she liked you."

Oh, well. I don't know why it was so important to my self-esteem to be liked by this old battleaxe. Perhaps it's like being interviewed for a job, where you desperately grovel to people whom you would cut dead without a second thought if you met in real life.

I looked at him intent over the steering wheel. Was it imagination, or could I really see Maw with her sleeves rolled up in her pinny, ready to run down any pedestrians limping on their left feet? I still knew nothing about him but guessed or rather hoped he inherited most of his traits from Sandy.

"You can call me Eck if you like."

"No, thanks."

With that avenue blocked for now, he began to open up and tell me a lot more about himself. Even on the A8's triple-death lanes I found it absorbing. Superficially mister nice-guy, he was a lot tougher inwardly and shrewder than Dermot. He had mapped out his life and career with a clear eye, and I could picture him plotting graphs measuring achievements so far. On the table beside him would be Dale Carnegie's little gospel. For Archie, who had been so deliberate in wooing me, there were no maybes. We were driving past the Old Ingliston Golf Course when he told me how wasted I had been on Dermot. Clearly I had a role in his plans. Nothing as straightforward as lusting after me, or even liking me, cut any mustard for him.

When I tackled him about this later in our relationship he came admirably clean. His background he realized was a formidable handicap.

"Look, I love Maw and Paw and that, but..." I knew what he was thinking. "How can I explain this to a stuck-up snob. I mean they are not Queen Street."

"More like Glebe Street," said I snobbishly.

"There you go, Moira." This mention of the domicile of the cartoon Broon family of Scotland's favorite Sunday drove him wild.

"Everybody talks aboot you, ken, and your fantasies. You label everybody as if they're either Oor Wullie and the Broons out of The Sunday Post, or Blandings Castle and that. That guy you call Algy. You talk about him as if he were Bertie Wooster. Yer aff yer bunnet!"

"So why do you take me out?"

"Because of what you are."

So here we had it, the real Archie. He possessed the drive, cunning and capabilities to make his mark in the world, but didn't know his alimentary tract from his elbow as far as passing the Port round the table. With me around to provide the je n'sais quoi and my Sunday Supplement vocabulary, he could suck up to the boss's wife, no bother.

"You"—he meant to say this seductively, it came out as a snarl— "don't come from Glebe Street, or sit on a bucket. You don't eat fish suppers wrapped in newspaper."

"No, we sell them." I was catching his drift.

His brass neck flabbergasted me. Although when I thought about it, everything about his approach showed nerve. That he was open about using me aroused me in an odd sort of way I found difficult to explain, and still do.

Next week, at another eatery, he illustrated his grand design through the medium of comestibles. As we munched our way through his future, he outlined his plan. The soup and bread roll were his parents: nice to have but they spoilt your appetite for the big course. The meat and two veg: these were the exams, and qualification needed to attain Nirvana; the wine was climbing, which gave the meal its character. And me? I was the dessert, the catalyst that would give him lift-off into the world of posh restaurants and cigar-smoking gentlemen's clubs.

When he told me that, I felt that frisson of fear and delight all girls know when an exciting question is on the horizon. The question, simply by being posed, forces itself as a possibility onto your agenda. So that was it. There I was, not just the icing on the cake but the cake itself. And the big question, well it came with the bill.

Chapter 25

The Old Parish Kirk

Today was to be my day of days. I was luxuriating in what specialists in this field call a long soaky bath. This hedonistic phrase had been appropriated from the catalogue of a lingerie company with whom I had entrusted the purchases of my trousseau. Wallowing in the fragrant froth of my bubble bath, I was utterly happy. By my bedside was my suitcase, packed and ready for our flight to a secret honeymoon destination, some far away haven of romance. It wouldn't be Largs, as I needed my passport.

Any eleventh hour doubts had been talked out of me in the long hours of the night by my chief and only bridesmaid Rosie, once again my best friend. Her sojourn with Dermot had been of fairly short duration, and we had made up soon afterwards. I reasoned it out thus: if you never fell out with your best friend and got together again, how could you tell if she really is your best friend? But as to this more serious business, it was not a matter of whether I had picked the right guy—that had to be taken as read at this late stage—but whether I had chosen the right church for the occasion. Had I committed a heresy in going apostate and marrying in the local parish church? My reasons were purely aesthetic. Father Doherty's church and congregation were no doubt blessed by the Holy Spirit, but were housed in what I once uncharitably called a consecrated Nissan hut. On the other hand, the Old Parish Kirk, secure in both history and architecture, was founded in the reign of King David I by the ancient family of Forrester, of whose castle not a spar remained. Tucked into an alcove on the eastern wall of the Kirk was a perpetual light, kept burning from the middle ages to guide to safety those lost on the marshy road from Edinburgh. The symbolism was not lost on me. Not a furrow length away stood a dovecote built by monks in the reign of Good King Robert. In its grounds grew an elderly sycamore whose multilayered branches made a hardy alternative airport for the homing pigeons. Underneath, in its moon shadow, a phantasmic nun known locally as the White Lady trysted with her long dead lover. Was I her latter-day corporeal manifestation? An entertaining thought, swiftly dismissed in the hurly-burly of wedding preparations.

Somewhat less plausibly I claimed that the Old Parish Kirk had been part of the Universal Church as long as it had been sundered from it. Perhaps so. Perhaps all these fancy reasons. The fact of the matter was the groom's mother had put her foot down. No son of hers would step anywhere near a den o' papedom, as she very prettily put it. Yes, my secret was out. I was abandoning the faith of my fathers to satisfy the whim of a Ranger's supporter.

Father Doherty had been hurt, but true to his nature had been more disappointed than angry, and for the sake of my family was prepared to give us his blessing.

As to any other reasonable doubts, Rosie soon assured me I was not marrying just for spite. "That Dermot is as dead for both of us as Julius Caesar." The object of my non-spite had lately taken to phoning, telling me I was marrying for the sake of a new semi-detached down at Silverknowes. He was quite wrong. Although I had to admit that on a bored Sunday Archie and I had gone to look at the show house near the Forth, and rather to my own surprise I found myself measuring the rooms for carpets.

Was I in love with love? Certainly I went giddy with delight chatting with Rosie about the ritual and paraphernalia of that blissful day. My dress was modeled on that worn by Queen Guinevere in her Pre-Raphaelite representations, with eighteenth-century Cinderella undertones manifested in the fullness of the wild silk dress and the bows and furbelows that popped up in rococo abandon. My veil was a romantic wisp of Nottingham lace. Rosie was all set to look gorgeous in a billowing pink confection. But I had no fear she would outshine the radiant bride as I made my egress in a mist of white silk and satin to the tune of Glazunov's wedding march—no common or garden Mendelssohn here. The best man, Archie's brother—an almost illiterate football hooligan chosen for his Bacchanalian talents to lead an exuberant stag night for the almost-never-drunk stag—would have the greatest difficulty in carrying out the rhetorical component of his task, and I suspected a ghost writer at work on his speech, for all the punchlines were written in big letters. His notes had been submitted to me for vetting. No sniggering smuttiness was going to alloy these proceedings.

They had been passed clean except for a hinted allusion to underwear, which I excised with a firm red pen. In case you are interested, this was it: "The bride is a bit of a blue-eyed girl. The bridesmaid tells me she is wearing a Ranger's strip that's borrowed and blue." Strip was printed in capital letters amongst the other inanities. You must agree I was right. Anyway, my eyes are green, but they would never accept that.

So why was I being summoned by Mamma out of an ecstatic daydream to the phone? It was a puzzled sounding Archie: "I have got a telegram here." I was a trifle annoyed that my beloved should call just now. I was dripping in a towel and not radiant in my taffeta, and was it not bad luck for bride and groom to communicate before splicing the knot?

"Well, give it to your brother to read out."

"This one's different. It's in Latin." The dripping water began to chill. There were only two Latinists that I knew, and Miss MacPherson, whom I would never be able to call Bella, was invited to the ceremony. "I've worked out the first bit; but I still don't get it. It says, 'Maria virgo non est.'" The voice was puzzled with a worried edge to it. As well there should be. "When's your birthday?"

"You should know. April the first."

"But that's not Virgo, so whoever sent it got that wrong."

I had to muffle my sigh of relief over the mouthpiece. Incredible as it may seem, Scottish maidens in the sixties still believed in a fate worse than death, and some men honored that credo. Archie told me the reason he had never tried it on with me was that he set great store in marrying me unspoilt. Maw had said anything else was shoddy goods: "You might as well buy yin at the Barras," she told him in her usual no-bones-about-it manner.

So the first hurdle had been cleared. In an almost cringing whisper I asked what came next. It was bound to be nasty, but with luck I could bluff it away. He enunciated with difficulty, "'Memento Bosworthium proelium.'"

"Remember Bosworth Field," I translated. "The man's crazy."

"'Gladium sanguinem ex vagina deripuit.'"

"'He ripped a bloody sword from its scabbard.' It's a quote from Virgil's Aeneid, Book Four," I lied through my now chattering teeth. The word vagina, although I had given its correct meaning, was a dead giveaway.

"Paddy is totally tapped." For there was no doubt who was the author of the telegram. "He's been at the Bushmills again. Don't let it spoil our day, darling. Tear it up and chuck it." In other words don't let your mother read it. Even she

287

wouldn't need Miss MacPherson to prise out the not-so-hidden message. I put down the phone, shaken but relieved. Some guerilla action had been expected from my old Celtic China, but him being too clever as always, the damage had been minimal. Now I could relax and have a quick cup of tea in my dressing gown, before I adorned myself in my bridal raiment.

About an hour later I was ready, give or take the minutes Rosie and I swirled around in a merry rustling froth of pink and white, taking narcissistic peeks in the mirror and hugging in mutual admiration.

"Bellissima!" my mother cried, fussing and weeping unashamedly over me, evidently relishing the "having lost a daughter" role. Dad himself was dry-eyed but only just.

"My own beautiful Maria Theresa." For the last time I gave him an unashamedly filial kiss. Realizing the solemnity of the moment, both of us prolonged the hug till my taffeta was in danger of being crushed. Only Freddie and I remained with composure intact, and with me it was only for cosmetic reasons.

Dad escorted me down the garden path saying to calm both of us, "What a bonnie day. Even the weather is dancing for my wee darling." The day was gorgeous and I was gloriously serene, despite Dad's arm shaking. We got into the bridal car, a glittering Rolls Royce placed at our disposal by Freddie's quasi-Mafiosi friends. As I adjusted the billows of my dress in the confines of the car, I briefly wondered if it had doubled as a hearse. My nerves started at the bottom of Kirk Loan by the entrance to the churchyard, passed onto me by the agitated flutterings of Dad and Rosie setting my train. Deliberately I set my mind wandering to regain what I hoped was regal serenity. The old baronial hall—where Bonnie Prince Charlie was reputed to have had a refreshment break before entering the capital—was just across the road; well, it would be if you took a hop, step and a jump as well. This afternoon it would grace our reception.

I recovered my stately poise on our progress through the churchyard, along a winding path surrounded by ancient gravestones. All of Corstorphine's finest were laid to rest there. Perhaps one day...I chased away these dismals as an incredibly dirty ragamuffin popped up behind a moss-carpeted gravestone. The face inspected me carefully, its cheeks dilated by an enormous lollipop. Then it grinned and gave me a friendly wink. In return I gave a gracefully regal smile to the whole tribe of urchins hiding behind the tombstones in expectation of a liberal poor oot. They yelled out a ragged cheer, not being aware that I was only practicing my smile for inside. I heard one say, "Yer awfy bonnie, missus," which funnily enough reassured me more than anything. I hoped Archie's pockets were well filled with silver. Like the Roman Plebs, they could turn hostile if there was insufficient largesse.

We stopped at the massive Norman wooden doors. The rusty rivets, mute witnesses of the entire gamut of Scotia's bygone days, those grim annals of murther and foul play, stared out unblinking. Today's happier event should offer some light relief. Dad gave a nervous cough, jarring me back to the present. It was the first time he had entered the portals of the heretic, and now he was surrendering his only daughter there. The deacon smiled pleasantly. I nodded. The nod was passed on to the organist, who without any preliminary puffs and groans from his machine broke into an adaptation of the slow movement of Beethoven's ninth symphony. Slowly, majestically, I floated down the aisle.

As we came out of the blinding sunlight, a gratifying gasp of awe drowned the swishing of our dresses. In the gloaming I could only just discern dusty columns redolent of Scotia in ages past from the parti-colored light falling in soft dusty beams from the mullioned windows illuminating my friends and well-wishers. They were all there; all eyes on me, admiring and bidding me Godspeed on this day. At the back of the church was an unclaimed group of sniffing old ladies. I remembered the Sunday Post had done a little feature on "the angel who found her true love in the snow." For them I gave an especially ethereal look.

There was Algy blinking through his monocle, resplendent, as befitting the senior member of his clan, in the dress tartan of the MacBeths. Who was to be his lady? Next to him was Miss MacPherson looking imposing and elegantly fetching, as all Roman matrons should. If she should be his unclaimed prize I wished them both luck. They were more than a match for each other. On their right was Duncan, up from Spain especially. He was traveling incognito, but his dark glasses made him more conspicuous in the twilight that pierced the stained glass windows. In front Father Doherty, ecumenical for the day, had both feet encased in slippers. I couldn't help smiling at this omen of blissful domesticity. Rab was looking up at the organ to check if it needed mending. Esme turned to smile at me. She looked quite nice, and her tubby paramour was at least outwardly sober, although you could tell he was just itching to get his hands on a cigarette. I suspected that there was a tube of lager in his pockets. Who was that smiling from ear to ear in an encouraging fashion, chic, improbably handsome in a pin-stripe? It was Basil, difficult to recognize out of his climbing gear. Seeing him in mufti made me realize that he must cut an imposing figure in the world of affairs. I gave a start. Who was that lurking behind a pillar? Och, it was only Jamie, almost forgotten from the past, who had managed to sneak in. I didn't need a Kirby pin to protect me now.

I was moving forward, glorying in my moment of triumph. Dad was tugging at me, anxious to get on with it, but I was reveling in the slow, solemn pace, my dress swaying to the rhythm of my hips and Beethoven's music. Dermot's ill-conceived telegram was after all only the slave whispering into the ear of the triumphal general, "Remember you are mortal."

At the front my beloved turned round to see his vision in white, his Buddy Holly specs gleaming in my reflected glory, while Maw, looking more than ever like a belligerent navvy, scowled in her Sunday best.

The minister's sombre colors muted the scintillating

moment just a teeny bit. The rites according to the Church of Scotland were, I fear, rather prosaic. After all, I had been used to the full-blown glories of the Tridentine Mass, now sadly extinct. But there was no denying his full-throated, gravelly voice ensured sufficient solemnity to the proceedings. As with every wedding, there was a breath of excitement when the minister thundered out to the assembled to speak now or forever hold their peace. There came a sound like a drain being flushed, which brought an audible sigh of relief from the congregation. After this reverent clearing of the throat the service could continue.

The Sunday Post readers at the back were taking longer than necessary to settle down. Some latecomers must be pushing their way along the pews. I wished they would shut up. They were distracting everybody and detracting from the splendor of the occasion. If it were not in church these noises would sound suspiciously like a scuffle.

Then I heard an unmistakable voice raised. "Tis the lady, I am telling you." My cheeks brimmed with anger. There was no doubt about it. It was that bastard Mulvaney, drunk as a tink! Perhaps it made my peach-like complexion even more becoming.

"Tis the lady is a whore, I am telling you!" He was roaring away at the congregation in his stupid stage-Irish voice. No one was moving to stop him. The whole high-vaulted innards of the Old Parish Kirk were petrified by embarrassment; even Algy was gawping open-mouthed in amazement, the round of his mouth making a perfect "O" to match his monocle.

"I rogered her meesell." He was stumbling up against the glassy-faced individuals in the pews, not mock drunkenly. "You don't believe me?" he bawled at his stunned audience. "You can see for yourself. Why, I left her kellies hanging on King Richard's grave!" That was a lie. The Great Hunchback's last resting place is unknown.

King Billy's right-hand woman was now hauling her son and heir away from me. He looked pleadingly at me as the harridan pushed him into a pew by the side—Orpheus and Eurydice in reverse. "I am no haeing nae son o'mine merryin' nae pape hoor," she bellowed out with horrible grammar, but (according to her rights) with impeccable theology. I turned and, smiling sweetly for the benefit of the congregation, rammed my bouquet straight down into her Ranger's-supporting gob. Her mouth, open preparatory to howling some Ibrox chant, received the full volume. For a moment she stood there stock still—a human vase filled with carnations, roses, and lilies arranged in a pleasing nosegay.

I could hear her choking, but my attention was elsewhere. There was fear in the Irishman's eyes now as he saw the full force of my wrath bearing down on him. He quickly took to his heels. He had come prepared for flight, wearing a pair of gymshoes, and had the length of the aisle as an advantage, but I was sober. I ran down the length of the church, rustling in my silks and taffetas like a speeded-up Cinders at the stroke of midnight.

"Whit's going on here?" This was outside.

"Come and see this. Thon wifie's chasing her man and they are only just merried!"

"Gie her a rolling pin, Jeanette!"

He was trying to force his way through a crowd of kids, who were clutching at him shouting, "Dinnae be a miser, mister. Gies a bob or a tanner!" Flash bulbs were popping away quite unnecessarily in the bright sun. This was the gentlemen of the press determined to wring the last teardrop from the Snowmaiden story. Tomorrow their readers would be in for a rude shock.

Little girls were clinging to my train. "Please missus, can we be bridesmaids?" I controlled myself enough to swear at them in Italian. It looked as if the swine was going to get away. In front of the church an old man totally self-absorbed, smoking his pipe, was strolling past. He was looking forward to his game of bools in St. Margaret's Park. Without a word I snatched the bowl bag away from him. Dermot had emerged from the crowd and was stopping for breath across the road outside Ma Scobie's Sweetie Shop. The first bool I hurled caught him in the ankle.

He said, "Oh!" in surprise, and clutched his leg.

Now all the urchins were cheering me on. "Get him in the coconuts, missus!"

I missed, but hit his head and knocked him over. Now he was a sitting—or rather groaning—target. With all this encouragement my aim was improving. I brought the third bool back up to my shoulder and cocked one eye just to give the professional touch. I paused. He was lying there at my mercy.

"No! No! Moira! Please help me, someone. Stop her! She's a dangerous lunatic!"

I let fly. The weighted cannonball landed with full force dead amidships, hitting him right in his courting tackle. I heard a high-pitched scream that will stay with me all my days—a rare moment to cherish. There was still one piece of weighted ivory left in the bag, but I let it drop. The last thing I needed on my wedding day was to be indicted for murder.

The next day I became a national celebrity for the last time. And I can tell you notoriety is no worse than glory. At least I wouldn't have to act coy or simper for the press. Gone was the Madonna of the Snows. There were some surprisingly good shots of my bowling action hindered not at all by veil and bridal gown, with the usual puerile captions ranging from the possibly libelous "her maiden over" to the incomprehensible "she bowled a duck," but then I am not a cricket fan. The one I enjoyed most of all, though not really funny, was a picture of myself looking positively radiant, about to discharge my final missile. The story was entitled "New Bowling Fashions Emerge in Corstorphine," and was all a play on people meeting and yet not meeting their match. It appeared under the Scotsman's Log, not normally a sporting or fashion column.

Chapter 26

The Roman Spring of Miss Fiorelli

"Miss, your hands are freezing! Your face is white as a sheet! Have you seen a ghost, miss?" I was tucking the girls into their hotel bedrooms. The encounter with Dermot had unnerved me. Shutting myself in my room, I poured a large dry sherry. My hand, unsteady for once, made an involuntary libation on the carpet. It's funny how a chance meeting can so suddenly unravel the years and make you forget how different you've become that what's in the mirror comes as a shock. Ten years crumpled into a black hole. I had to force myself to remember that those years had been filled out in a more enterprising manner than was my wont. I had taken a grip of myself after the fiasco of the "wedding" and opted into life instead of skimming round its edges. To reassure myself, I sat on the edge of the bed and recounted the milestones leading towards... What? My redemption, or at least my rebirth. Night classes in that poky corporation school; then the Higher Certificates I had missed out on in school popping through the post; surprising and briefly impressing my nearest and dearest; finishing up with a Classics degree and a post as Latin teacher at Tamworth Girls' Academy in the English Midlands. I never saw Miss Macpherson again, but I suppose I must have paid subconscious homage to her by adopting her teaching style, dated before I even left school. Though still in my thirties, it made me look fuddy-duddy as well as schoolmarmish. Twin-set and pearls hovered dangerously on the horizon. But then, the more fustian I became the more I divorced myself from that part of my life, tainted forever with its association with Dermot. Edinburgh and mountain climbing were relegated to the storehouse of memory.

If I sounded more bitter than hitherto, you have the reason. Bitterness was my albatross. I was a good teacher; my exam results said so. Respected by my colleagues, although conversations tended to drift off like leaves in a breeze whenever I entered the staff-room. The pupils obeyed me; they did not love me. I lacked that kernel of huggability that makes for the beloved teacher. Few hung around my desk when the lesson was over. Quite the contrary; their exodus was as swift and impersonal as motorists leaving a motorway.

There was a knocking at my door. I groaned. It would be Lindsey, the attention seeker, with another nightmare prompted by the great furry shoals of cats that constantly prowled through the nooks and crannies of this creaky Roman hotel.

No.

"Please miss, there's a funny man wants to see you." It was Bellaine, a little bossy-boots, who sergeant-majored the girls from pillar to painting, nipping naughtiness in the bud.

He had changed somewhat over the years; alcohol and an insecure life had exacted their toll. But within minutes he was exactly as I had last seen him writhing on the ground, waiting for the bool to fall. I had spared him that for I might have killed him, but how often had I regretted that small mercy in the intervening years. Age had not cured him of his impudence.

"'I'll see if Miss Fiorelli is receiving.' That's what the kid said. Made me wonder what Morningside Lady you had turned into."

"Oh, and what do you see?"

"Pianos and kippers. Not my Moira at all."

"Your Moira, as you call her, was killed off ten years ago. I think you know the murderer. He was so spoilt he wouldn't let anyone else play with his dolly."

He let that pass for a moment, and slumped down in the armchair.

"You should be grateful to me."

"Why, because you saved me?"

"Sort of. Maybe."

"Oh, I see. Well how about this: saving me from marrying for spite rather than love?"

"Something like that," he mumbled. Years ago I had prayed for this moment. Now his abject form only provided me with mild amusement.

"Oh and how is my favorite Ranger's supporter?" He looked up, not quite sure of the plot. "Archie."

"Archie?"

"Yes. Archie."

"Surely even you must have heard?"

"No, heard what?"

"Married to Rosie. Six years now."

So that was it: a double betrayal. I tested my emotions. They still worked, but it was only a dull unease, on a par with revisiting a now spoilt haunt of youth. Instinctively I tried to fling it back in his face to cover my hurt.

"That must have annoyed you?"

"Not at all. When you have looked into the face of beauty once, all else..." He let his words hover. Outside, the crepuscular pulses of the city were fading. We were marooned, washed up in our own island in time. It was all my eye of course, but I still liked to hear his voice no matter how much he tampered with the truth.

"Don't think you can restore the old fires with me. It's over, Dermot." And that is what I said.

He was in my lair. For the first time in my life I had the initiative over him. We were both silent. "Do you remember, Dermot, a long time ago you called me a Peter Pan? You had just destroyed one of my childhood idols," I made this a casual afterthought. "Well, your words have taken root as you can see." He nodded quite as if he was taking me seriously. "I grew up." For the very first time he was listening to me. "Yes, Dermot, my dear one." My voice shook just a shade even though its timbre was firm. He was grinning from ear to ear, the irritating bastard. I turned round to avoid facing him. "There comes a time when you must put away childish things. I have a career, a little niche to carve. You got lost on the way. Don't try to pull me back with you." That seemed to flatten him. In the moment of silence I looked down over his head; the thick copper quiff that used to bounce like a speedboat cresting the waves now showed light through the thatch, the whole structure shored up with hairspray. His presence was making me uncomfortable. I could never re-member him silent for so long.

"Have you thrown away your climbing gear?"

"Of course not!" It had been one of his old saws that no one ever retired from the hills. It was getting late. Knowing him, he would be sure to try and chance his arm. I was not sure of my power of resistance, but if he hoped he was going to get a leg-over amidst a boatload of nosy little virgins, he had another thing coming, or so I said to myself.

"I think you'd better go now. We've got a long day tomorrow."

"Okay, Moira."

He stood up to go. On an impulse I turned my head to kiss him, placing my palms flat across his collarbone. I saw the little light of triumph in his eyes.

"Still think we are a charmer, don't we?" I said and

pushed him ever so gently towards the door. "Please go."

"Okay, but if you fancy going climbing give us a call."
He thrust a ragged scrap of paper at me.

"Ciao, Dermot."

Back in the lounge I threw the scrap of paper in the
wastebasket. An hour had elapsed since he had left the room.
Something within me had died; or perhaps it was his visit
that made me realize I had been dead for the last ten years.
I tested my reactions. Only the palest ember was flickering
amongst the ashes. Was it hatred? I should have hated him,
truly hated him—hated him for jilting me, hated him for
drunkenly destroying my happiness at the altar, but most of
all for the dull, dried-up spinster staring at me across the
room from the mirror. But then, it is the driest leaves that
make the best tinder, for the spark to flicker into flame. Revenge, topped by unexpired love, makes the warmest fire.

Chapter 27

Pieta

In the grey dawn we padded up the snow from the Nevis hut. Now and then the curtain of cloud would roll back to reveal grey ice-speckled rock and formations of ice in an entire spectrum of all the shades of grey, from dirty-white sinking down to almost black. Then the mists wrapped all away. On this dim and dismal day, an invisible sun was pushing the night back as raw spits of rain spattered through the snowfall.

"Dermot, I don't like this. It's miles above freezing point."

"Dinnae be daft." His feet creaked through the packed snow as if it was cardboard. "The higher we go the better it gets. See when you get up to me."

Sure enough, when I reached him the snow was harder, though still damp to the touch; at least it didn't creak so ominously.

"You're sure Observatory Ridge will go in these conditions?"

"It's easy seen you have been away for a long time. Trust me. Anyway we're safer on a ridge than in a gully."

It was mid-February. A week wallowing in nostalgia on the Ben was long enough to cure me of it; and as for revenge, the nearer we got to the sticking point, the less it featured. After all, it wasn't really in my nature to keep hatred on the boil so long. Meanwhile, just being in the hills was rekindling an older love.

The ferocity of the weather surprised me most of all, blowing the crust off these memories of still, deep-blue-sky days in the hills. Forgotten were numbed fingers in the wind tunnels of frozen gullies, and the techniques on which I had served my apprenticeship were now as obsolete as fountain pens. Where we had crafted subtle steps up snow and ice, people now clawed their way up using crampons and axes as prehensile tools. It was faster, but vastly more demanding on the nerves.

We cruised up the steep bay of snow to the point of attack. With almost every step, conditions were getting better, and I began to revel in the stabbing and kicking upward rhythm. The warm work cheered me up, even though I could see little in this whistling murk.

Dermot was stamping out a hollow in the snow. "There you go." Handing me the rope, he pointed towards a snowy shelf leading up to the right. I crab-crawled along, accompanied by little cascades of poorly consolidated snow dislodged by my picks. Should I ask him again if he was sure it was safe? I stopped myself, afraid of seeming cowardly. "Commitment," I muttered to the rock and snow in front of me. Running out the whole 150 feet of rope, I belayed right below a steep slab wrapped in a cellophane covering of ice. When my rope-mate arrived at the stance I said nothing, merely cocked a glance at the slab and looked at him.

"Here goes." Holding my breath, I watched as he climbed up to the bottom of the slab, tapping lightly with his hammers at the smear of verglas licking the stone. Kicking in the normal fashion would smash the thin membrane on the slab, so his crampons just delicately grazed the surface. I had often seen my partner climb well, at times brilliantly well, but today's display took my breath away. I was gripped. Too much pressure would cause the whole pitch to collapse; too little penetration and he would peel off. He tiptoed up the steep slab with balletic grace, the tips of his front points clicking as he grazed the ice with the quiet persistence of an electric typewriter. So minimal was his contact with the surface of the mountain that from down below it looked as if he were floating upwards. When he reached the belay and safety, it was I who gave a deep breath of relief.

He hammered in a rock piton and passed a sling over a flake of rock, clipping them to karabiners to make a sound belay.

"Okay, up you come."

"Tight rope." I stepped onto the slab. "Keep it real tight." Jesus! It was thinner than seen from below. My crampons kept slipping off the ice with a horrible metallic screech. My arms were shaking, holding all my body weight. "Tight," I repeated and he bodily hauled me up the pitch.

"Jesus! Well led!" I gasped, reaching over the top, scrabbling up all arms, elbows, and knees, and dignity thrown to the winds. The tension came out in that breath. Had I held my breath all the way up the skinny pitch?

He pointed up to the right, my pitch a steepish gully choked with ice. I hacked my picks in deeper than necessary to make assurance double sure. It was hard work, and the adrenalin pumping through my body and the thump of my heart added to the labor of punching and kicking the ice. The sinister, swirling mist masking and then revealing the scarifying drop hundreds of feet below made me tighten my grips on the axe shafts till my fingers went rigid with cramp.

So it went on all day: his lead neatly and quickly executed, followed by my tentative efforts. Every time I embarked on a pitch I would fumble for an ice screw, not be able to get at it, so back down I went. Then, after placing the peg, I would finally tackle the sea of ice. Dermot was unbelievably patient during this performance, actually saying nothing. Then he took over, tapping hand and footholds, steadily and surely as a crab on a familiar shore. Every now and then the grey murk would swirl away to reveal Tower Ridge on our right, looking like a snowbound switchback railway. Over to our left lay the mighty Orion face, with micro-dots of climbers stretched out on it as tiny and insubstantial as flecks on a lace curtain.

At long last the cloud blew away, and I found myself climbing up towards an azure sky on pale-blue snow ice. Little spikes of brown rock stuck out from the snow, handy for runner placements. I stabbed my way over the top to see beyond the crest the whale-back of a gentle snow ridge. The climb was in the bag.

"Come on up." Beside me the rope lay in a neat pile of hairy matting. I glanced around at the silken snowfields. The odd rock that lay uncovered seemed to be blushing under the unaccustomed sun, while to the east on Carn Mhor Dearg some stray clouds were still clinging to the ruddy-tinctured summit ridges. Sometimes my mental faculties were unable to connect, and it took Dermot to point out that the glowing Pre-Raphaelite colors meant the onset of evening and a serious chance of benightment. We had been caught out.

We moved quickly now up the snow ridge. There was a last rocky step before what seemed a gentle slope of snow and broken rocks. Dermot quickly turned it on the right. "Off you go." He nodded me through to lead the last wall. I waited. He had taken off his gloves to sort out the mess of the rope, now a ball of frozen knitting.

"No time for that. Keep climbing. I'll make sure you've enough rope." Goaded, I put on a spurt, jabbing and hacking my way upward. It was steep, manky and incredibly dangerous. The snow had softened, changing its texture till it was worse than the slurry at the bottom. Plonking my picks gingerly into this butter-like substance, I scraped upwards, keeping my tools at chest height and pressing down on them. I had no trust in the snow. A piton appeared, its black eye winking at me from behind the ice. My knotted calves, trembling with tension, relaxed when I clipped into the little anchor. By tilting back my head I could see just above my helmet the ridge rearing up for its last few feet. Beyond that lay an easy slope to the summit plateau.

Right by me, a steeply canted slab thinly coated with a shattered windscreen of ice glinted dully in the half-light. I had to step out of the hollow chimney and bring my boot flat on that slab, pushing the weight of my body over to the right. Stretching to the limit of my reach, I could just about get the front four points onto the edge of the slab. My boot stopped firmly, but would it stay when I pushed down on it? I thumped my axe into the snow above me. It seemed secure. It had to be. The hammer in my left hand sank into a floury morass. I leant out, my arms straining. My heart was thumping against my ribs. The splattered ice under my right crampon wouldn't hold much more. I glanced down below to see Dermot still trying to make sense of his knotted ropes. Soon the dusk would turn to night. Around me the wind was whistling like grey shades in torment.

I had to move and now. I muttered "now" to myself between gritted teeth and pulled up all my weight over my right leg. Sparks flew from my crampons screeching off the slab. The pick sliced through the snow as if it was hot butter. I was off! The peg will hold! Then a sharp "ping." The peg was ripped from its moorings. I hit a snowy bank with a wallop and then bounced off, floating freely through the air.

In no time at all I was spinning up and down at the end of the ropes.

Dermot was cursing and swearing. The rope's abrasion had torn his ungloved hands to shreds. "Moira! Moira, are you all right?"

My up-and-down motion stopped, but I was still penduluming gently. I heard the urgent hammering of a peg above me that gradually faded into the distance as the snow turned black in front of my eyes.

"Moira, Moira," I woke from a pleasant dream of canoeing on the River Sence. "For God's sake say something." Snowflakes were gently blanketing my face. I wiped them away with soaking mitts. Dermot was hauling with all his might, trying to drag me up bodily.

"Don't Dermot, you can't. It's hopeless."

The effort he was making would wear him out, and we needed every little bit to survive the night. At last I managed to make him hear me. "I'll have to prusik."

"I hear you. Take care."

Shakily I tied two slings to the rope, stood in one and clipped my waist-loop to the other. The knot, designed to lock under strain, was for getting out of crevasses in the Alps. This was the first time I had used it in earnest. Above me I could just make out the rope cutting into the gloom. Driving snow was plastering everything. Every foot gained had to be twice fought over as the prusik knots jammed repeatedly on the snow-rimed rope and had to be retied with fingers shrieking with pain. It was pitch dark when I rolled onto the belay.

"You're a great lass, Moira," he said, hugging me. I looked at his bloody hands. Angry welts ran in deep channels like lightning scars. His gloves were sitting uselessly in the snow beside him. He must have been in agony. I was bruised and shaken after the fall. We were a pretty pair. But at least we were both alive. Frantically scooping out a hollow in the snow to protect us from the howling blizzard raised our temperature fractionally. As in our vigil in the snow cave, every second passed in slow motion in those long, dark hours. We sat in our rucksacks, our head and shoulders covered by a black poly sheet, listening to the wind crackling across its fabric interwoven with the constant blast of snow. He kept digging his hands in the snow in a fruitless effort to lessen the pain. From the expression on his face I could see that it was a waste of time.

Our situation was desperate. Neither of us was fit enough to climb out. The fresh snowfall was already purring and hissing in miniature avalanches, masking every belay point under the new snow. Alone on that bare mountain, our cries for help echoed back at us plaintively. There was no answering cry, for the summit acres were as desolate as the Sahara. Trying to keep warm by rubbing each other's hands and backs was pointless; everything was damp from the wet snow. So we just shuffled about. At one point he lay across my lap like an infant.

"This is where we met again."

"What?"

"St. Peter's, the Pieta, in Rome."

"Oh, sure. Serendipity." Never sure if he was mocking, I replied sarcastically, and wondered if we had ever had a proper honest conversation. On that note we both dozed off.

I dreamt I was choking in a smoky room, and woke shivering into that still dawn to find slabs of snow slithering off in sugary crusts. Clumps of cloud still clinging to crags and buttresses were thinning, opening patches of blue. The mist drifted away to disclose a fairyland of virginal snow, beautiful and hellish, all the previous day's landmarks blotted out under a powdery white cover. Briefly I allowed myself the luxury of examining my conscience. The terrible beauty of the mountain laid waste by the storm plus the terror of our predicament purged me of malice, leaving me as innocent of intent as a newborn babe. Sweet-toothed revenge was a hothouse creature that had wilted and died long before that night. It was a Monday morning. No one else was about to get us out of this mess.

We stood up to shake the snow off and bring some life into our bodies. Our clothes were stiff, encased in hoar frost. His face, grey with cold, was empty of animation. I looked down and saw a few rocks.

"We'll have to abseil." He nodded absently. "Are you going to be okay?"

"Got to, haven't we?" Without further ado he started sorting out the ropes, which lay in a twisted heap covered by layers of snow. The frozen cords played agony with his raw hands. Every minute he stopped to blow some warmth in them, grimacing in pain. The knotted ends of both ropes were frozen solid onto the rock; I had to prise them free with the axe. I took a knife from my pack and scraped the ice off the rope to make sure the knots would hold, then tied the ropes round the anchor point while he was stamping his feet and slapping his hands to bring back some circulation. Our breath sent out chilly smoke signals. I watched anxiously as he made the first short abseil onto the easy snow ridge. It would be curtains if his wrecked hands lost their grip on the rope.

"Okay, on you come. It's easy." He unclipped. I followed quickly and soon both of us were tugging at the rope lodged in the snowy groove. Luckily it slithered free. If it had stuck we would be right up the creek.

Soon we were over the easy ridge, setting up the next anchor down the steep buttress—not easy as it was snow-covered. The state of Dermot's hands meant he could only work for short spells. I was so totally knackered that just scraping away at the snow did me in. Bone-weary, we committed ourselves to rappel after rappel, screwing up concentration each time; any slight relaxation under these circumstances would be fatal.

"Wakey, wakey, Dermot." I looked at him in alarm. He was slumped like an old man dropping off by the fireside. Keeping my eye on him, I threaded the ice-glazed rope through the anchor and coiled it into big, stiff loops. I threw it down. It slapped against the snow and slithered as it uncoiled, bringing down little rivulets of powder in its wake.

Dermot went first, his technique getting sloppier by the minute, knocking down mini-avalanches, leaving me with an easy snow chute to follow. A few anxious tugs and then the rope came down like a great white whip.

We had passed over my ice-choked gully and were now above the thin slab, almost unrecognizable under its thick new mantle. Dermot collapsed. I lifted and tied him to the belay by a surge of strength from I-don't-know-where. A snowball wiped over his face brought him round enough for the job in hand. Like an anxious mum dressing the kids for the first day at school, I got him set up for the abseil.

"Off you go!" I said, and with a gentle push from me, off he went. Meanwhile, the early-morning blue skies were being invaded by clouds seeping up from the Allt a'Mhuillin. From the west, a great mass of cloud driven across the summit plateau was steadily, slowly dripping over rock and icefield towards us. Once again the snow came on, at first with the steady pattering of flakes beloved of Christmas cards, then picking up momentum till soon we were in the wake of a strong Ben Nevis blizzard. At this point we swapped over and I went first, landing easily on a capacious ledge. Anxiously I watched as he poked and shuffled his way down in a series of jerky steps, his expression switching from dopey to agonized when the rope burnt into his raw hands. Nothing was safe, nothing secure. At any moment I expected the pain to be too much, and he would let go. My limbs shook, but not with cold. I was desperately struggling to stay in control of a rapidly unraveling situation when the rope jerked as Dermot leapt over a small overhang, pulling the knot into a crack where it jammed solid. Trying to prise the knot free with my ice axe, I was crying with frustration. There was no give. Finally I cut it free with the knife, still attached to my wrist, and then retied the knot before I rappelled down. Only a short length had to be given up. It's probably still stuck up there.

"Moira, I cannae feel ma hands." His eyes were glazed, beyond caring. I took his gloves off and saw bloodless blocks of wood peppered with purple blisters. The fingertips were black, far gone with frostbite. His hands were useless. He would have to make a short abseil with one of the ropes doubled while I held him on a safety rope, playing him out till he reached the ledge below. I had to let out the rope very gently, as he could hardly control it with his hands. I abseiled down to see a face totally washed out; gaunt eyes staring into nothing as he tottered about trying to fix the belay. And as I did so a well of affection, dormant these ten years, bubbled up inescapably. We were almost there. Only one final rappel stood between us and a safe haven.

I looked down into the boiling clouds, my face sprayed with up-flung snow. The clouds parted and then closed like a hurried curtain call at the theatre, long enough to see a huge abyss dropping away for hundreds of feet and, tantalizingly close, the snowy bay that marked the start of the climb. The key was a long pendulum to the right—a piece of cake normally. But now? His mood was so unpredictable I had to lash him to the belay in case he launched himself off the cliff.

"I apologize missin' yer wedding." Like a drunk clinging to a lamppost he gripped the belay.

"What?"

"You and me made a great team on the rope."

"Yes, sure, Dermot."

"Maybe we should tie a permanent knot."

Timing is everything. Ten years ago that would have been the world. But now? I shook my head at this classic sign of exposure. Did he know where he was and what he was doing? I doubt it.

"It's the last abseil. Once we are down. It's cracked." He looked at me vacantly. Did he realize I could not steer him, for we needed both ropes to reach the deck?

"Can you manage?" He nodded, at least. The double fisherman's knot was tied, and I tested it with a sharp tug before handing over. His hands were not able to manipulate the stiff hawser, so I had to feed it through the descendeur and twist it over his arms as if I was adjusting a child's clothes. His cagoule was encased in snow and ice. There would be little friction there to slow him down.

"Make sure you go down to the right. Wrap the rope around your arms to slow you down." Sotto voce, I added, "My love." He didn't hear.

Without any warning the old Dermot flickered briefly. "It must be opening time," he laughed, and jumped off the stance. Immediately I saw his hands lose their grip on the icy rope. Without any resistance the rope whirred through the descendeur like a high-speed machine belt. Soundlessly he parted company with the rope. Handsome, debonair, feckless to the last, Dermot plunged down over the cliff to his death.

For half an hour I couldn't move. Then slowly, stiffly, I rappelled down to the ledge where we had started the climb. As if to mock me, I could still see the remains of the stance Dermot had kicked in the snow yesterday. Without thinking I pulled down the ropes. They snaked down the cliff with silken ease. Stuffing them in my sack, I stumbled down to find the spot where Dermot lay.

It did not take me long. The heavy rope I dumped. It would provide a marker for the mountain rescue. He was lying peacefully in the snow, propped up on some rocks like a baby across his mother's lap, asleep in pleasant dreams. One glance told me that he was dead, as dead as Julius Caesar. I stood there unable to speak, unable to say even, "Rest in peace, darling," unable to bring together any suitable thoughts in requiem. The shock of death was registered in the sharp creases and corrugations of his clothes, but even now the falling snow was gently enshrouding him, smoothing out the ugly wrinkles under the mask of white into graceful folds sculpted in marble, recalling Michelangelo's Pieta of that fateful school trip. I smiled, wondering how Dermot would treat that comparison.

Chapter 28

Under the Fiery Cross

What the good people of the mountain rescue didn't realize was that a girl in deep shock will act a little strangely when she has just seen somebody killed in front of her eyes. My alcohol-fueled hysteria in the Jacobite Bar was interpreted as more than just bad taste.

"What's the fastest way down a mountain?" I said to a bar full of appalled faces. "Sliding down an icy rope!" In the background to the pall of silence that was laid on the room, there was a scuffle and the distinct: "That murdering hoor!" Someone more sensible than the rest grasped me firmly by the elbow and led me out into the fresh air. I was violently sick down the front of his ski-jacket, and then started weeping as hysterically as I had been laughing a minute before.

It was not long before it was noticed that the two ends of the rope had been freshly cut. In the small inward-looking community of mountaineers, gossip spins faster than a Chinese whisper, and the old slander about Whymper's descent of the Matterhorn was dug up and cited as precedent. Twice-scorned and bent on revenge, I had cut the rope of my cheating lover. According to rumor, immediately after my miscarried wedding I had disappeared into Purdah, nursing my vendetta for ten years till the opportunity to get even arose. No one took account of the fact that I had openly pursued a successful career during my "lost" decade. But of course, why upstage a good tale with that spoilsport, truth?

Every day, fresh talebearers came eagerly to tell me how my tantrums were now legends in themselves. In a fit of rage, I had attempted to burn to death all the members of the Bannockburn Mountaineering Club after being slighted by my erstwhile lover.

The fact that the police had no interest in prosecuting was easily dismissed, since I had gulled them with my Lucrezia Borgia wiles. The interview desk in the Lochaber police station, where I sat later on that awful Monday, was a fairly ordinary place for their very first mountain-murder inquiry. As the sergeant said, "No case to answer," slamming the filing cabinet home as if a whole chapter in everyone's life was shut. I had never realized until this moment how final was death, so many loose ends unresolved, and half-completed conversations closed irrevocably.

No one asked the fairly simple question: If I had cut the rope how did I get off the mountain? Anyone who knew me could have told them that I didn't have the ability or nerve to descend the ridge without the aid of rope or partner. But a murderous Messalina who could cold-bloodedly catapult her former fancy man into extinction would find no problem in casually soloing down grade-three ice pitches. You see, if you have a particular slant on a problem, you can always overcome any awkward issue of facts.

After a time, the cause celebre faded away but it was never entirely extinguished, and I was left with that most unsatisfactory verdict of our legal system: "Not proven," which to most people reads as "Guilty, but not proven."

During this lonely period I had plenty of time to reflect. I'd got nothing right in my life. Worst of all, my approach to mountaineering was childish. My estrangement from ortho-doxy was heightened by my Rip-van-Winkle reemergence from a ten-year sleep. All this business of Pre-Raphaelite colors was just mawkish tosh. The hard school of mountain writers saw their rocks as the most skeletally austere of ar-chitecture. Caledonia, land of mountains and flood, was to these arbiters of taste the most laughable of kitsch.

The way it was enacted in the pages of the glossies held no appeal for me whatsoever. Shinning up the wall in a gymnasium epitomized the spiritual level of modern rock climbing, straining up to a fixed point in an otherwise blank wall, then dropped down like a bag of flour, without any affinity with the mountain or concern for the sculpture of the crag. The mountain rambler, once the most unaffected of hill-folk, was now infected with competitive peak-bagging. What impoverishment of the soul to boast of doing all the Mamores and Grey Corries in one day? What knackered limbs and wearied feet would relish stuffing themselves with such a Lucullan feast that the connoisseur would linger over for three days? In my exile from the main forum of mountain debate, I considered my father—in his ragged breeks, with his piece and flask in his sack, strolling up Carnethy Hill—closer to the spirit of the hills than the computer-assisted assailants of a Himalayan giant. You see, I was hopelessly out of tune with the times.

W.D., a hangover from another, better age, was retiring. It was the end of an era. The post of housekeeper was eagerly sought after by the spinsters of Edinburgh South, while the committee rooms of the Scottish Mountaineering Club could once again return to their cloistered hush. He had always seemed one of the timeless ones, in an active career that spanned the rise of Hitler up to the emergence of Jimmy Carter as protector of the free world. Easily a match for any of the young tigers of each transient generation, his only concession to the passing years was that his axes grew shorter and his beloved tricounis had been retired in favor of adhesive rock slippers. His loud bellow of "Up you come. It's as easy as picking daisies"—dreaded by seconds everywhere and as familiar to the Victorian figures of the Pre-War Alpine Club as it was to the habitués of Jacksonville—would no longer echo round the hallowed walls of Glencoe.

At the age of seventy he had refused to use chalk, denouncing it not on ethical or aesthetic grounds, but surprisingly because it reminded him of school. "Wretched place. They fed us like pigs at swill. The masters were great black crows flapping round in their Oxbridge gowns"—a poor testimonial of gratitude from the scholar who had been the first to realize the Homeric influences on the Old Testament. Many would be relieved that the Old Colossus would no longer be striding his favored hills, but there were others who felt that his departure would usher in a new Dark Age in Scottish mountaineering. His farewell party coincided with the bleak news that the vandals of the local council had torn out the amorous tree at Lynwilg in the name of road improvements, symbolic as anything of the uprooting of old values.

And then I came home to Pappa, alone in his room, a cold old man wrapped in blankets and his memories. On the gramophone, Gigli and Caruso endlessly sang of Bella Italia and passions in a land running over with sunshine and brio. Here were echoes of the last days of Bonnie Prince Charlie, broken, lonely, drowning his sorrows in that deceitful comforter, wine. Rejected by kings, he who once would be king was left alone to molder. At nights he would break open a bottle and sing laments for those Highland men who had loved and followed him. Those tear-sodden melodies were the only epitaph for those who had died for that impossible dream.

Dad also had a dream. I could see it flickering weakly

in his eyes like a candle in the wind. What was it? To see Naples once again and die, perhaps. Or to be once again in that steamy kitchen with the chips sizzling in the fatty fryer, cod and haddock battered and ready in the front shop, in line with those ambrosian mince pies—all waiting to be clothed in the Sunday Post or Edinburgh Dispatch for the happy hungry punters of a Saturday night. What it was we shall never know, for his voice was silent both of song and speech.

That afternoon I had a rendezvous with an old friend in the Blairlogie Arms. To rekindle old memories, I decided to walk part of the way. The old Palais de Dance was still there, a forgotten monument that had survived a transmutation as a Bingo Hall, and was now looking forward to a further reincarnation as a supermarket; only the neoclassical columns on the front remained of the original impulse for the building. Its reawakening was to be presided over by a fulsomely dentured celebrity of the little box, without whose ritual "Shazaam" no food emporium could be brought to life.

I remembered the evening there with Esme. I, a stranger from another country, stared in amazement at the finger-clicking caballeros of Fountainbridge. In their drapes and drainpipes, gyrating endlessly with their Debbie Reynolds lookalikes, they had been the paradigm of Edwardian youth. Where were they now? Could this be them standing anxiously by the closed pub doors, their thinning hair still greased in a half-hearted imitation of their youth, cigarette cupped in brown, stained fingers, the giveaway pose of the underdog sneaking a fly fag at work? They watched the inheritors of their wasted dreams go laughing by: punks, greasers, mods and rockers—they had seen them all in their own bright hour. Sadly they shook their heads and entered to drown the sorrows of another day.

Entering the Blairlogie at the appointed time I surveyed the terrain. The room was done out a la Tartan Trash, strips of plaid representing old and famous clan names hung side by side in harmony. Old enmities had apparently been laid to rest for the sake of the brewer, for few of those placed cozily next to each other had in real history been on speaking terms. Targes, scabbards, sabres and two-handled swords cluttered up the rest of the vertical space in case of sudden attack by Redcoats. The clientele scattered round the leather-bound alcoves lived in something more commodious than the lonely shieling in the Glen, exuding a prosperity that distanced themselves from their ancestors more surely than if they had turned their coats at Drummossie Moor.

And there was Archie. For him, time marked time—the ebb and flow of hair and stomach yet to commence—but now prosperity glowed from every pore, while the hair had a patted sheen that had nothing to do with the wind on the hill.

"Well, Moira, what can I get you?" There was no trace of the hinterland of Ibrox stadium in his voice. In fact, if I did not know him I would have assumed he had been brought up near the foothills of the Pentlands in one of Edinburgh's posher suburbs. At first I thought his "pianies and kippers" accent was facetious to put me at ease, but no, it was all part of his social uplift. I noticed the non-alcoholic lager he was drinking, another aspect of his self-improvement.

Never the one for small talk, Archie fiddled with his beer mat, which advised him to "think before a drink." I was just pondering on that when Archie presented his plan for me. It was an updated version of the blueprint for life he had outlined many years ago. But first things first. In one respect, Dermot had been out of date. The marriage with Rosie was over.

Mephistopheles himself could not have laid out a more dazzling project; a house in the Marina by Leith Docks, fast car, time share in Tenerife, American Express card and an account at Jenners. I toyed with the idea as a way of getting my own back on twice-trecherous Rosie rather than for the enjoyment of the advertised creature comforts. Although the idea of a reversal of the double betrayal had a certain mathematical neatness, the idea of marriage as an act of revenge, even by proxy, was dauntingly committing. In addition, with one of the players in our eternal quadrilateral now dead, my heart was no longer in it.

Poor old Archie; little did he realize that all he had on offer in that scintillating vista was stultifying boredom. Anyway, there was no sense in digging up the past.

I took his hand across the faux stretch of MacAlpine tartan tablecloth. "Archie, my lad, I am not like that. I'm plain loaf, home baked—not your type at all, really. You know where I'm at my happiest? With my elbow deep in chip fat." I lied of course. You would scald your arms doing that. "And now," I looked at my watch, pretending another appointment, "I really have to go. It's wonderful seeing you again and knowing you've not really changed." I stretched out my hand for him to shake. As he looked at me, baffled by my refusal, I could tell what he was thinking: "From the altar steps to a farewell handshake."

I turned away from my sleekit Laird of Cockpen. Whatever he had I had no wish for now. I had little appetite for anything now; life had lost its savor. As I walked out I looked again at the lounge lizards. Naturally I despised all these pseudo-clansmen with their small talk and small minds, but I was pleased to note that my presence was still sufficient to command all their eyes and attention as I headed for that exit. "A Lauriston Lady," said Miss MacPherson in the days when her word was law, "is always a leader, a Patrician—never a Helot."

M.G. ANDERSON is a Scottish mountaineer and writer who has climbed extensively in Europe and the Americas, while until recently pursuing a career as a teacher of Latin in a private school in the US. This is the author's first novel.

Learn more at www.MGAndersonAuthor.com